Jude Deveraux is the author of twenty-two *New York Times* bestsellers, including *Sweet Liar*, *Remembrance*, *The Heiress* and *Legend*. She began writing in 1976, and to date there are more than twenty million copies of her books in print. Jude Deveraux has homes in Cambridgeshire and New York City.

### Also by Jude Deveraux

# Jude Deverayx

## An Angel for Emily

POCKET
BOOKS

LONDON · SYDNEY · NEW YORK · TOKYO · SINGAPORE · TORONTO

First published in Great Britain by Simon & Schuster, 1998
First published by Pocket Books, 1998
An imprint of Simon & Schuster Ltd
A Viacom Company

Simon & Schuster Ltd
West Garden Place
Kendal Street
London
W2 2AQ

SIMON & SCHUSTER AUSTRALIA
SYDNEY

A CIP catalogue record for this book is available from the British
Library.

1 3 5 7 9 10 8 6 4 2

ISBN 0-671-01777-2

Printed and bound in Great Britain by Caledonian International Book
Manufacturing, Glasgow

# Chapter 1

## The Mountains of North Carolina, 1998

*I* AM GOING TO KILL HIM," EMILY JANE TODD MUT-
tered; then, her voice rising, she said louder, "Kill
him! Murder him. Tear him limb from limb!" She
pounded her fist on the car steering wheel, but even as
angry energy filled her, she felt it leave as she remembered her humiliation of tonight. And the embarrassment renewed her anger.

"Did they just give me the award because I'm going
to marry Donald?" she said out loud as she swung the
car around a sharp curve in the road. When one wheel
hit the gravel of the shoulder she took a deep breath
and told herself to slow down. But even as she let up
on the gas, her foot came back down on the pedal
harder and she took the next curve even faster.

When she whizzed too close past a tree in the
darkness of the moonless night, she felt tears cloud

her eyes. This night had meant a lot to her. Maybe being honored by the National Library Association was nothing to Donald, but it was everything to Emily. So maybe delivering free books to rural areas in the Appalachian Mountains was nothing to a big-deal newscaster like Donald, but it's what took up a lot of Emily's time—as well as nearly all of her money—and she had been thrilled to have someone notice what she was doing.

As the tears started to obscure Emily's vision, she dashed them away—sure she was smearing her mascara, but who was to see it now? She was driving back to a romantic little inn that had sherry and date cookies in each room. There were antique chests and flowered bedspreads, and the room had cost her a fortune. But she was going to spend tonight there *alone!*

"I should have known that everything was going wrong when they gave me a room with two beds," she said aloud, then heard her car hit the gravel shoulder again. "It was the beginning of the worst week and in—"

She broke off because as she came around another sharp curve in the road, trees closing in on her on both sides, standing smack in the middle of the road was a man, his hand shielding his eyes from her headlights. Emily swerved. With all her might, she swung the wheel to the right trying not to hit him. She'd rather wrap herself around a tree than hit another human being, but suddenly, the man seemed to be between her and the side of the road. She swung to the left, back toward the center of the road, but she was going too fast for the car to respond.

When she hit the man, she felt a sickness inside her such as she'd never felt before. There was no sound in the world like that of a car hitting human flesh.

Emily felt like it took hours instead of seconds to get the car stopped, and her seat belt unfastened before she leaped out and started running. The headlights provided the only illumination in the blackness and her heart was pounding. She could see nothing.

"Where are you?" she choked out, feeling frantic and very frightened.

"Here," she heard a whisper, then she went tearing down the side of the steep embankment that ran alongside the road. Her long, beige satin dress caught on every fallen branch, and her high-heeled sandals sunk into the soft leaf mold covering the floor of the woods, but she kept going.

He had fallen—or been knocked—several feet down the hill, so it took Emily a while to find him, and then she almost stepped on him. Dropping to her knees, she had to feel him to see what part of him was where, since the trees blocked the light from the car above. She felt an arm, then his chest and finally reached his head. "Are you all right? Are you all right?" she kept asking as she ran her hands over his face. There was dampness on his face, but she couldn't tell if it was blood or sweat or from the moisture of the forest.

When she heard him groan, all she felt was relief. At least he wasn't dead! Why, oh, why hadn't she purchased the cell phone Donald had wanted her to get? But she'd been selfish and said that if she had a phone in her car, Donald would talk to everyone but her.

"Can you get up?" she asked, smoothing his hair

back from his forehead. "If I leave you here to go call for help, I'm afraid I won't find this place again. Please tell me you're all right."

The man turned his head in her hands. "Emily?" he said softly.

At that, Emily sat back on her heels and tried to look at him. Her eyes were adjusting to the darkness somewhat, but she still couldn't see his face clearly. "How do you know my name?" she asked, and every horrible news report she'd ever heard Donald give on TV went through her head. Was this man a serial killer who faked injuries in order to lure women to their doom?

Before she knew what she was doing she had shifted her body to run back up the hill to the car. Had she left the engine running? Or had it stalled when she'd stopped so abruptly? Could she get away from him if he made a grab for her?

"I won't hurt you," the man said as he tried to sit up.

Emily was torn between wanting to help him and wanting to run away as fast as she could. Suddenly, his hand gripped her wrist and the decision was no longer hers to make.

"Are you hurt?" he asked, his voice hoarse. "You were driving very fast. You could have hit a tree and been hurt."

Emily blinked at him in the darkness. First he knew her name, now he knew how fast she was driving. I must get out of here, she thought, and again looked up the hill toward the car. She could see a tiny ray of light through the trees. Would the headlights drain the battery too much for the car to start?

Still holding onto her wrist, the man tried to sit up, but Emily didn't help him. There was something very strange about him that just made her want to get away.

"This body feels awful," he said as he raised himself into a sitting position.

"Yes, being hit by a car is indeed dreadful," she said, her voice rising as her fear increased with each second.

"You're afraid of me," the man said, his tone one of disbelief. It was almost as though he expected her to know him.

"I . . . I'm not really afraid . . ." she began, thinking that she should pacify him.

"Yes you are. I can feel it. It shines from you. Emily, how could you—"

"How do you know my name?!" she half shouted.

He was rubbing his head as though it hurt him a great deal. "I've always known your name. You're one of mine."

*That does it!* she thought, and with a sudden wrench, she pulled away from his grip and started running up the hill toward the car.

But she didn't get very far before he caught her about the waist and pulled her into his arms to hold her close. "Ssssh," he said. "Be calm. You can't be afraid of me, Emily. We have known each other too long."

Oddly enough, his touch began to calm her, but at the same time, his words disturbed her.

"Who are you?" she asked, her mouth against his shoulder.

"Michael," he said, as though she should have known that.

"I don't know any Michael." Why wasn't she struggling to get away? she wondered, even as she leaned against him. Who was it who had been hit by the car, anyway?

"You know me," he said softly, his hand entangling in her hair. She'd had it put up for the awards ceremony tonight, but it had come down and was now hanging in a mass about her neck. "I'm your guardian angel and we have been together for a thousand years."

For a moment, Emily stood where she was, safe in the circle of his arms, and didn't move. Then what he'd said began to penetrate her brain—and laughter began to bubble up inside her. Laughter was what she needed after this horrible day. What should have been a great honor for her had turned into a great humiliation and had ended with her hitting a man with her car.

A man who now claimed he was her guardian angel.

"An angel, are you?" she said, pulling away from him. "So where are your wings?" She didn't know whether to laugh or run away in terror.

"Angels don't really have wings. It's something you mortals invented. We appear in them sometimes so you can identify us, but we never have them when we are in mortal bodies."

"Ah, I see," she said, smiling, as she stepped away from this insane man. "Well, look, I can see that you're not hurt and, besides, I guess you can fly out of here. That is, if you decide to put on your wings." She was backing up the hill toward the car, which was no easy feat considering that she was wearing a full-length evening gown and high heels. "So I think this, uh, ah, mortal will be leaving now."

He caught her at the edge of the tarmac, his hand going about her waist.

Enough, she thought, and whirled on him. "Look, mister, whoever you are, *what*ever you are, keep your hands off me." With that, she walked to the driver's side of the car and got in. And as soon as she was seated, she saw him standing in the headlights. For someone who'd just been hit by a car, he could certainly move quickly.

For just a second, as she closed the car door, she had a look at him. He was tall, broad shouldered, with a great mass of black curly hair. But he also had eyelashes that were so thick and heavy that she wondered how he could see out from under them. His clothes were dark and they seemed to be stained, but she wasn't going to stay and find out what the stains were.

The car engine was still running, so what had seemed like hours must have been minutes. She meant to drive around this crazy man, but the second she put her hand on the wheel, he crumbled to the ground in front of her, lying in the beam of the headlights as though he were dead.

Cursing under her breath, Emily was out of the car in seconds as she went to him, slid her arms under his and helped him to stand. "Come on, I'll take you to a hospital," she said wearily.

He leaned against her. For someone who had just run up the steep bank of a hill, he now seemed peculiarly helpless.

"I knew you couldn't leave me," he said, smiling down at the top of her head. "You have always been a lollipop for a wounded man."

She helped him into the passenger seat, fastened his seat belt and then got behind the wheel before she thought about what he'd said. *Lollipop?* she said to herself, then, *Oh. A sucker.*

She drove into the tiny mountain town where she had a room at what had to be the most romantic inn on earth with a crazy man beside her. She'd defy anyone to come up with a worse weekend than she was having! Yes, she thought, she was indeed a lollipop of a sucker!

"I can't find anything wrong with him," the young doctor was saying to Emily. "Not a scratch or even a bruise on him. Are you *sure* you hit him with your car?"

"You don't forget a sound like that," she said, sitting in the chair across from his desk. It was two o'clock in the morning, her new dress was torn, she was dirty and tired, and all she wanted to do was go to bed and forget that this day had happened.

"Well, either you are both very lucky or . . ."

He didn't have to say it, but she could tell that he thought she may have been drinking, or sniffing some sort of fairy dust. What kind of drugs did angels do, anyway? Wasn't there something called angel dust? Or was that angel hair, and it went on the Christmas tree?

"Are *you* all right, Miss Todd?" the young doctor asked, staring at her.

"What about his saying that he's an angel?" Emily snapped. *She* was not the patient.

For several seconds, the doctor blinked at her, then looked down at his clipboard. "Michael Chamberlain, aged thirty-five, born in New York, six-foot-one, one hundred ninety-five pounds, black hair, brown—"

"Where did you get that information?" she snapped, then apologized. "I'm sorry, it's been a long night."

"It has been a long night for all of us," the doctor said, letting her know that he didn't usually see patients at two A.M. on a Saturday morning. "His driver's license," he answered. "Everything we needed was on it. Now, I really would like to go home and get some sleep. I have patients coming into the clinic at eight A.M. I suggest that if you want further tests done on Mr. Chamberlain, that you drive him to the hospital in Asheville. Now, if you don't mind . . ." he said pointedly.

Emily hesitated, wanting to insist once more that this man must be at least slightly hurt.

But the doctor's raised eyebrow was enough to make her keep her mouth shut. In his view, she had dragged him out of bed to look at a man who was in perfect physical health.

Except that Emily knew she had hit him with her car hard enough to knock him thirty feet down the side of a mountain.

"Thank you," she managed to say quietly, then slowly made her way out of the office and into the waiting room.

She expected the crazy man to be sitting there waiting for her, but there was no sign of him and she breathed a sigh of relief. Why couldn't insanity be seen, like a scar or a birthmark? she wondered.

Sometimes you had to know a person for years before you realized he or she was crazy.

As Emily reached the door to the outside, she was beginning to relax. Whatever was wrong with her? The man had just been hit by a car! It was no telling what a person might say after being knocked down a mountain. Maybe she'd misheard him and what he'd really said was that he felt his guardian angel had protected him. Yes, of course, she thought, smiling. Believing in guardian angels *was* all the rage lately. Having one meant a person was personally watched over by Heaven. A guardian angel could make a person feel very special.

She was musing on this idea so intently that she didn't see him until she was inside the car and buckled in her seat.

"Now I see why you mortals sleep so much," he said as he gave a bone-cracking yawn and Emily nearly jumped out of her skin. He was sitting in the passenger seat.

"What are you doing in my car?" she half screamed.

"Waiting for you," he said, as though she'd said something odd.

"How did you get in here? It was locked and—" She cut him off before he could say another word. "And so help me, if you say that you're an angel and that's why you can open locked car doors, I'll . . . I'll. . . ." She never had been very good with threats. Instead, she opened her door and started to get out.

"Emily," he said as he caught her arm and drew her back in.

She snatched out of his grasp. "Keep your hands off of me!" She drew a deep breath and tried to calm herself. "Look, I don't know who you are or what you want, but I want you to get out of my car and go back to wherever you came from. I am very sorry I ran into you but the doctor says you're fine, so you can go home. Do I make myself clear?"

He gave another of his huge yawns. "This isn't your town, is it? Do you have one of those . . . mmmm . . . what do you call them? Places where you stay overnight."

"A hotel?"

"Yes," he said and looked at her as though she were a genius. "Do you have a hotel room where we can stay?"

"We?" she asked, anger just below the surface. She was no longer afraid of him, just fed up.

Leaning back against the headrest, he smiled. "I can read your mind, Emily. You're thinking about sex. Why do mortals think about sex so very much of the time? If you people just used a little restraint—"

"Out!" she shouted. "Get out of my car! Get out of my *life!*"

"It's that man, isn't it?" he asked, turning toward her. "He let you down again, didn't he?"

For a moment she had no idea what he was talking about, then she nearly exploded. "Donald? You're asking me about the man I love?"

"Isn't there something in this country named that? Or is that in Persia? Now, what was that? Oh yes, a duck. He's—"

At that, Emily doubled her fists and lunged at him

11

as though to beat him in the chest. But he caught her wrists in his hands, then looked at her for several moments nose to nose. "Your eyes are quite nice, Emily," he said in a low voice that made her hesitate before jerking away to lean back in the driver's seat.

"What do you want?" she asked heavily.

"I don't know," he said. "I really don't know why I'm here. Michael told me there was a serious problem on Earth that involved you, and he asked if I'd be willing to take on a mortal's body so I could solve it."

"I see," Emily said tiredly. "And just who is *this* Michael?"

"Archangel Michael, of course."

"Of course," Emily said. "Whatever was I thinking? And I guess Gabriel is your very best friend."

"Heavens no. I'm only a level-six angel. Those two are. . . . Well, they don't even have levels where they are. But when Michael asks you to do something, you do it. No questions asked."

"So you came to earth to help me do something—"

"Or to help with something involving you."

"Yes, of course. Thank you for correcting me. And now that that's straightened out—"

"Emily, we are both tired. These mortal bodies are certainly awkward, heavy things and—what is it you say?—I'm asleep on my head."

"Feet," she said wearily.

"Your feet? Did you hurt them?"

"Asleep on my feet. I am asleep on my *feet*."

"Me too," he said. "But I think I'd really rather be asleep on my back. Could we go to your hotel now? I got you one with two beds, didn't I? Or did they disobey me? Sometimes making mortals actually hear you is difficult. You people don't listen very well."

Emily opened her mouth to speak but closed it again. Maybe if she slept, when she awoke she'd find out this was all a dream. She put the key in the engine, started the car and drove to the inn without saying another word.

# Chapter 2

WHEN EMILY AWOKE THE NEXT MORNING, HER FIRST feeling was of panic. She was going to be late for work or she was to meet someone to talk about town business or she had to. . . . It was with disbelief, then blessed relief, that she realized she had the whole weekend off. She didn't have to do anything at all until next Tuesday, and this was only Saturday.

Turning over under the heavenly down comforter, snuggling deep into the lovely white sheets, she thought, What a strange dream I had last night, of brown-eyed angels and car wrecks and. . . . She drifted back to sleep without finishing her thought.

Sunlight shining in her eyes woke her, and as she squinted up at the window she seemed to see a man standing in front of the bright light. She couldn't see his face, but he seemed to be wearing a huge set of white wings. "I'm not awake yet," she mumbled and moved back under the covers.

"Good morning," said a pleasant male voice.

Ignoring the voice, Emily kept her eyes closed.

"I brought you breakfast," the voice said. "There are strawberries just picked from the landlord's garden and tiny muffins made with carrots. And there's cold milk and hot tea and I had the landlady make you an egg, just barely cooked so the yolk is firm. That's the way you like eggs, isn't it?"

With each word she heard, the night before came back to her. Of course what she remembered couldn't possibly be true. Cautiously, she pushed down the comforter and looked at him. He had on the same dark shirt and dark trousers from last night, and now in the light she could see that they were dirty and stained.

"Go away," she said and tried to snuggle back under the covers.

"I've made you sleep too long," he said as though observing a scientific experiment. As though next time he'd know to put a little less so-and-so into the formula.

Emily knew that sleep was no longer something she was going to get. "Don't start that again," she said, groaning, pushing the covers back and her hair out of her eyes. Now that she was waking up, her body felt awful. She didn't seem to remember much about last night after she drove away from the clinic, but she must have fallen into bed in. . . . A glance down confirmed that she was still wearing the remains of her beige evening gown, and, no doubt, the remains of her makeup.

Holding the covers closely about her, Emily sat up in bed. "I want you to go," she said firmly. "I've done my duty so now I want you to leave. I never want to see you again."

He acted as though he hadn't heard her. "The tea is very hot so don't burn yourself," he said, handing her a pretty porcelain cup on a saucer.

"I don't want—" she began, but stopped at his look. There was something compelling about his eyes, she thought as she took the cup and began to sip the tea. He put the tray of food across her lap, then sprawled on the bed with her.

Compelling eyes or not, this was *too* much. "Of all the presumptuous—" she began as she set the cup down and started to get out of bed.

"I talked to a man downstairs who is with—what did he say?—the police, and he is investigating an auto accident the doctor reported to him."

Emily halted, one foot on the floor, and looked at him.

"The policeman said that if I didn't press charges there was nothing he could do about the accident. However, if I were to file a complaint and they found out that you were, say, driving too fast—or worse, that you had been, say, to a party and had drunk a glass of champagne or two—well, there could be serious consequences."

Emily stayed where she was, frozen into ice, as she stared at him and her mind began to comprehend what he was saying. Immediately, visions of jail cells and public trials for drunken driving danced before her eyes. She remembered that police could look at skid marks and tell how fast a car was going. And as fast as she was driving last night, she was sure that she had left skid marks that would be there even after the road fell apart.

"What do you want?" she whispered through a throat suddenly gone dry. In spite of herself, she could feel little shivers of fear run through her body.

"Emily," he said, reaching out his hand to her, but she pulled back abruptly. He gave a sigh. "I. . . ." He hesitated as he looked into her eyes, and Emily had the feeling that he was trying to read her mind. Let him! she thought and glared at him.

He gave a tiny bit of a smile and relaxed on the bed. "Come on, have a muffin. And your egg is getting cold."

"What do you want?" she repeated, her voice angry.

"Let's start with something easy," he said, spreading butter on a muffin. "How about spending the weekend with me?"

"You're sick," she said, then put the other foot on the floor and stood.

He was in front of her in seconds, and when he put his hands on her shoulders, she began to feel calmer. "Emily, what if I were to tell you that I don't remember who I am? That I don't know why I was on that road last night or how I got there? What if I said that I remember nothing whatsoever from about two minutes before you hit me with your car?"

She looked up at him, no longer afraid of him. "Then you should go to the police and—" Again the idea of an investigation flashed before her eyes. They'd want to know who hit him with a car, then they'd ask her lots of questions and, yes, there had been champagne at the awards ceremony last night, and, yes. . . . She thought of Donald's political career and his involvement with a convicted drunken driver.

"What do you want me to do?" she asked. At least he was no longer saying he was an angel, she thought, so maybe there was hope that he'd remember who he really was. Surely someone was looking for him. Maybe a wife, she thought, looking up into those heavily lashed eyes.

"There, that's better," he said, smiling. "Now why don't you climb back into bed and eat? I can feel that you're starving, so eat."

She did feel much calmer and was no longer afraid of him. If he'd lost his memory, maybe he was frightened himself.

"Emily," he said, holding back the covers for her as she slipped under them and he put the tray over her lap. "I need your help. Do you think you could spend this long weekend helping me? The innkeeper said you had paid for the room in advance and you'd lose the money if you went home now." He handed her a buttered muffin. "I know you must have many things you want to do, things you planned to do with . . . with Donald." It was as though the name caught in his throat. "But perhaps you could find a bit of time to help me." He gave her a tiny smile of hope.

Emily looked down at the food and didn't answer him.

"I don't remember anything," he said. "I don't know what foods I like or how to buy clothes or what interests I have. I know it's a lot of trouble but maybe you could help me figure out what it is I like and—"

Emily couldn't help herself, but she began to laugh.

"Am I supposed to believe this pathetic story?" She began to peel her egg. "What is it you *really* want from me?"

He gave her a grin that was dazzling. "Find out who the hell dropped me in the middle of nowhere last night and left me to die. I know the doctor said nothing was wrong with me, but I have a headache that would kill lesser mortals."

"We should get you to a doctor," she said at once, starting to fling back the covers.

But he put the comforter back into place. "I don't want to draw more attention to myself. I. . . ." He looked up at her. "I think perhaps someone was trying to kill me."

"Then you should go to the police."

"Then I'd have to tell them about you, wouldn't I?"

"I guess so," she said and began to eat again as she thought about what he was saying. If she were involved with the police, she might as well say good-bye to her future life. Would the NLA withdraw their award?

"I really don't think I'm the type of person to help solve a murder," she said. "Maybe you should hire a private detective. Really, I mean it. I'm not one of these courageous women who secretly desire to wear a gun and sneak around dirty warehouses at night. I'm more of a, well, a librarian type. My excitement is secondhand. And I like it like that!" she said with emphasis.

"I'm not asking you to help me find the people who tried to kill me; I'm just asking you to help me get my memory back. I doubt that killers were so stupid as to leave me outside a town where I was known. In fact," he said as he unbuttoned his cuffs, "I think I may have been tied up and put into the trunk of a car."

As he held out his arms before her, she saw what looked to be rope burns encircling his wrists. "There's more on my ankles."

"And you don't remember anything before last night?" she asked, finishing her milk. "Nothing?"

"No, but this morning I seem to know a bit more. I don't like Spanish omelets."

Emily had to laugh. One minute he was talking of murder and the next he was talking of Spanish omelets.

"Spend this weekend with me," he asked, his eyes pleading. "I want to try all the food, see all the sights, do everything there is to do and maybe something will make me remember who I am."

"Other than that you're an angel, that is," she said, unable to resist teasing him.

"I remember that, all right," he said lightly, looking down at the bedcovers.

For a moment Emily thought he was going to start in on that nonsense again, but instead he got off the bed and went to the antique dresser across the room. "Look at this," he said and proudly handed her a wallet. "It has some interesting things inside."

Emily wiped her hands with her napkin, then took the wallet and looked at it. Yes, there were some "interesting" things inside. For one, there was thirty-five-hundred dollars' cash. There was a gold Visa card signed on the back by Michael Chamberlain, and there was a driver's license from New York that, oddly enough, had no photo on it. But it did have an address.

"The policeman had already called it this morning," Michael informed her. "That's one of the reasons he was here, because the information the doctor had didn't plaid out."

She blinked at him. "Plaid? Oh, I see. Check out. What you told the doctor didn't check out. I think that English must be your second language."

"At least the second," he said, smiling. "Will you help me?"

For a moment Emily's mind whirled with all aspects such a decision would cover. Donald would, of course, be furious if he found out. But then, Donald had stood her up. In fact, if she hadn't been so angry at him for not showing up when he had sworn that he would, she might not have hit this man in the first place.

And, too, there was the question of what else she had to do if she told this man to go away—told him no, she was not going to help him. Forget that that might cause her to spend the next twenty years in prison; she would have a very boring weekend ahead of her. One of the reasons she liked Donald so much was that he always had ideas about what he wanted to do. He was not one of these men who stood around and let the woman in his life plan everything.

Irene said Donald "dragged Emily around as though she were his lapdog," but Emily liked the excitement of being around Donald and the whirlwind of activity that always surrounded him.

So now she could go home and have to answer a thousand questions about why she'd returned early, or she could stay here alone all weekend. Alone.

Speaking to no one. Wandering about by herself. Alone.

"I hear there's a craft fair in town," Michael said. "Do you know what a craft fair is?"

Emily's blue eyes brightened and she smiled. "People from all over the area bring things they have made and sell them in booths."

"Sounds boring," he said, glancing out the window.

"Not at all! American crafts are wonderful! There are baskets and wooden toys and jewelry and dolls and . . . and just everything you could imagine. And the people are so nice and—You're laughing at me." Her smile left and her lips tightened. "I'm sure you'd rather see a football game."

"I have no idea. I wouldn't know a craft fair from a football game. I was just thinking that you are beautiful."

Emily did not take that as a compliment. Whenever men told her she was beautiful they wanted something. And she knew very well what that was!

"I don't think this is going to work," she said softly. "I am engaged to be married and you—"

"And I have no idea who I am or what I am," he said, smiling at her. "Look, Emily, you are very pretty and I think you have a very kind heart. What woman would consider helping a stranger as you're doing?"

"One who wants to stay out of jail?" she asked, making him laugh.

"Well, maybe I said all that just to get your attention. Anyway, I was about to say that, for all I know, I might have a wife and half a dozen children somewhere. How would it be if I found her then had to tell her what I'd done when I wasn't with her?"

"I'm not sure married men in America, or any-where else for that matter, are faithful," she said under her breath.

"Maybe I am. I don't know. What about The Duck? Is *he* faithful?"

"You call him that one more time and you're on your own. You understand me?"

Michael smiled. "I guess that means you won't answer my question about his faithfulness."

"Let's get a couple of things straight right now," she said forcefully. "I'll help you try to regain your memory, but there are some ground rules."

"I'm listening."

"First of all, my private life is off-limits. And my body is off-limits. Keep your hands to yourself."

"I see. You are in the harem of another man."

"I am in no harem and—" She narrowed her eyes at him. "Stop that right now. I can see very well what you're doing. You're trying to annoy me, make me angry. I don't like that."

"But you look like an angel when you're angry. Your eyes flash and—"

"I mean it! You either stop these personal com-ments or there's no deal. Understand?"

"Perfectly. Any more earth rules?"

"Ground rules. They are called *ground* rules. And that's another thing. I don't want another word about this angel business. I don't want you to tell me that you're an angel, that I'm an angel, or that . . . that. . . ."

"That we're all angels, just that some of us have human bodies and some don't? That sort of thing?"

"Exactly. And today we look for you another room.

You can*not* spend another night in the same room with me. Now, do you agree to all this?"

"Of course. Easily. Only, you must promise me one thing."

"Such as?"

"That if you *want* me to discard any of these rules, you will let me know. If you want to talk about your private life, would like to have me touch you and would like to hear about angels, you must promise to tell me." At that he held out his hand to shake hers. "Is it a bargain?"

Emily hesitated, feeling that she should tell him to get out of her life, but she shook his hand. And, again, the moment she touched him, a feeling of peace came over her. She felt that everything was going to be all right and that her life would be the way she wanted it to be.

She snatched her hand away from his. "Now I want you to leave so I can get dressed. I'll meet you downstairs in one hour, then we're going to buy you new clothes and find you someplace to spend the night. Other than in here with me, that is," she said.

"Thank you, Emily," he said, smiling. "You're an angel."

She opened her mouth to protest, but closed it when she saw the twinkle in his eyes. "Get out!" she said, but she was laughing. "Go!" And he left the room.

Emily was on her way to the shower when the telephone rang.

"Hey! My little love muffin, are you mad at me?" she heard Donald's voice. "Would you forgive me if I told you I was up all night covering a fire? A really big fire and that I'm sorry from the bottom of my heart?"

Emily sat down on the bed, glad to hear a familiar voice. "Oh, Donald, I've had the most horrible time of my life. You couldn't believe what's happened to me. I hit a man with my car!"

For a moment Donald was silent, and she could imagine the lines that were creasing his forehead. "Tell me everything," he said solemnly. "Especially about the police report. What did the police say?"

"Nothing. The police weren't called into it. I mean they weren't last night. This morning they told Michael—he's the man I hit—that he could press charges and put me in jail for life but—"

"Emily! Slow down and tell me everything from the beginning."

She did the best she could, but Donald kept interrupting and asking the same questions about the police. "Donald, if you don't let me tell *all* of the story I'm going to think that you're only interested in what this could do to your career."

"That's absurd and you know it. I've asked if you were hurt."

"No, not in the least, but I was going too fast on a winding road and I'd had at least two glasses of champagne."

"But this guy isn't going to press charges, right?"

Emily's lips tightened as she took a deep breath. "No," she said calmly, "but he's demanding that I perform unspeakable sex acts with him."

Donald didn't miss a beat. "If you learn anything, be sure and show me."

Emily was not amused, because he obviously thought that the idea of a man demanding sex from her was a joke. "Actually, this man, Michael Chamberlain, is gorgeous and he's staying in the same room with me. I bought a black silk teddy."

"That's a good idea," Donald said. "Let him stay with you so you can observe him for any signs of injuries. And be sure people see that there's nothing wrong with him. We don't want this jerk to come up with some phony charge later."

"Donald!" Emily said angrily. "He's not a jerk and I spent the *night* with him."

Donald laughed in a very secure way that made Emily even more angry. "Emily, my love," he said. "I trust you, and you've never owned a black silk anything in your life. You're much too practical to waste your money like that."

"Well, I might!" she said, her lips still tight.

"Yeah, and I might start driving a Volvo. I have to go. You stay and have a good time with your stray cat. Love ya!" He hung up.

For a moment Emily sat there and stared at the receiver blankly. He had just hung up on her. There had been no mention of his driving up to spend the rest of the weekend with her, and he hadn't heard a word she'd said about spending time with another man. An angel of a man, she thought as she dropped the receiver into the cradle.

She got up and took a shower, and all the while she was cursing Donald. Practical, she thought. What woman wanted to be thought of as *practical?* And what woman wanted to be told that she'd never owned anything black silk in her life, even if it was true?

Out of the shower, Emily looked into the chest of drawers against the wall. She'd unpacked yesterday while she was waiting for Donald to appear with roses and apologies. Not that he ever did show up with roses, but he often nearly drowned her in apologies.

Everything in the drawers was "practical." She was a conservative packer, so everything she'd brought matched everything else—and all of it was washable. "Practical," she said with disgust and pushed the drawer shut.

Slung on the end of the bed were the remains of her beige silk evening gown, but even that was eminently practical. Or at least it had been until she'd run down a ravine in the middle of the night, and now it was merely shreds.

She pulled on a pair of dark blue trousers, a pale pink blouse and a very ordinary blue cardigan, then looked at herself in the mirror. Her hair, her best feature, was scraped back from her face with a blue scarf, and the few cosmetics she wore were guaranteed to make her look "natural." But that's the way Donald liked her. He said he couldn't abide what he called "painted ladies." Irene said that he couldn't abide anyone being prettier than he was.

But no, as she looked in the mirror, she saw that she wasn't the type of woman to whom mad, exciting adventures happened. She was pretty in a calm, unexciting way, with big brown eyes, a small nose and a rosebud of a mouth. Even with lipstick she'd never possess the full-lipped, seductive mouth of a model.

Only her hair, a dark chestnut brown, thick and full with just a bit of a wave, hinted at any sexiness.

But sexiness didn't suit her job as town librarian, she thought, then gave a sigh. No, her quiet prettiness, her neat, trim figure, and her wardrobe suited her as she was.

"Natural and practical," she muttered as she left the room.

# Chapter 3

MICHAEL CHAMBERLAIN WAS WAITING FOR HER BY THE front door, sitting quietly in the sun, his eyes closed, his head back and smiling.

She plopped down beside him. "Do you think I'm a practical woman?"

He didn't ask her to explain what she was talking about as anyone else would, he just answered her question. "Emily," he said softly, "I think you are the least practical woman I have ever looked after. I mean, that I have ever met. You are a great romantic. You love inappropriate men, you dream of adventures no one else has ever imagined and you are utterly fearless."

Emily gave a little laugh. "Me? Fearless? You are a great liar, aren't you?"

"If you aren't fearless, then why aren't other women traveling into the backwoods of Appalachia, *alone,* just so she can give books to children? When was the last time you could get anyone to go with you?"

"Never. A few people said they would but. . . ."

"But they backed out. The hills and hollows scare them, right?"

She looked away, then turned back and smiled at him. "I never thought of myself as brave before."

Michael smiled, then stood and held out his arm to her. "Well, my brave princess, where shall we go?"

"To a men's clothing store," she said, making him laugh, for he still wore what he had on last night, and in the sunlight she could see how dirty and raggedy it was.

"And afterward, we will go to a woman's dress shop and I shall dress you."

Emily started to protest, but ever since hearing Donald's words her drab navy outfit had seemed hopelessly dowdy and stuffy. But oh so practical, she thought with a grimace. "Yes," she said, laughing. "I would like to do some shopping for myself."

They were sitting in an ice cream parlor that someone had spent a great deal of money on to make appear old-fashioned. There were tiny round tables topped with white marble and little wire chairs with red seats and heart-shaped backs. Before them were two huge banana splits, Emily's dripping chocolate syrup, but Michael's plain—just nuts and no other topping.

They'd had fun this morning in the clothing shops, and it had been nice to choose clothes for a man.

Donald always knew exactly what he wanted to wear and how he wanted to look, so Emily never so much as bought him a tie. But Michael had let her choose sweaters, shirts and trousers, then coordinate them all. He was a willing mannequin as she held up clothes against his body to see how they'd go with his dark hair and eyes.

He paid for everything with his credit card, then allowed Emily to pull him into a barbershop to have his mass of curls trimmed and tamed. "With all that hair you look like a street thug," she had said, laughing.

"Maybe I am," he had answered. "If I don't remember who I am, I could be anyone."

"Even an angel?"

"Even an angel," he had said, smiling.

With his hair cut properly and combed, his appearance had changed a great deal, showing Emily that he was in fact a lot more handsome than she'd originally thought. When he saw the way she was looking at him, he smiled at her in such a way that her neck started getting warm.

"Stop it!" she hissed at him so the barber wouldn't hear. "Come on, get up from there and let's go find you a room."

"I have a room," he said as he stood, then looked at himself in the mirror. "This body's not bad, is it? I'll have to thank Michael."

She gave him a sharp look.

"Sorry," he said, but he didn't look sorry. Instead, he was grinning at her in a way that made her think, Room! *Must* get him a room.

Once they were outside the barbershop, she led the

way toward the end of town opposite from her inn. Wasn't there a place he could stay out there?

"Emily," he said from behind and she turned to look. He was standing before a store window and staring at women's clothing. "There." He was pointing toward a store dummy to her left. "That one." The next thing Emily knew, she was in a dressing room trying on a heavenly outfit.

And now they were sitting in the ice cream parlor— Michael had ignored her protests that a banana split was not a proper lunch—and she was wearing a cream-colored silk challis dress with a beautiful pattern of flowers and a tiny rust-colored jacket. The dress was belted with a three-inch-wide, rust-colored leather belt with a mother-of-pearl buckle.

And Emily was aware that the dress was the most impractical thing she had ever worn in her life. The light color would get dirty easily and the bodice was . . . well, the bodice didn't have a button on it. Instead, it was crisscrossed so that if she bent in such a way, well, a great deal of her top half would be exposed. And, as well, the bodice was altogether too tight—it showed a bit more of her shape than she wanted shown.

"You look beautiful," Michael said. "So stop worrying. I like your hair down like that. Much better than pulling it back. Scythian women always had beautiful hair and when you were an Elizabethan—"

"When I was a what!" she said.

"I, ah, I mean, you look . . . How's your ice cream?"

She looked down at the enormous boat of ice cream and smiled. "I've had a good time today," she said.

"Me too. I didn't embarrass you too much with my mala. . . ." He looked thoughtful. "It means 'bad' in Latin."

She smiled. Not many people today had studied Latin, but "mal" meant bad. "Malapropisms."

"Did I embarrass you?"

"Of course not. Everyone likes you." And it was true. He had a way of making people feel calm. At the clothing store the cashier was quite rude; at first she couldn't be bothered with ringing up their sales. But Michael had looked her in the eyes, and Emily had seen that as he'd handed her the items they were to buy, he'd twisted his hand in such a way that his fingers touched hers. And the instant he touched her hand, she calmed and started smiling at them.

"How do you do that?" she asked. "When you touch someone, they become quieter, more at ease, more—" She stopped and glared at him. If he started telling her he was an angel, she'd walk out.

But he just smiled at her. "Thoughts are very strong. You can make a person feel what you're feeling. Here, give me your hand. Now try to make me feel an emotion. Any emotion at all."

She took his strong right hand in hers, looked into his eyes and sent what she was thinking directly to him.

After just seconds, he laughed and dropped her hand. "All right I get your message. You're hungry and you want no more holding hands. I guess The Du—" Breaking off, he smiled. "I guess the man you love wouldn't like for you to hold the hand of another man, stay in the same room with another man, spend—"

"Would you mind!" she hissed as she started to get up. "I think it's time we found you your own room and—"

She broke off because a pretty little girl, about two years old, came running up to Michael, her arms opened wide, and Michael caught her.

With wide eyes, Emily sat back down and watched the two of them hugging and kissing, the child clinging to Michael as though he were the love of her life and they hadn't seen each other for years. I guess he got his memory back, she thought, and was disgusted at the sadness that shot through her. Now she'd either have to return home or spend the rest of the weekend alone. Selfish Emily! she told herself as she looked up to see a young woman who was obviously the child's mother hurrying toward them. Was this Michael's wife?

"Rachel!" the woman gasped. "What has come over you? Oh, sir, I am so very sorry. Usually she'll have nothing to do with strangers. I don't know why she's—"

Emily refused to pay attention to her feeling of relief that this was not Michael's family.

"Please, sit down," he said graciously. "You look tired. How about some ice cream and a friendly ear?"

Emily ate her banana split and kept silent as she watched the scene unfolding before her. The child was still sitting on Michael's lap, snuggled up to him as though he were her father, perfectly content.

As soon as the child's mother was seated, the waitress appeared and Michael silently held up two fingers for more ice cream, and without the least bit of encouragement the child's mother began to pour out her heart to Michael. She felt sure her husband was seeing another woman and she was going crazy with anger. "I try to be a good mother, but Rachel misses him so much."

And so do you, Emily wanted to say, but she didn't.

The ice cream arrived, the woman kept talking, and Michael began to feed the little girl from a spoon as though she were six months old.

"Your husband Tom is a good man," Michael said at last, and only Emily seemed aware that the man's name had never been mentioned. The woman didn't seem to notice. "And he loves you. But now he's afraid that there isn't any room for him in your heart since Rachel was born."

The woman dropped her head. She'd been able to keep the tears back, but now they were beginning to form. "I know how he feels. Rachel is a high-need child."

To Emily's consternation, this statement made Michael laugh. "Is that what you're calling it this generation? Hear that Rachel, honey, you're driving your parents crazy." He looked back at the woman. "She is cantankerous," he said, smiling fondly at Rachel, "because she's missing something in her life."

"We give her everything we can afford. She—" her mother began defensively.

"Music," Michael said. "Rachel is a musician. Take her to a music store. Buy her a flute or one of those. . . ." He made a playing motion on the table with his free hand and looked to Emily for help.

"Piano," she said softly.

"Yes, exactly," Michael answered and looked at Emily as though she were a genius.

35

"Get Rachel something to make music with so she can translate what's in her head," he told the mother.

"But don't you think she's a little young to be playing music?"

"How old were you when you first fell in love with the ocean?"

The woman smiled at Michael so warmly it's a wonder her untouched ice cream didn't start steaming. "I better go. I can just make it to the music store before they close. Come on, Rachel, we have to go."

The child threw her arms around Michael, obviously never planning to leave him.

Standing, the woman looked down at Michael in wonder. "She seems to love you, yet she's never met you."

"Oh, we've known each other a long, long time and she's so young she still remembers me. Go now, sweetheart, go to your mother. She'll give you your music and you can stop shouting at her. Your mother will listen now." With that he kissed the child's cheek, gave her one last hug and set her to the floor, and she went to stand beside her mother and hold her hand.

"Thank you," the woman said, then bent and kissed Michael's cheek. Smiling once more at him, she left the ice cream parlor.

"I don't want to know," Emily said as she finished her ice cream. "I don't want any explanations of a word you said or what you knew. I don't want to know *anything*. Do you understand me?" She said the last while glaring at him.

"Perfectly," he said, smiling.

Emily stood. "Look, I think this has gone far

enough. It's obvious that you're not hurt from the accident and I have a lot of work piled up at home, so I think I should leave."

"You aren't going to help me find out who I am?"

Her lips pursed. "I think you know very well who you are and it seems that a lot of other people also know. I don't like being the object of your little jest."

"Just minutes ago you were glad that wasn't my family, that I wasn't going to desert you to spend the weekend alone and—"

"Clairvoyant!" she snapped at him. "I don't know why it's taken me so long to figure it out. Do you work at one of those psychic hotlines? Do you tell people that the love of their life is just around the corner?" Grabbing her handbag, she turned to leave, but he caught her arm.

"Emily, I haven't told you one lie. Well, except maybe a few that you made me tell you. But the basics are true. I really don't have a home, don't have anywhere to spend tonight."

"You have cash and credit cards and I've seen you use them."

"I learned by watching others." He put his hand on her arm. "Emily, I don't know why I'm here. I don't know what I'm supposed to do and I need help. All I know for sure is that my life is connected to yours and I need you if I am to complete my task."

"I've got to go," she said, suddenly wanting to get away from him as fast as possible. She liked her life as it was and she had a feeling that if she spent even ten more minutes in this man's company, her life would change in a way that she didn't want it to. "It has been very nice meeting you and I thank you for . . . for the dress," she said hesitantly, then before he could say another word she ran from the ice cream parlor.

And she didn't stop running until she got back to the inn.

"Miss Todd," the young woman behind the desk said. "I have a package for you."

Emily's first thought was, He couldn't have. He couldn't have sent something to her so quickly. Even an angel—Stop that! she ordered herself. Stop that now! He is *not* an angel; he is merely a very strange man. A strange man with strange powers.

She took the express package from the woman, thanked her, then went to her room. It wasn't until she was inside that she saw that the waybill said the package was from Donald.

"Dear Donald," she said aloud. Dear, plain Donald, who was a local celebrity because he was on TV. Dear Donald who spent his weekend at the site of a fire. At the moment, a fire seemed so very normal compared to a man who knew a woman's husband's name without ever being told. And knew that a child liked music and said that he had known the child for a long, long time.

She tore into the package and withdrew a flat white box. Inside was a gorgeous black silk teddy. Holding the lovely thing in her hands, she thought how she had never felt such softness, much less owned something like this.

With trembling hands, she read the card. "Please notice that the label says it's hand-washable," was written in Donald's handwriting. "Your practicality and my sense of the absurd. May they always work together. I love you. Again, I'm sorry about the weekend. Watch the five o'clock news tonight. I'm on . . . With you."

The note brought tears to her eyes. Just when she was sure that Donald was the most vain, selfish man alive, he did something like this. Holding the silk to her face, she fell on the bed and cried a bit from missing him, and from something else that she couldn't understand. She wished she didn't hear the voice of her friend Irene in her mind asking pointedly, "But is this really a gift for you or for Donald?"

"That odious man," she said aloud, thinking of the dark-haired Michael. Since she had nearly run over him her life had been turned upside down, and she knew that the only way she was going to get herself back to the way she should be was to get rid of him.

Grabbing her suitcase off the rack in the closet, she began to throw her things into it. She had to leave now, right this minute. The sooner she put this town behind her and went home, the sooner her life would get back to normal.

But as she was packing, she glanced at her watch. It was already 3:00 P.M., and if she left now she'd miss the five o'clock broadcast, miss seeing whatever her dear, beloved Donald wanted to show her. But what if *he* came to the room? What if he again tried to get her involved in whatever strangeness that was his life?

But somehow she knew he wouldn't. She'd not known Michael Chamberlain for even twenty-four hours, but she sensed that he had great pride. He wouldn't come to her again, wouldn't try to force himself on her.

Good, she thought, as she put the last of her clothes

in her suitcase. Emily didn't like driving at night, but she'd leave immediately after the broadcast, because although maybe Michael didn't plan to bother her, she was very aware that she felt that she was leaving behind a helpless kitten.

Ridiculous! she said to herself, then looked at her watch. Ten after three. Less than two hours to go. Piece of cake. She'd. . . . What would she do for these two hours? She hadn't seen the craft fair, something she'd been longing to see, but if she went outside she might see *him.* And she knew that if she looked into those big, dark eyes, she'd succumb. She'd promise to help him do whatever it was he thought he had to do.

She looked at her watch. Twelve minutes after three. If she saw him she'd probably even try to help him figure out whatever it was that Archangel Michael wanted him to do, she thought with a little laugh. Yes, that was good. Thinking of the ridiculous things he'd told her would help her keep her perspective. Were *all* the angels named Michael? she should have asked. Or did escapees from mental institutions name themselves that?

She looked at her watch. Fourteen minutes after three. *I think I'll go out. I think I should buy Donald a gift.* With her mouth set, she left the room.

# Chapter 4

H ER ARMS LOADED DOWN WITH BAGS FULL OF GIFTS, Emily ran into her room at one minute to five. "Perfect!" she said, dropping her bags as she turned on the TV. Donald didn't usually do the weekend news, so she was dying to find out what he was up to. She was calmer now that she'd been out and hadn't so much as seen a trace of the odd man who had entered her life last night. And she was glad he was gone. Now she could think about her real life, the one that didn't have even one wing-wearing person in it, she thought with a smile.

The broadcast came on. She was greeted by the sight of Donald and immediately relaxed. How well she knew his blond good looks, knew the twinkle in his blue eyes. They'd been going together for five years now, engaged for nearly a year, and they'd had some wonderful times together.

Watching him now, he didn't look real. He was dressed perfectly, his hair sprayed into place, and he was as remote as though he were computer-generated. Many times when he was wearing old sweats that hadn't been washed in weeks and he had a three-day stubble on his chin, she'd asked, "Is *this* Mr. News?" teasing him about the name the station had coined for him. "Is this the man who is being groomed to be the next governor?"

She loved the way he'd grin at her and tell her to get him another beer. "I don't think the First Lady fetches beer," she'd say, then Donald would leap on her and start tickling her, and quite often one thing would lead to another and they'd end up in—

Emily hadn't been aware that her reverie had taken up nearly the entire thirty-minute broadcast, but now she came out of it—because there on the screen was a video of *her!* She was wearing her evening gown and she was walking up to the podium to accept her award of special merit from the National Library Association.

"And now we come to our Angel of the Week," Donald was saying. "Miss Emily Jane Todd was honored last night for her selfless devotion to the cause of donating reading matter to disadvantaged children in Appalachia. Miss Todd purchases children's books with her meager salary as a small-town librarian, then spends her weekends driving into the mountains and giving the books to children who can barely afford food, much less a 'banquet for the mind,' as this reporter knows Miss Todd calls her gifts."

Smiling into the camera, he lifted a little gold statue of an angel that she knew the station gave out every Saturday. "Something to boost the ratings on a week-end," Donald had told her when they'd first started the award program. "So here's an angel for you, Emily," he said.

"And now, for something a little less uplifting, but certainly as unearthly," Donald said, still smiling. "We have just heard that the FBI has lost the body of one of the most notorious killers this century has ever known."

Emily was about to turn off the TV when, to her shock, an out-of-focus picture of Michael appeared behind Donald's head. She sat back down on the end of the bed and watched.

"Michael Chamberlain, a suspected killer with or-ganized crime connections, has been wanted by the FBI for more than ten years, but the man has rarely been seen, much less caught. As far as anyone knows, this is the only photograph ever taken of the notorious alleged killer. When a man was brought in for ques-tioning on a domestic charge, a visiting FBI agent identified the man as one of the top-ten-most-wanted criminals and ordered him held for questioning. Seems that Chamberlain may know where *all* the bodies are hidden."

Here, Donald paused for effect. He always hated doing the weekend news because he said it was little more than a comedy routine. No one wanted to hear serious news on the weekend, so the newscaster had to be a clown on Saturday and Sunday in order to get the

ratings up. The last segment was always played for
laughs.

Donald continued. "Even though Chamberlain was
put into a private cell with a twenty-four-hour armed
guard while he awaited the arrival of the Big Boys, in
the morning he was found dead, his chest full of bullet
holes, and one round in his head. He was immediately
pronounced D.O.A. by the coroner."

At this point Donald looked down at his papers for
a moment, then back up at the camera with a bit of a
smile. Emily knew that smile well: he used it on her
when he thought she'd done something dumb but was
being too polite to tell her so.

"But it seems that the FBI has lost the body,"
Donald said. "Even though Chamberlain was very
definitely dead, it seems that he stole some clothes
and walked out, and there is again a warrant for his
arrest."

Donald's smile broadened. "Should anyone see this
man, uh, walking about, please contact the FBI. Or
perhaps your local mortuary."

Folding his hands over the papers on his desk,
Donald smiled into the camera. "And that's it for the
news tonight, the end of our tales of angels and
zombies. This is Donald Stewart wishing you the best,
and I'll see you on Monday."

For a moment Emily was too stunned to move. The
man she'd run into with her car might be odd, but he
was no killer.

Suddenly so many things began to whirl about in
her head: the headache Michael said he had, his
disorientation and—She sat up straighter. And his
use of a credit card.

She grabbed the telephone, called the TV station and hoped she caught Donald before he left. Holding her breath, she listened to the rings, then had to wait while someone went to try to find him.

Maybe he knows something, she thought as she waited, for Donald wasn't just another pretty face on TV—he was a top-notch investigative journalist and he knew a lot of people. More than that, he knew a lot of secrets. Emily had used her access to the documents of the world to help him research some astonishing stories.

"Hey Muffin!" he said when he picked up the phone. "Did I make it up to you? You're the prettiest angel—"

"Donald," she said, cutting him off. "My nose is itching."

Immediately, he quit laughing. "What about?"

"The last story you did, on the man who was killed in his cell. There's more to it, isn't there?"

Donald's voice lowered, and she knew he was making sure no one was listening. "I don't know. The story was handed to me to read. Let me make a few calls. Give me your number and I'll get back to you."

She did, then hung up.

Her "evil detector"—that's what her father had called her nose, because a couple of times her itchy nose had saved her family's lives. Like the time she was six and she and her brother were going on a Ferris wheel with their father. But Emily had started screaming, saying her nose was itching and they couldn't go on the ride. Her brother had been angry, but her father was amused, so he'd agreed to wait until the next run of the ride. But there was no next run—

the Ferris wheel broke a gear minutes later and four people were killed and several injured. After that, the family listened when Emily said her nose itched.

When her family told Donald the stories, he hadn't laughed at them as her other boyfriends had but had asked her to warn him any time she needed to scratch. A mere three months later she'd told him. They went to a party where Emily was introduced to a man considered by all to be a great guy. He owned the television station that had just hired Donald as news anchor, and Donald adored the man. But Emily said the man made her nose itch, so Donald did some investigating and found out that the man was up to his neck in land scandals. He was arrested six months later, but by then Donald was out and clean. And the day of the arrest, Donald broke the story, scooping all the other news media. It was his first big story and it established his reputation as a hard-hitting journalist and not just a handsome newsreader.

Emily was a nervous wreck while she waited for Donald to call back, fidgeting, pacing. When the phone rang, she pounced on it.

"I owe you roses."

"Yellow ones," she answered quickly. "Now tell me what's going on."

"They may have arrested the wrong man. His name is Michael Chamberlain, all right, but now they're not sure he's a hit man."

"So why wasn't he released?"

"After the FBI had leaked it to the press that they'd finally caught this notorious criminal? Not likely. They were going to put him in jail until the case died down, then release him."

"So who shot him?"

"Take your pick. Could have been the FBI, who didn't want anyone to hear of their mistake. Or maybe it was the Mafia who wanted this guy dead to take the heat off the real killer. Or his wife."

"His wife?"

"Yeah. I hear that's the reason he was arrested in the first place. His wife was holding a gun to his head screaming she was going to kill him when a neighbor called the cops."

"What for?"

"What for what?"

"Why was his wife trying to kill him?" She could hear the laughter in Donald's voice.

"I'm no authority on marriage, but my guess would be infidelity. What's your guess?"

Emily was not in the mood for joviality. "So you're telling me three people want to kill this man, who may or may not be wanted for murder?"

"Well, when you count all the FBI, all the Mafia, which includes a hit man who'd like some pressure taken off himself, plus an irate wife, I'd say that adds up to more than three people. Personally, my money's on the wife. She'll find him first. If the poor schmo is alive, all he has to do is use his credit card once and he's dead. Anybody with a modem will know where he is."

"So if this man's not guilty, how does he clear his name?"

Donald was silent for a moment. "Emily, do you know something?"

"What could I know?" Even to herself, her laugh sounded insincere. "Really, Donald." Her voice was rising. "How could you ask such a question? I'm just a simple little librarian, remember?"

"Yeah, and I'm going to do local news all my life. Emily, what the hell are you up to?"

She took a deep breath. She wasn't good at lying . "I think I saw this man today. Here in a store." She could risk that because if Donald was right—and he usually was—soon everyone would know that Michael Chamberlain had been shopping in the same remote town where Emily had spent the weekend.

"Call the police!" Donald said vehemently. "Emily, no one knows for sure this man *isn't* the killer. He's slippery; he's a liar; at the very least he's a con artist. Emily! He could well be a cold-blooded killer. Emily, are you listening to me?"

"Yes," she said, but her mind was elsewhere. It had been hours since Michael had used that credit card.

"I want you to call the police," Donald said firmly. "Now. Do you understand me? Don't take the time to *go* to the police, *call* them. Then I want you to get out of there. Now! Am I making myself clear?"

"Yes, perfectly. But, Donald, what will happen to this man?"

"He's dead, Em. A walking dead man. Whoever tried to kill him in jail will come back and finish the job. That is, if someone else doesn't get to him first. Lord! Emmie, I want you out of there now. If that man is there it will be known in minutes, and that town just may turn into a bloodbath."

Abruptly, he paused and his voice changed. "I have to go."

"You're going to call the FBI, aren't you?" she said frantically.

"If he's innocent maybe the FBI can save him."

"They'll never get here in time."

"Emily," Donald said, his voice full of warning.

"Okay, I'm going. I'm packed anyway. I'll call you when I get—"

"Em!" He cut her off. "What happened with that man you hit with the car?"

"Oh him," she said as lightly as she could manage. "He was fine. No injuries. He went home to his family when he realized I wasn't rich."

There was a long pause from Donald. "When you get back we're going to have a long talk."

"Oh," she said, swallowing. "Good. I'll. . . ." She lowered her voice to try to sound sexy. "I'll wear my new gift from you." Maybe if she reminded him of black silk, he'd get his mind off—

"Like hell you will! I'm going to put you inside a cardboard box while I talk to you. But afterward we can have a little show-and-tell."

She looked at her watch. "I think I better leave now. And don't forget the yellow roses." She was trying to sound lighthearted.

"Sure. Lots of 'em. Call me the second you get back."

"Yeah, sure, and talk to your machine."

"He loves you nearly as much as I do."

"The feeling is mutual. Bye."

For a moment, Emily stood looking at her suitcase in indecision. She should obey Donald and get out of there. Yes, that would be the sensible thing to do. But the next second, her hand was on the doorknob, her suitcase on the floor by her feet. She had to find him and warn him!

She never got a chance. When the door flew open, nearly hitting her in the face, there stood Michael Chamberlain—and it didn't take much to see that he was enraged.

He looked from her to the suitcase then back to her face again. "You were going to leave me, weren't you?" he said under his breath.

Emily backed up. "How did you get in here? That door was locked."

"Making doors open seems to be one of my powers," he answered in dismissal as he advanced toward her, his jaw set. "It's bad enough that you don't recognize me, don't remember me, but you were going to *leave* me as well."

"You are insane, you know that?" Her back was against the dresser and he was still coming closer. "And for your information, I was planning to find you and warn you."

Just as he got so close that she could feel his breath on her face, he turned away. "I saw this body on your—"

"Television."

"Yes. Someone wants to kill me."

"No, they have already killed you," she said, then couldn't believe what she was saying. "But you're innocent. I talked to Donald about you and—"

"You did what? You told someone about me?"

"Only Donald. Listen, I can draw you a map and tell you how to get to an abandoned cabin up in the mountains. I'll even give you my car, and you have money so you can buy yourself groceries and you can hide out there."

"And how long do you think it will take your police

to find out that you were with me? Ten minutes? Fifteen?"

For a moment he ran his hand over his face as he tried to calm himself. "Look, Emily, I don't know what I'm supposed to do here on Earth, but it has something to do with you and I've spent all the time I can spare in courting you so—"

*"Courting* me! Is that what you call this? You threatened to charge me with drunk driving if I didn't let you—"

She broke off because Michael, in one swift movement, grabbed her in his arms and put a hand over her mouth. Emily tried to squeal in protest but his grip was too strong. A second later, a knock sounded on the door. Squirming with all her might, Emily tried to get away, but Michael held her tightly.

"Miss Todd," came a man's voice.

Michael started pulling Emily toward the window as though he meant for her to climb out of it, but she grabbed the sides of the frame.

"They think you've helped one of the ten-most-wanted criminals," he said into her ear. "What do you think they'll do to you?"

As soon as Emily thought about those words she quietened. Neither she nor Donald wanted the publicity that would be generated by her being found with this man. Michael removed his hand from her mouth to push the window up higher.

"But I'm innocent!" she hissed, then tried to push past him to get to the door.

"So was Michael Chamberlain," he said into her left ear.

Emily hesitated only a second before she climbed

out the window onto the tiny balcony, Michael right behind her.

"Now what?" she asked, her back pressed to the wall. "Do you spread your wings and we *fly* to the ground?"

"Wish I'd brought them," he said seriously, as though she hadn't made a joke. He was looking at the building. "No wings, but we can go down that," he said, nodding toward a drainpipe that ran down the side of the building.

"If you think—"

But Michael had already lifted her to the balcony rail and was bending her backward as he studied the drainpipe. "Put your foot there and hold onto that ledge."

"And then what?"

Looking back at her, his eyes twinkled. "Then you pray *very* hard."

"I hate angel jokes," she said under her breath as she stuck out her foot. Getting over the balcony was easier than it looked, thanks to the building's fancy carpentry, which was a veritable lacework of beading, molding and curlicues that seemed to protrude everywhere.

However, when Emily was on the ground, she found that she was shaking so much she had to sit down on a large stump to steady her knees.

"Catch!" she heard, and looked up in time to miss being hit in the face by two full laundry bags.

Within seconds Michael was on the ground beside her and he had another bag in his hand. "I couldn't carry the suitcase so I put everything in these."

Opening one bag she saw her clothes and toiletries

jammed inside. For a suspected killer he certainly could be thoughtful.

"Let's go," he said, then grabbed her hand and started running toward the parking lot.

As soon as they reached her car, Emily panicked because she didn't have her handbag. "I'll find it," Michael said, dumping first one then another laundry bag out onto the back seat.

Emily was so annoyed at his reading her mind that she didn't protest the mess he was making, but just got into the car and waited until he got in beside her and handed her the keys. "Where to?" she asked angrily. Her ankle was hurting and there were three bleeding scratches on her hand from some thorny branch that grew alongside the hotel. Besides that, she was tired and very frightened.

"It will be all right," Michael tried to reassure her as he reached for her hand, but she jerked away from him.

"Sure it will," she said as she backed out of the parking lot. "I'm about to be arrested for harboring a fugitive but everything will be just fine."

She didn't look at the man beside her as she pulled up to the entrance of the hotel, and she didn't bother asking him which way he wanted to go. No doubt he'd start that angel business again and tell her he only traveled north and south.

Emily drove east, the opposite direction of her hometown, down what looked to be a farm road. Immediately, she began to think how much she hoped she'd be able to go to work on Monday. Beside her, the man sat quietly, not saying a word. But she was very aware of his presence.

Emily's mind was moving rapidly, filling with thoughts of how to get rid of him. Had that been the **FBI at the door** of her room? Or was it room service? Had she ordered anything? Maybe Donald had called someone. For all she knew, the person behind the door had been her savior, not her enemy as this man had made her think. Maybe—

"Stop here," Michael said softly.

Glancing at him, Emily saw that he was frowning deeply. There wasn't much light, but she could see that he was deeply worried. Ahead of them were the lights of what looked to be a terrifically sleazy motel/cafe. Maybe he wanted to get something to eat.

"No! Here," he said forcefully. "Let me out here."

"But—"

"Now!" he said, and Emily nearly screeched to a halt by the side of the road, then watched as he got out of the car. "You're free, Emily," he said softly. "Free to go. Tell anyone who asks the truth, that I kidnaped you and forced you to go with me. Tell them I did it at gunpoint. You mortals love guns. Good-bye, Emily," he said, then shut the door.

Emily didn't waste even a moment getting away from him. A great rush of relief filled her as she pulled back onto the pavement. But she made the mistake of looking into her rearview mirror and saw him standing there by the side of the road, watching her drive away. He was all alone in the world. How long would it take the FBI to find him? Or would the Mafia find him first?

As she watched, he turned away and started walking down the side of the road in the opposite direction she was going.

Even as Emily turned onto the gravel of the motel, she was cursing herself. "Damn, damn, damn," she said under her breath, using the strongest language she allowed herself. *A doormat,* Irene called her. And Donald laughed about her "stray cats," referring to the aimless people she got involved with.

She drove slowly along the road, but Michael was nowhere to be seen. Had he gone into the woods that lined both sides of the road?

When she'd traveled about a mile and a half, she turned around and headed back, this time more slowly, her eyes searching the dark night for any sign of him. Had she not been looking so hard, she wouldn't have seen his crumpled body lying in the gravel not more than a couple of feet from where she had let him off.

She pulled the car to a halt just in front of him, then jumped out and ran to him. "Michael," she said, but he didn't answer. Bending, she touched his face. When he still didn't respond, she put both her hands on his head and said louder, "Michael!"

At that she saw his smile, illuminated by the car taillights. "Emily, I knew you'd come back. You have the biggest heart in the world." He didn't open his eyes and he made no effort to get up.

"What is wrong with you?" she demanded, using anger to cover her fear. Fear of what, she didn't know, since the man was nothing to her but a great nuisance.

"My head hurts," he whispered. "I hate mortal bodies. Oh, no, you don't like that word. Human bodies? Is that better?"

Emily ran her hand over his head as though she

could feel the cause of his headache. She had some aspirin in her bag but she'd need water and—

Just then she noticed a round, hard object protruding from Michael's head. Had he fallen when he got out of the car? But she felt nothing wet to indicate blood.

"I have to get you to a doctor," she said as she started to help him up.

"They will kill me," he said, smiling. "That will make it two times."

There was truth to his words: Donald had said the man on the news was a walking dead man.

Putting her arm under his shoulders, she commanded him to help her get him into the car. He did the best he could, but she could tell that he was in too much pain to give her much help.

Once he was in the car, the only thing to do was to get him somewhere safe. Maybe she could call Donald and—And hear him tell her to leave the man and get out as fast as she could, she thought.

She pulled into the parking lot of the motel, then drove to the back where her car couldn't be seen. Inside, the place was even sleazier than outside and the man watching TV from behind the desk looked as though he hadn't had a bath in a while.

"I'd like a double room, please," Emily said, and for a moment the man just stared at her without speaking. He was looking her up and down and taking in her clothes, making her feel as though she were wearing couture at a drag race.

"Only people stay here are people that cain't afford no better, local high school kids, and. . . ." He smirked. "And *ladies* like you that's doin' somethin' she ain't supposed to be doin' with somebody she ain't supposed to be doin' it with."

Emily didn't feel like talking to the man or explaining anything. What could she say anyway, except that he was right? "How much to keep your mouth shut?" she asked tiredly.

"Fifty cash."

Without another word, Emily paid the money, took the key to a room at the back of the motel and left. Minutes later, she had Michael in the ugly motel room stretched out on the none-too-clean double bed.

As far as she could tell, Michael was still near to being unconscious, but as she straightened up he caught her wrist. "You have to take it out," he whispered.

"What?"

"The bullet. You have to take the bullet out of my head."

Emily stared at him. "You've been watching too many cowboy movies," she said. "I'll take you to a doctor and—"

"No!" he said, lifting his head with the force of his voice, then falling back on the pillow in agony. "Please, Emily. In remembrance for the things I have done for you."

"For me?" she gasped. "And what would that be? Making me climb down a drainpipe? Putting me on the Most Wanted List? Or—"

"When you fell in the pond, I called your mother," he said softly.

At that Emily backed away from him, for the story was one of the great ones in her family. Even though she had been forbidden to go, Emily had been collecting tadpoles by the edge of the pond and had fallen in. Within seconds her mother had been there to fish her out. Later her mother had sworn that "someone" had told her to go get her daughter.

"Who are you?" she whispered, backing away from him.

"Right now I am a man and I need your help. Please, Emily, I do not think this body can stand this much pain for very long. I do not want to be recalled before I have done what I was sent here to do."

"I . . . I don't know what to do. I have no knowledge of medicine. I know nothing."

"Those things you use on your eyebrows. . . ." he said, his voice very weak and his eyes closed.

"Tweezers. But a pair of tweezers couldn't remove something as big as that . . . that thing in your head." She sat down on the bed beside him and smoothed his hair back from his face. "I would like to help you but only a doctor can do what you're asking. A person can't just take a pair of pliers and pull a bullet from someone's head. There would be blood and infection and. . . ." She smiled down at him even though he couldn't see her. "Your brains would leak out through the hole," she said, trying to make him smile. "I must get you to a doctor *now;* we'll worry about the FBI later."

"Yes, pliers," he said. "Yes. You have them in your car. You must get them and remove this thing."

Emily started to get off the bed. There was no phone in the room and she knew that it would take an ambulance longer to find this place than it would for her to drive him back into the town to the clinic. Or maybe she should take him into the city to a proper hospital.

Michael grabbed her hand. "You must, Emily. You must remove this thing. To take me to a doctor means taking me to my death."

Once again she had that feeling of calm that seemed to come over her whenever he touched her. As though she were in a dream, she got up, picked up her keys, went to the car and got the pouch of tools that she kept there. Back in the room, she unrolled the pouch and extracted a pair of flat-nose pliers.

It was almost as though she weren't in her own body as she moved to sit on the bed, her back against the headboard, and then pulled the man's head onto her lap. The bedside lamp was all the light there was in the room, but she couldn't see much anyway, for her eyes didn't seem to focus clearly. Some part of her knew that if she weren't in this odd trance-state she would never be doing what she was. How in the world could she, a librarian, pull a bullet from a man's head?

Using her fingertips more than her eyes, she easily found the bullet and put the end of the pliers against it, then pulled. The first time, the pliers slipped off, so the second time she used all her strength to hold them together and pull. It was as though she suddenly had the strength of a dozen strong men, and when she pulled the bullet came out.

Lying across her outstretched legs, she felt the man's body go limp, and she knew he had fainted. She could not let herself imagine the kind of pain she had just caused him.

*Jude Deveraux*

Part of Emily expected blood, but another part of her knew that there would be none. And she was glad, for she didn't think she had the energy to cope with more trauma than she'd already experienced in the last couple of days.

With her head back against the wobbly headboard, the man still sprawled across her, the pliers still in her hand, she fell asleep.

# Chapter 5

WHEN EMILY AWOKE SHE DIDN'T AT FIRST KNOW where she was, but she did know there was something she didn't want to remember, so she snuggled back under the covers and closed her eyes.

"Good morning," came a cheerful male voice that Emily instantly recognized. And it made her bury herself even deeper under the thin covers.

"Come on, get up. I know you're awake," he said again.

She turned her face toward the wall. "Head all right?" she mumbled.

"What was that? I couldn't hear you."

She knew very well that he heard her perfectly but he was pretending not to. "Is your head all right?" she shouted without turning to look at him.

When he didn't answer she turned over and glared

61

at him. His hair was damp and he was wearing nothing but a towel about his waist. It made her even more infuriated that she couldn't help noticing that his broad chest was well muscled and his skin was a lovely honey color.

Michael grinned. "They did a good job in choosing a body for me, didn't they? I'm glad you like it."

"It's too early for mind reading," she snapped, pushing the hair out of her eyes.

He sat on the bed and looked at her. "Sometimes I can understand the attraction you mortals have for each other's bodies," he said softly.

"Touch me and you die."

At that he chuckled but he didn't move off the bed. "Look at this," he said, then ran his hands over his chest. "I didn't see all that on your TU but—"

"TV, short for television."

"Ah, yes, TV. Anyway, didn't they say this body was shot in the chest?"

"I really wish you'd stop referring to yourself as 'this body'," she said, looking away from him.

"I am making you uncomfortable," he said, but he didn't seem to have any real remorse for doing so. "You know, Emily, if we're going to work together, we must make some earth, ah, ground rules." He looked at her as though he wanted praise for having remembered something she'd taught him, but Emily wasn't going to give him anything. "You can't fall in love with me," he said.

That loosened her jaw. "I what?"

"You can't fall in love with me." Taking advantage of Emily's speechlessness, he got up and walked away, his back to her. "While I was in that waterfall, no, don't tell me, that shower, I—" Turning, he looked back at her. "You know, it is quite one thing to watch mortals and their toilet habits but quite another to experience them. I find them a great nuisance. In fact, I find most everything about these bodies a nuisance."

Emily was glaring at him. "So why don't you just fly off to where you *really* belong?"

His smile broadened. "I have offended you."

"How could you?" she asked sweetly. "You have made me into a fugitive wanted by criminals as well as law enforcement agencies, not to mention your wife, but you tell me I'm not to fall in love with you. Tell me, oh please do, how do I refrain myself?"

Michael laughed, then again sat down on the bed beside her. "I'm just telling you in case you feel so inclined. Once my mission here is done, I have to go home."

"And home is Heaven?" Emily asked, one eyebrow raised.

"Yes, exactly. I'll go back to keeping you from drowning in ponds and tickling your nose whenever I see trouble ahead."

At that Emily drew the covers up around her neck. "I would like for you to get out of my life," she said quietly. "You appear to be in good health now so I'd like for you to—"

"Here, feel my head," he said, bending toward her, ignoring her words.

Emily wanted to remain aloof but she was curious as to what had happened after last night. She put her hands in the damp curls of his hair and felt all of his scalp. There wasn't a wound or dent or any sign that last night there had been a fat, round piece of lead sticking out of his scalp.

"And look at these," he said, sitting up and again roaming his hands over his chest.

She saw what could be healed-over scars from what could have been bullet holes.

"And here," he said, turning around so she could see his back. "Two of them came out the back."

She couldn't help herself as she ran her hands over the scars that did indeed look like bullet holes. Donald had said that the man had been killed in his cell, "his chest full of bullet holes, and one round in his head."

Turning back around, Michael picked up the piece of lead from the bedside table. "This was causing me horrible pain, but after you took it out I was fine. Did you sleep well?"

As he spoke he handed the bullet to Emily, and for a while she sat there looking at the horrid little thing. Last night she had pulled this from the man's head with a pair of pliers, and this morning there wasn't so much as a cut on his scalp to show it had been there.

She looked up at him. "Who are you?" she whispered. "How can you open locked doors? How can you have something like this taken from your head and not bleed? How do you know so much about me?"

"Emily," he said softly, then reached for her hand.

"Don't you dare touch me," she said. "Every time you touch me odd things happen. You . . . you hypnotized me last night, didn't you?"

"I had to. Otherwise you were going to call a doctor. But expending the energy to calm your mind was more than I could do last night," he said. "I became unconscious."

"You are creating a diversion," she said, "and you are not answering my question. Who are you?"

"I seem to remember that I told you I would not talk of, well, of angels unless you asked me to."

"Oh, so now I'm to beg you to tell me. . . ." She looked away and suddenly her eyes filled with tears. These last days had been too much for her.

"Are all mortal women so illogical?"

"Of all the chauvinistic things I have ever had said to me, that is the worst!" she said as she flung back the covers and discovered that she was in her underwear. Her slacks and shirt were laid neatly across the back of a chair at the other end of the room.

"Did you undress me?" she said, seething as she glared at him.

"You seemed to be uncomfortable and I wanted you to sleep well." He seemed to know that he had done something wrong, but he wasn't sure what.

When she continued to get out of bed, he caught her hand, and, as always, she calmed. "I will tell you everything I know if you'll listen. But I warn you that I don't know much. You must believe me when I tell you that I'm as confused and disoriented as you are. I'd like to go home as much as you do. I don't want to be chased by people, shot at or have to climb out windows. I have duties and work to do just like anyone else."

"Just your work happens to be in Heaven," she said, pulling away from his touch.

"Yes," he said simply. "My work happens to be elsewhere."

"What you're asking me to believe is impossible."

"Why?" He took a deep breath. "Mortals never believe in what they can't see. You don't believe an animal exists until you actually *see* it. But whether you believe in something or not has no effect on what is or is not. Do you understand me?"

"I understand you; it's just that I don't *believe* you."

Michael looked at her a moment, then blinked. "Oh, I see. You believe in angels, you just don't believe *I* am an angel."

"Bingo!"

At that Michael laughed. "What can I do to prove it to you? Other than sprout wings, that is?"

She knew he was making fun of her but she wasn't going to allow herself to get angry. Instead, she just sat there and glared at him.

After a while he got up and walked about the room. "All right, you've seen some things but not enough to make you believe that I am what I say I am. What do you think has been the cause of what you have seen?"

"You're a magician and you have some clairvoyant powers. You're very good with locks."

"And bullets," he said, smiling at her, but she didn't answer so he sat back down on the bed.

"All right, Emily, I'm asking for your help as one mortal to another. My, uh, clairvoyant powers have told me that there is a situation that needs solving and it involves you. But I have no idea what the problem is so I have to find it before I can solve it."

"What kind of problem is it?" She could have bitten off her tongue when she said it, but when he presented the situation this way she was intrigued.

She loved helping Donald research stories. In fact, she just loved mysteries in general.

"I don't know, but what would be so big that an angel would need to be sent to earth?"

"Evil," she said. "True evil."

At that Michael's face lit up. "That's right. That's what it must be. I haven't had much time to think since I got here, but evil must be the answer." He leaned toward her. "So what evil surrounds you?"

"Me? In a small-town library? You must be kidding." She was back to normal now, and she could keep this good-looking man at a distance. But why did they always seem to end up alone in bedrooms?

Again he stood and began to walk about the room. The towel was slipping lower over his hips and Emily suddenly wished there was a telephone in the room. If there were, she'd call Donald right now.

"That's just what I thought. That town you live in is quite without interest and, as always, your life is without excitement and—"

"I beg your pardon!" she said. "My life is *not* without excitement. For your information, I happen to be engaged to a man who plans to be governor of this state and maybe even president."

"No," Michael said solemnly. "He always has grand plans when he's young, then spends his old age telling everyone what he could have been if someone hadn't hindered him."

"Of all the—" Emily said, flinging back the covers.

"Ah yes, I forgot that you never could take the truth."

At that Emily sat back down. "I can take the truth as well as the next man." She arched an eyebrow at him. "And the last I heard, God gave us lowly mortals free will. Even if Donald has been what you say in the past—which, by the way, I don't believe, since I don't believe in reincarnation—then he could change in this lifetime. Am I right?"

"Very right," Michael said with a smile, and Emily gave him one back. "I stand corrected. Now, where was I?"

"Telling me that I am boring, where I live is boring and that the man I love is going to be a failure," she said sweetly. "If you're an angel, I'd hate to see Satan's imps," she said under her breath.

Michael laughed. "All right, maybe you and your town aren't exactly boring, but I don't remember seeing any evil around you."

"But then, maybe you'd already made up your mind about all of us and weren't looking. Maybe it says on your Rolodex that Emily is boring and whatever she does is boring and where she lives is boring, so you don't bother yourself to really *look.*"

For a moment Michael stood there staring at her, his eyes wide. "I think you may have something there," he said, astonishment in his voice.

"Me? Boring little me?" she said, for a second hating all men everywhere. First Donald tells her she's "practical" and now this man tells her she's too boring to attract evil.

Michael didn't respond to her sarcasm. "I really do think you have something. Good attracts evil."

"So now I'm 'good' too," she muttered. "Boring, good, practical."

"What is wrong with being called good? All of

Heaven likes good people and I can tell you that there are few enough of you."

She wasn't going to answer him because there wasn't a real answer. Her mother always told her good was good, but sometimes a woman wanted to be considered a bit wicked. "So how can you solve evil if you can't even find it?" she asked. "And I don't think there's much evil in Greenbriar, North Carolina. As you say, it's pretty boring."

Michael sat down on the end of the bed. "I'm trying to remember that town. I have to take care of several towns and cities and cultures are different. What is sinful in Saudi Arabia is not always sinful in Monaco, and what is sinful here in America is not necessarily sinful in Paris. Sometimes I get mixed up."

"I see. Not that you are one, but isn't there a guidebook for being an angel?"

"Is there a guidebook for being a mortal?" he shot back.

"The Bible?"

He grinned at her. "I've always liked you, Emily," he said. "And I find you even funnier in a body."

"My body is funny-looking?"

At that he laughed and bent forward and kissed her cheek, then drew back as though he were startled. "My, but that was pleasurable! Well, shall we get started?"

"At the risk of boring you with my boring question, could you tell me what we are to get started *on?*"

"Why, we're going back to your town and searching out the evil, of course."

"We? As in you and me?"

He just looked at her in answer.

"Did it slip your mind that you are wanted for crimes that you may or may not have committed and that a few hundred people are looking for you? Maybe Greenbriar is a backward place to you, but we do get TV and your picture has been all over it. Someone will see you and turn you in."

"Mmmmm. Yes, I can see that would be a problem. You'll have to hide me then."

"Oh no, you don't."

"I don't do what?" he asked, eyebrows raised in innocence.

"You don't involve me in this. And I am *not* going to hide you. In my opinion I have spent much too much time with you already."

"I can understand that. Or now I think I'm supposed to say that I can respect that. Is that right? Or did they make that rule in Thailand? No, I'm sure it was you American women."

She narrowed her eyes at him, not sure if he was making fun of her or not. "Why do I always get the impression that you're not really *hearing* me?"

He gave her a small smile. "Do you want a shower before we have breakfast?"

"Sure, let's just go have breakfast and have everyone in the cafe pointing at you and saying they saw you on TV last night."

"Do they do that to Mickey?"

She glared at him, knowing full well that he was referring to Mickey Mouse.

"Sorry," he said insincerely. "I have my cartoons mixed up. He's the other one. But isn't your Donald on television all the time? Do people stare and point at him?"

"If they do it's not because he's a criminal." With a start, she realized that he had done it again! Once again he had sidetracked her from the issue. "Listen to me and listen well. My involvement with you is at an end. I'm not going to spend another minute of my time leaping out of windows, climbing down drainpipes or listening to you tell me you're an angel. You're the most unangelic person I have ever met. Now, I'm going to get up from here, get dressed and I'm going *home.* Without you. Understand me?"

"Perfectly," he said cheerfully. "And I'm glad we have that settled, because I believe some of your federal mafia are pulling into the parking lot."

It took her a moment to understand what he was saying. Federal mafia? In the next second everything happened quickly. Michael grabbed his clothes from over a chair and disappeared out the door. Seconds later there was a knock, then a man telling her to open up. Emily called for them to wait because she was still in bed in just her underwear, but they didn't wait.

Three men opened the door that she was sure had been locked, and stood there staring at her for a second before they started to search the room. "Wait a minute," she said. "Do you have a search warrant?"

"No ma'am," one of the men said, then flashed a badge for just a second before putting it back into his coat pocket. "We are here to protect you. We had word that you had been taken hostage and were being held against your will."

Emily pulled the covers up higher about her neck.

"If I were I'd be dead now after the way you barged into this room, wouldn't I?" she said, glaring at the man. Actually, she was shaking under the covers; her bravado was just to cover her fear. How could *she* be involved with the FBI?

She gave a squeal of protest when one of the men ran his hands over the covers, all along her body, to see if she was hiding a man in bed with her. "Get away from me!" She took a deep breath and looked at the first man. "Would you mind telling me what this is about?"

The man showed her a photo of Michael, the one she had seen on TV. "Have you ever seen this man before?"

Emily didn't know what these men had been told, so she decided to be as honest as she could. For all she knew, Donald had told them everything she had told him. "Yes, I saw him yesterday in the town where I was staying."

"Did you spend the day with him?"

"What a ridiculous question. Why would I spend the day with a strange man?"

The three men, all of them standing, looked down at her and waited. "All right, I did. I ran into him with my car on Friday night, took him to the doctor, then the next day we spent some time together. He seemed perfectly harmless and I did feel a sense of obligation to him because I could have killed him."

"What happened last night?"

"I saw him on TV, then called my fiancé, Donald Stewart." She looked at the men to see if they knew him but not one flicker of recognition registered on their faces. "Anyway, Donald told me to go to the police and get out of there."

"And did you go to the police?"

Did they think she was going to believe they hadn't checked? Emily looked down at her hands on the covers and tried to bring a blush to her face. "Actually, no I didn't. I, uh, heard a knock on the door, got frightened and climbed out the window." She held up her hand for them to see the long scratch there. "There's a thorn bush growing up the side of the building. I, uh, even left my suitcase behind because I couldn't throw it down. I know it was silly of me, but after what Donald said, I was too frightened to do anything but get *out.*"

For a moment Emily held her breath, wondering if the men were going to believe her story.

"Your story confirms what we already knew, Miss Todd," said the first man, the only one of them who seemed to have vocal cords. "We're sure a man like Michael Chamberlain is long gone but if he should contact you again, show yourself to be as sensible as you have been and call us." He handed her a business card. "Call this number night or day and someone will help you. Good morning," he said, and as quickly as they'd arrived, they left.

Once the room was empty again, Emily fell back against the pillows and felt her body shaking all over. The FBI! Asking *her* questions! Her. Practical, boring, sensible Emily Jane Todd questioned by the FBI. And all because a man who said he was an angel was looking for evil.

Suddenly, Emily sat up straight. "The old Madison

place," she said aloud, and suddenly several things seemed to fall into place. If there was ever an evil place on earth, it was that horrible old house. And of course it had something to do with her, since she'd been researching it for years. She had a file on it that must be a foot thick. No one knew as much about the Madison house and all that had gone on there as she did.

Throwing back the covers, she had one foot on the floor when the door burst open and Michael came running in. "Emily, are you all right? They didn't hurt you, did they?"

He had his hands on her shoulders and was looking down at her nearly nude body as though she were in mortal danger.

"Why are you still here? Those men could come back at any second. They're probably watching this room right now." She was frowning at him.

Michael grinned at her. "You were worried about me, weren't you? So why didn't you tell those men I was hiding in the bushes outside and get rid of me forever?"

"Whatever you are, I don't think you're a killer. Nor are you an angel," she said before he could say another word.

"Ah well, you think that because you mortals have odd ideas of what we angels are like. Now, would you please get out of bed so we can get something to eat? This body is weak with hunger. What an annoyance this is. How often do I have to feed it?"

"Once a month," she said, smiling sweetly. "And give it something to drink every two weeks."

Laughing, he said, "Up! Get dressed." Then he

stood back and looked at her. "It's very strange seeing a person's body through mortal eyes. Usually, I just see spirits, but seeing you like that is quite interesting."

Emily flung the covers back over her body. "Go outside and wait for me. Keep hidden and don't let anyone see you."

"My wish is your command," he said then looked puzzled at his own words.

Emily couldn't help laughing. "Go on, get out of here," she said as she threw a pillow at his retreating form.

# Chapter 6

*N*O, NO, NO AND DOUBLE NO," EMILY WAS SAYING. SHE was sitting with Michael in a back booth at a truck stop eating blueberry pancakes. At least she was trying to, but he kept eating half her food as well as his. He said he was trying to decide whether strawberry pancakes or blueberry were better.

She lowered her voice. Not that anyone was looking at them. From the look of the men in this place, half of them were wanted by the FBI. "I am *not* going to take you home with me. I am not going to hide you. I am not going to take you to the old Madison place so you can snoop around. That house is falling down and it's dangerous. Not to mention that it's haunted."

"Haunted? What's that?"

"Ghosts! Stop that! That's my pancake. Yours are

on your plate. Look, it's not polite to eat off another person's plate. At least not if you aren't lovers."

Immediately, he looked hurt. "But, Emily, I've loved you for thousands of years. I love all the people in my care. Well, maybe I love some of them more than others but I make a supreme effort."

"We're not lovers. Actually, we're not 'in love,' either."

"Ah, I see. Sex. We're back to that."

"No we're not. We can't get back to something we never got to in the first place and *stop* doing this to me!"

"What?" he asked innocently.

She narrowed her eyes at him until he grinned.

"All right, back to the subject. Emily, love, I need to see that house. If it's as you say it is, then maybe it's what I was sent here to fix."

"What are you going to do? Perform a séance?"

She could tell by his expression that he had no idea what that was. "You sit around a table, usually with a person who is a spirit medium, then you call a spirit up and ask questions and—" She stopped because his mouth was definitely twitching in laughter.

"What have I said that is so very hilarious to you?" she hissed. "And you take one more bite of *my* pancakes and you'll lose a hand." She held her fork aloft, ready to jab.

"I'm just trying to understand what you said," he told her, and she could see that he was working hard to keep from laughing out loud.

"No you're not. You're not trying to understand anything. You just want to make fun of me." Grabbing her purse, she started to leave the table, but he caught her hand and instantly she calmed and sat back down.

"Emily, I don't mean to offend you—I really don't. Why can't you just look at me as though I come from a different country and my ways are very different from yours?"

"Another country?" she said. "You come from an insane asylum and I'm not going to help you do anything whatever on this earth."

She sat there with her hands folded across her chest, knowing full well that she looked like a sulky little girl, but she couldn't help herself. He seemed to bring out the worst in her.

"Hear that, Mr. Moss?" Michael said casually. "To talk to a spirit we have to sit around a table and call you up. You know, I think I remember seeing a few of those things. Emily, you loved them back in . . . when was that? I think it was about 1890. Or was it 1790? What do you think, Mr. Moss?"

"Very funny," Emily said, her arms still folded. "Talk to your imaginary friend and make fun of me."

"Are you going to eat that?"

"Yes!" Emily said, although she was full and didn't want another bite. But she stabbed what was left of her pancakes and put a huge bite in her mouth.

"Emily," Michael said softly. "I don't mean to make fun of you, but I think I see things differently than you do. There are spirits everywhere. It's just that some have bodies and some don't. There really is no difference."

"And I guess you can see the ones without bodies," she said, her voice dripping sarcasm.

Michael didn't answer but looked down at what was left of his pancake.

"Well?!" she demanded. "Can you or can't you?"

His head came up, his eyes fierce. "Yes, of course I can. And it amazes me that you can't. Can't you see Mr. Moss sitting right here beside me?"

In spite of herself, Emily glanced to his right, then back at him. "I guess you're going to tell me that this truck stop is haunted and there's a ghost sitting next to you."

"Mr. Moss says he is. . . ." Michael paused, then smiled. "I don't understand this but he says he prefers to be called 'anatomically challenged.' He's a very nice man, and he says that the next time we come here we have to try the sausages. Maybe we could order some now."

"No!" Emily said. "You're going to get fat. Would you please stick to the subject?" She would have died rather than ask him such a dumb question, but she couldn't resist. "Are you telling me that you're talking to a ghost right now?"

"Well, more listening. He says it's been a long time since anyone's been in here who can hear him. He says this modern world is really sad because no one believes he exists so when he tries to talk they don't listen. The only people who listen are ones who are crazy or on lots of drugs." Michael leaned toward Emily. "He says being a ghost in modern America is a very lonely life."

"Well," Emily said slowly, looking about the restaurant. "I think I need to use the ladies' room, then we'd better head out."

"What's a powder?"

"A what?"

"Mr. Moss says you're going to take a powder."

"That's right. I'm going to go to the powder room."

"He says you're going to run away and leave me here because you think I'm crazy. He says he sees it all the time. If that's so, Emily, I wish you well in your life and hope you have every happiness."

"You are a truly horrible person," she said, glaring at Michael. If he'd protested or demanded that she stay, she could have walked out, but how could she leave a man who wished her happiness? "I'm going to the rest room now and I want you to pay the check while I'm gone, and when I return I don't want to hear one word about Mr. Moss."

Michael turned to his right. "Sorry. Maybe next time."

Emily didn't respond but turned on her heel and walked toward the rest room.

When Emily returned, Michael was waiting for her outside the restaurant. It annoyed her that he was becoming so familiar. Sometimes she felt like she had spent more time with this man than she had with Donald. But then she and Donald were always working on one of his stories.

"I think we need to talk," she said seriously, planning to start with the speech she had written in her head in the few minutes they had been apart. He couldn't go home with her, so she had to leave him somewhere else. They just had to figure out where was safe.

Safe for a man wanted by the FBI, the Mafia, an

enraged wife and the media. Not to mention bounty hunters and—

"Worried about me, are you?" Michael said, and seemed to be extraordinarily pleased at this idea.

"Not in the least," she answered, walking through trucks parked in front and back of the restaurant. She had parked her little white Mazda more in the woods than in the lot, hiding it behind the trailer of an eighteen-wheeler that looked as though it hadn't been moved in many years.

"It's just that we have to figure out what to *do* with you. You can't possibly go home with me, so we have to come up with somewhere else you can go. Or someone you can call to help you. Or maybe you can—"

"No!" Michael said sternly as Emily reached out to put her key in the car door lock.

"You don't have to unlock every door," she said in disgust. "I know you want to practice your magic but—"

Abruptly, harshly, Michael pulled her away from the car, and with her back against his chest, she could feel his heart pounding. A glance up at his face revealed that he was glaring at the car as though it were something malevolent.

"W-what is it?" she whispered looking back at the car. Her own heart was beating hard and fast.

"There's something wrong with that machine," he said. "It has dark colors around it."

It took her a moment to realize what he meant. "An aura? Machines don't have auras."

He didn't bother to answer. "I want you to go into those trees—far into them—get down on the ground, cover your head and wait for me. Do you understand?"

He had his hands on her shoulders, and when he looked down at her, his eyes were burning; all Emily did was nod yes. Then he released her and she walked quickly toward the woods, giving her car a wide berth. And once she hit the tree line, she couldn't stop herself from running until she stumbled and fell against some shrub oaks. Obediently, she got down on the ground and covered her head with her arms.

It seemed like hours went by, but when she dared lift her head so that she could look at her watch, she saw that only a few minutes had passed. When fifteen minutes went by and she'd heard nothing, she began to feel foolish. What in the world was wrong with her? Why had she so blindly obeyed the orders of a man she knew to be insane? A car having bad colors around it, indeed! Did he think she was born yesterday?

But in spite of her reasoning, she stayed where she was. When she heard a noise in the bushes, she put her arms over her head again.

"It's me," Michael said, "and I think the danger is past. Is this a bomb?"

Emily looked up to see Michael standing there. In his hand appeared to be sticks of dynamite with wires dangling from them. "I . . . I think so," she said. "But my experience with bombs is limited. Shouldn't you, ah, get rid of it?"

"How, exactly?"

"I have no idea. Did you find it on my car?" She almost choked on the last word, as her throat was suddenly very dry.

"Hooked to the bottom. Mr. Moss told me which wires to cut so the machine wouldn't explode."

"And you," she said, looking up at him.

"No, I'm afraid I didn't know which wires so he—"

"No, I meant that you would have exploded as well as the car."

"Ah, yes, this body would have." He took his eyes off the thing in his hand to look at her. "That would have been a shame, since I would have been sent back to work without finding out what evil is around you."

"I think maybe you're holding the evil," she said. "Couldn't you get rid of that thing?"

"Yes. Mr. Moss says there's an old mine shaft around here that needs filling up. If I throw this down it, it will explode and fill the hole. Emily, stay here and stop worrying about me. Mr. Moss knows what he's doing."

"Great," she said. "A ghost showing an angel what to do with sticks of dynamite. I can't imagine what I was worried about."

Chuckling, Michael went off into the trees while Emily stayed on the ground and waited. It seemed like a long time before she felt the earth rumble under her body and knew that the explosion had taken place. Only after Michael reappeared and she knew that he was safe did she get off the ground. Even then, her legs betrayed her, and she would have fallen if he hadn't caught her.

"It's all right," he said softly, holding her in his arms while he caressed her hair. "Really, Emily, we're both safe now. You can relax."

"Who did that? Did they want to kill you that much?"

"That bomb was for you, not me," he said softly.

It took her a moment to comprehend what he was saying. "Me?" She pulled away from him. "Are you telling me that someone wanted to blow *me* up?"

"Yes."

She stepped away from him, and the absurdity of his words gave her her strength back. "So I guess it had my name on it and that's how you know. Of course, the fact that you're wanted by every criminal in the country could have nothing to do with a bomb, could it?"

"You'd think that," he said, frowning in thought. "But I could feel that the bomb was meant for you. Who would want to kill you, Emily?"

"No one. Absolutely no one in the world, that's who." Turning, she started back toward her car. Right now she didn't care whether there was another bomb attached to it or not.

Michael caught her arm. "You can't go home alone, if you're thinking of leaving me here. Emily, someone wants to kill you, and whether you believe that or not makes no difference. I know the truth."

"Release me or I'll scream," she said.

"Then what will happen?" he asked. She could see that he was not being facetious, but merely curious.

"Aaarrgh!" she growled. She jerked away from him, then started walking again.

But when she got to the car she hesitated before putting her key in the lock.

"It's safe now," he said from the other side. "Really, the machine has a nice clean color around it now."

Emily gave him a look of disgust, then put her key

in the lock and turned. She didn't realize she'd been holding her breath until she let it out. Since all doors opened when hers did, Michael slid into the passenger side and put his seat belt on.

"You can't go with me," she started. But he wasn't listening to her; he was staring out the window. "Looking at dead people?" she asked nastily. "Remind me not to visit any graveyards with you."

"Every spirit leaves a part of himself at his grave," Michael said absently, then looked at her. "Emily, how long does it take to drive to your house?"

"An hour and a half."

"Is there another route that will take longer?"

"Through the mountains can take all day, but I want to go home!" she said fiercely, not thinking about what she was going to do with *him* if he was still with her.

"Then let's go the long way. I think we need to talk."

"About what?" she asked warily.

"I want you to tell me everything about yourself. Everything mortal that you can think of. We have to find out who tried to kill you."

"First of all, no one has tried to kill *me*. I'm the one who is practical, boring, sensible and unadventurous, remember? Who in their right mind would want to kill me? And, besides, why would it matter to an angel if I were killed? Not that you are one, that is. But people die hideous deaths every day, so what does one small-town librarian matter?"

"I don't know," he said thoughtfully. "I'm beginning to ask those same questions myself. Why was I sent here? What evil surrounds you that would compel an archangel to send someone down to look into it?" Turning, he looked at her profile. "But something is very wrong if anyone would want to destroy such a lovely person as you. Emily, you are a good, kind person. Maybe I shouldn't say so, but I have always liked you the best of all my people. You've done so many good things in your life and have loved and helped so many people that you've attained quite a high level, you know."

"No, I didn't know," she said, part of her thinking that what he was saying was ridiculous, the other part flattered. Maybe when an angel said you were good it didn't mean the same thing as it did when they called you that in seventh grade when you refused to smoke what they were offering.

Emily swung the car a hard right when she saw a sign that said SCENIC ROUTE. They did need time to talk, so maybe a trip through the mountains was as good a time as any.

# Chapter 7

By the time they reached the little grocery store in the mountains, Emily felt as though she'd been cross-examined in a murder trial. Michael sure could ask questions! And in spite of herself, she was becoming involved.

Once she got over her anger at thinking of the absurdity of someone trying to kill *her*, she began to look at all of it as the plot to a murder mystery. Except that, try as they might, they could come up with no reason for anyone to want to murder her.

"No, no," Emily was saying as she picked up a red plastic basket at the front of the little store. Except for a man dozing behind the counter, there was no one else in the wooden-floored country store, so she felt free to talk to Michael over the shelves. "I still think you're wrong," she said fiercely. "I think *you* are the target, not me." She glanced at the man behind the counter, but his head was back against his chair and his mouth was open.

"I know what I know and I know that bomb was meant for you. What's this?" he asked, holding up a bottle of heavily sugared fruit juice.

"Nasty, horrible, vile stuff. It'll rot your teeth on the way down."

"Sounds great," he said, dropping it into her basket. "The problem is that you have your mind made up and won't look at alternatives."

"Okay, so what would be the motive of anyone wanting to kill me rather than you? I'm not rich and have no chance of an inheritance. I certainly don't *know* anything that would make someone want to kill me. I've never seen a crime. So why would anyone want to knock me off?"

"Jealousy?"

At that Emily smiled broadly. "Right. My two lovers are ready to kill each other over me. Put that back! Why do you always pick up the most non-nutritious things in the store? That pink icing will make your intestines glue shut."

Michael gave a one-sided grin then dropped the cakes into her basket. "Look at this! It's cold in this case. What's in these cartons?"

Emily sighed. "Get one of them that says 'frozen yogurt,' not the other kind."

"Ah, I see. Emily, I'm beginning to think that this word 'cream' is a curse word to you. Now, where were we?"

"You were telling me that someone was trying to

kill me to keep me from publishing the Duke's love letters."

Michael looked puzzled for a moment, then grinned. "You want a title in your next life? I could arrange it. Usually it's not considered a reward. Lots of temptation and lots of responsibility. And not a whole lot of love."

"No, I don't want a title. I want—" She narrowed her eyes at him. "So why don't you want to talk about this anymore?"

"I think we just have to find out who wants to blow you up and no amount of talking is going to figure it out. It does amaze me that you don't *know* something like that."

She put the filled basket on the counter while Michael looked at the candy bars and gum in front of the cash register. "Those are all good for you, so get as many as you like," she said sweetly as she started to empty the basket. "Not all of us have the advantages that you have of being able to see what's not there. We poor mortals live our boring little lives and don't see evil spirits everywhere."

The man behind the counter woke up and started to ring up the purchases as Michael put half a dozen candy bars on the counter. "What's this 'caramel'? If you're referring to Mr. Moss, he wasn't any more evil than . . . than this man," Michael said, smiling at the man behind the counter, then he dropped another four candy bars onto the counter. "And, Emily, dear, you are the worst liar I have ever seen," he said companionably, referring to her attempt to get him to not purchase the candy bars.

An hour later, they had pulled over at a rest stop and were eating their sandwiches—Michael was sampling the junk food he'd bought—when Emily turned to him and said, "If those men found you—or me—at that truck stop, then they must know who I am and where I live."

"Yes," he said gently, stretching out the coconut-covered pink icing of a cake he'd bought.

She sat down at the picnic table heavily. "They're sure to be following us," she said, knowing without a doubt that *he* had blocked her from seeing this very obvious fact.

"No, not anymore."

"And you're sure of that, are you?" she said, leaning across the table from him. "You act like you know what's going on, but you didn't know that my car was being fitted with a *bomb.*"

"True, I didn't." He looked at her, now having discarded the icing but enjoying the chocolate cake inside. "The truth is that I have no idea what I can and cannot do. I know my powers when I'm at home because I've had years of experience, but here I find I'm extremely limited. For one thing, I can't see the future." A frown creased his brow as he looked off at the view that the picnic table overlooked. "I was frightened this morning because I couldn't see that everything was going to be all right about that bomb. I could feel that something was wrong with the car, but I didn't know what it was. For all I knew it could have had a broken. . . ." He made a back-and-forth motion with his hand.

"Windshield wiper."

"Yes. But then I don't think something so minor

would have made the aura of the car turn dark like that. But what do I know? I'd never ridden in a car before I went with you."

"But now you can sense that no one is following us, right?"

"Yes. They put the bomb on your car and they left. I could tell that much." He smiled. "So far, my powers seem to be limited to being able to do things with you. I can make your car door open, but I tried to open other locked car doors and couldn't. And only *your* hotel door opens to me. Isn't that odd?"

"Being able to open any locked door is odd," she said. "And being able to see auras is odd. Not to mention ghosts. And then there's that little girl at the ice cream parlor. And the bullet in your head, plus the ones in your body. And there seem to be a million things about everyday life that you don't know. And—"

"Be careful, Emily, or you'll be telling me that you believe me."

"I believe that you *think* you can see ghosts and you *think* you can—"

"So what would you do with me if I really were an angel?"

"Protect you," she said without thinking. But when she said it she blushed and looked down at her half-finished candy bar, which she couldn't believe she was eating in the first place. Angels were protectors, not the other way around.

"So what would make you believe? A miracle? A vision? What?"

"I don't know," she said as she stood and began putting food away and avoiding his eyes.

"What is it called when a person stands by the roadside and asks others for a ride?"

"Hitchhiking," she said quickly, then gave him a stern look. "And don't you think about doing it. It's dangerous."

"If you leave me somewhere I will hitchhike to your town and look for the evil that surrounds you on my own. No one will know you've ever met me."

"And you'll be reported to the police within ten minutes of stepping into town," she said abruptly. She put the food into the trunk of the car, but Michael didn't move. Instead, he sat at the table and looked at the view, sipping his awful, sugary fruit drink that she could tell he didn't like but wasn't going to admit it.

I should leave him, she thought. I should just drive off and leave him now. He is not my responsibility and I don't need more complications in my absolutely perfect life. For that's the way she saw her life—perfect. She had everything she wanted: a job she loved, a man she loved, friends—and she'd just been honored by the National Library Association. The only thing left that she wanted was to marry Donald and have a couple of children.

But she didn't leave the man sitting at the table; instead, she went back and sat at the opposite end of the bench and stared at the view.

"Maybe you could find out something about the Madison House for me," she said slowly. "You see, I'd rather like to write a book about what happened there. I've done a lot of research already, but something is missing."

"So what's the story?" Michael said as though he

weren't interested at all. "Mortal spirits always have a reason for not leaving this earth."

"I've heard the story all my life. We children used to frighten each other with taunts that Old Man Madison was going to get us, but in the last years I've . . . well, I don't know, I've become more compassionate."

"You've always been willing to help people."

She opened her mouth to tell him to stop pretending that he'd known her a long time, but why should she turn down a compliment? "It's a simple story really and one I'm sure happened many times in the past. A beautiful young woman was in love with a handsome, but poor, young man and her father refused them permission to marry. Instead, the father forced the girl to marry a friend of his, a rich Mr. Madison—old enough to be her father. As far as I can tell, they lived together in polite misery for ten years, then the young man who loved the woman came back to town. No one knows what happened, whether she sneaked out to see him or what. But her husband killed the young man in a jealous rage."

"Unfortunately, I've seen that too often," Michael said seriously. "Jealousy is a major failing of you mortals."

"Oh? I can't wait to tell *Mickey* that," she said, pointedly, reminding him of just one of the names he'd called Donald.

Michael grinned. "So now I guess your old Mr. Madison haunts the house."

"Someone does. After the murder, there was a trial and a servant of the husband's testified that he'd seen his master kill the young man. It was his testimony that convicted the man, because the body was never found. Anyway, Mr. Madison was hanged, the servant later jumped to his death from a window of the house, and the widow never left the house again and finally went mad."

"So the spirit in the house could be. . . ." He trailed off, thinking.

"Could be the murdered young man, the old man who did the murdering, the unhappy servant who sent his master to his death, or the mad wife. Take your pick."

"Emily, what do you think this has to do with evil surrounding you?"

"I, ah. . . ." She looked down at her hands.

"Come on, out with it. What have you done?"

Her head came up and she glared at him defiantly. "I don't know really. But I've done *something.*"

When Michael saw the fear in her eyes, he pushed his bottle of juice toward her. She took a sip, then grimaced at the too-sweet taste. "All right, I think you should spill your intestines," he said.

"Guts. Spill my guts."

"Whatever. Tell me what you've done that has been horrible enough to bring an angel to earth to solve the problem."

She looked down at the bottle and absently started to peel the label. "Do you believe in evil spirits?" When he didn't respond, she looked up at him and saw that he had one eyebrow raised in disbelief.

"Okay, so you do. But most people nowadays don't."

"Yes, I know. You mortals now believe in 'science.' Most of you think the person who does funny things on the stock exchange is an example of evil." Michael's voice was loaded with contempt. "Go on, tell me what you did."

"I was going to talk to Donald about it this weekend," she said. "That was part of the reason I was so angry when he didn't show up. I felt I needed someone to talk to."

"If you think he'd be a better person to discuss evil spirits with than me, please do so," Michael said stiffly.

"How did you get to be an angel with your attitude?"

"I was made for my job. Are you going to get on with this or are you too afraid?"

She took a deep breath. "I went to the house. That's all. I just went there to look at the place. I took a sketch pad so I could make a floor plan of the house, because I am trying to write about what happened. It was full daylight and even though the windows are dirty, I could see quite well."

She took another sip of the awful drink.

When Emily didn't say any more, Michael looked into the distance. "Let me guess. You opened something that was sealed."

"Sort of," she said.

"A box? No? You. . . ." He looked at her very hard. "Emily! You tore down a wall?"

"Well, it was half falling down anyway and I could see something behind it. Whoever put that wall up was not a very good carpenter," she said defensively.

"So what came out?"

"I don't know," she said with anger. "*I* can't see ghosts. All I know is something whooshed past me and I nearly fainted from the nasty feel of it. It took me a while to recover myself, but when I could walk again I left the house."

He gave her a one-sided smile. "Walked out quietly, did you?"

"Make fun of me all you want, but since that day, about two weeks ago, some very unpleasant things have happened in Greenbriar. A house burned down, a couple with four children are getting a divorce, there have been three car wrecks just outside town and—"

"Do you think you can attribute those things to an evil demon?"

"I don't know," she said, standing. "It's just a feeling I have now that when I'm in the library alone at night, that I'm not alone. And I don't like who or what is in there with me. Sometimes . . . sometimes, I think I hear him, or her, laughing. And . . . and it just seems that lately everyone in town gets into arguments easier than they used to."

She fully expected this man to laugh at her. She knew Donald would. But that wasn't a reflection on his character, because she'd tried to tell Irene the same thing and her friend had howled with laughter.

"Aren't you going to say anything?" she asked, trying to sound angry, but not succeeding.

"I can't see what this has to do with someone trying to blow up your car with you in it. But then demons can agitate others to do dreadful things. Their stock-in-trade is chaos and confusion so maybe. . . ." He looked up at her. "Exactly what did you do to this fellow to make him follow you?"

"Me? Why would he follow me? As far as I can tell, he's after the whole town. And why would an evil spirit want to follow me? I'm practical, sensible and altogether quite ordinary. That is, when I'm not being *good,*" she said in disgust.

"From what I've seen of your life the last few days, you lead anything but an ordinary life. In fact, your life is so extraordinary that you've had an angel sent down to save you—and just in time, if I do say so myself. Why, Emily, if you were less good and sensible, you'd be shot for a spy."

What he was saying was so ridiculous that she laughed and felt much better. "Are you ready to go?" she asked.

"With you? I thought you were throwing me out. I thought you were going to make me hike all the way back. I thought—"

"Liar!" she said, smiling. "You know, I think I'm going to talk to God about His angels. I think you guys need some rethinking."

"Oh?" Michael asked. "I guess we should be like those angels you put on TV where we do nothing but mouth platitudes and talk in parables."

"I could use some parables," she said, opening the car door. "I could certainly use some angelic wisdom. Listen, why don't you tell me who some of your other clients are, or have been?" she said, then when he smiled, she narrowed her eyes. "Make it up, like you do all the rest of what you tell me."

Michael seemed unperturbed by her accusations as

he got into the seat beside her. "Let's see. I think you mortals like kings and queens, that sort of thing, right?"

"Stop trying to provoke me and tell me a story or two," she said as she started the car.

"Marie Antoinette. She was mine. Poor dear. She lives on a farm now and has half a dozen kids and she's much, much happier. She was dreadful as a queen."

"So tell me everything," Emily said as she pulled onto the highway.

# Chapter 8

GREENBRIAR WAS NESTLED INTO AN ODD LITTLE LAND formation—a tea cup someone had called it long ago, and the name had stuck. Unfortunately, most people now referred to it as in, "I can't wait to get out of the bottom of this tea cup." Whereas Emily thought of the place as peaceful, most everyone else thought of it as boring. The most boring town in America was what some called it. They made jokes that Sheriff Thompson's gun had rusted to his holster from lack of use.

The way into the town was down a steep slope and the way out was up a hill that only the hardiest of bicyclists could love. The other two sides were steep mountains that could only be scaled with heavy ropes and steel rigging.

At the bottom of this formation was Greenbriar, where two-hundred sixteen and two-thirds people lived (Mrs. Shirley was pregnant again), and everyone said that what made people stay there was inertia: They were just too lazy to move elsewhere. Except for the people who worked in the few shops in town, everyone else worked in the city. Often, they were like Donald and stayed away all week but came back to Greenbriar on weekends.

One of the few things in the town that drew outsiders was the library. In the last century, Andrew Carnegie had happened to visit the tiny town of Greenbriar, thought it beautiful and designated one of his beautiful libraries to be built there. And it was this lovely old building that Emily called hers, the place where she did what she could to harass state and federal governments to give her money to buy books for her little library. She wrote authors and begged; she constantly plagued publishers. She went to the American Booksellers Convention each year and lugged home masses of free books so she could share them with her patrons.

As a result of Emily's nonstop efforts, the Greenbriar Library was the best small library in the state. People drove many miles to hear storytellers, to listen to authors read from their books, to see displays of book art, and anything else that Emily could think of to attract people to her library.

Maybe to the other residents Greenbriar was a place they wanted to leave, but not to Emily. She loved the town and the people in it as though they were her family—which they were. With both her parents dead, no siblings, and no other relatives, all she had was Donald and this town.

But now she seemed to have the man sitting beside

her, she thought as she glanced at him. He was engrossed in the music on the radio and kept changing stations and asking Emily questions about everything he heard. She told herself that of course he was just pretending that he'd lived his whole life and never heard country-and-western, or opera, or even rock and roll.

As she drove into Greenbriar, it was late and she was glad it was dark, as she didn't want anyone to see her with this stranger in her car. It would be better all around if no one saw him—even if he weren't recognized—because, well, Donald might not exactly understand.

Her apartment was at the near end of Greenbriar and she was glad of that. It was in a large building, at least large for Greenbriar. The ground-floor contained a grocery store, a post office and a hardware store. The upstairs had been divided into two apartments; one was hers and the other Donald's.

Soon after they met, Donald had decided he wanted a place to get away from the city on weekends. He also knew it would look better on his political resume if he came from a small town—and you couldn't get much smaller than Greenbriar. So, he'd rented the apartment over the hardware store.

After he began coming to the small town on weekends, the two of them had been inseparable. Well, at least inseparable in Greenbriar. Only once had Emily been into the city with him to see where he worked, to see his city apartment with its walls of mirrors and to meet the people with whom he worked. That once had been enough. She had felt out of place and useless, what with all those tall, thin women wearing black suits with wide-shouldered jackets and tiny skirts. Emily in her brown-and-white dress had felt out of place, a bit like a milk maid who had wandered into a palace.

After that, she and Donald had never spoken of it, but it seemed to be agreed between them that she'd stay in Greenbriar and be there when he came home on weekends. "My weekend wife," he often called her. "Just so there isn't a Mrs. Week*day*," she'd joke. Then he'd say that Emily wore him out so bad on weekends that he needed all week to rest, and they'd laugh together.

So now she was entering her apartment, with Donald's just across the hall, with a man who was actually a stranger to her. Except that, sometimes, she looked at him and felt that she'd known him forever.

Driving the car to the back of the building, she parked in the deep shadows. It would be better if no one in town realized that she'd returned. After all, she was supposed to be spending a long, romantic weekend with the man she loved. It had been long, all right, and anything but romantic—unless one counted bullets and bombs and leaping from windows as romantic.

"Yes, this is it," Michael said. His voice was almost reverential. "I've seen this place a thousand times as you've driven in here. Or when you walk home from the library."

"You've never been here before," she said more sternly than she meant to, but at the moment she was feeling a bit nervous. Whatever had made her bring this man home with her? And now that she had him, what was she going to do with him?

"It will be all right," Michael said as he put his hand over hers, and, as always, Emily instantly felt calmer.

Turning, she gave him a bit of a smile before getting out of the car.

In spite of his words, she was not prepared for Michael's reaction when he saw the apartment. He nearly pushed past her at the door, reached exactly the right place to turn on the switch for the table lamp, then started walking about, his eyes wide with wonder.

"Yes, yes," he said, "it's all here. It hasn't changed at all. There's your desk where you write letters to your mother. Emily, I was sorry for your pain when she died, but she's waiting for you and you'll see her again later. Oh, and this is the table where you beat out that man at the auction. You were so happy to get it. And here are your own books. I see you sitting. . . ."

He turned about the room. "Where's that long thing you lie on to read?"

Emily's mouth was a grim little line. "I put the chaise in Donald's apartment. Look, I don't like that you've been spying on me. I think—"

"Spying on you? Why, Emily, that's the farthest thing from my mind. I take care of you, and how could I do that if I don't watch over you? Oh, this," he said, picking up a glass paperweight. "I remember when you bought this. You were thirteen and you thought—"

"I was twelve," she said tightly, taking the paperweight from his hands and putting it back onto the table.

But he seemed oblivious to her growing anger as he

moved to the bedroom. For a moment, Emily stayed where she was, not sure whether to be angry or to be amazed.

When she heard him open a drawer in her bedroom, she made her decision. With hands on hips, lips tight, she stalked to her bedroom and saw he was looking into her closet, running his hands over her clothes.

"Get out of there," she snapped, then shut the door so quickly she almost caught his fingers.

Michael was unperturbed. "You should wear that red dress, Emily. It looked great on you. I was the one who got you to buy it."

"Do you spy on *all* your clients like this?" she said, then started to correct herself. "Not that you have clients but—" It was difficult to be furious when you had to add so many qualifiers to every statement.

Abruptly, he stopped moving and looked down at her bed. For a moment he touched her white quilt that she'd bought years ago at a tiny country store high in the mountains. "Emily, I feel odd. I feel very strange. I feel. . . ."

When he turned to look at her, there was no mistaking the heat in his eyes.

Instinctively, she backed away from him. "Look, I think you'd better leave. Or I'll leave. Or—"

Turning away, he hid his eyes from her. "So that's what it's like," he said softly. "I understand you mortals a bit better now."

There was no mistaking what he was referring to. "I don't think you should stay here."

His head came up and his eyes burned intensely.

"Emily, you'll never have to be afraid of me. I promise."

As quickly as his expression had become hot, it changed back to cool and he smiled. "Now, let's get some rest. These bodies of yours are weak. They constantly need refueling and resting."

"Where are you going to sleep?" she asked, her voice betraying her nervousness.

"Not where I'd like to," he said, and his grin was so cocky she laughed and the laugh made her relax.

*"Stop* flirting with me. I'll pull out the sofa in the living room and you can sleep there. And tomorrow morning we'll go see the house. And after that, you can leave."

"Of course, Emily, I'll leave whenever you want me to. I never want to impose on you."

"Stop it," she half shouted. "So help me, if you don't stop this saintly act of yours, I'll—"

"I'm no saint, Emily," he said, eyes twinkling. "I'm an—" He broke off, then grinned. "I'm a very sleepy man. Now don't you mortals do something to the couch before sleeping on it?"

As Emily went to get the sheets, again she asked herself what she was doing.

She woke to a hand on her hair, and instinctively she snuggled up to it. She had barely opened her eyes when she saw a handsome, dark-haired man with enormous wings framing his body. "Michael," she whispered, then smiled as she felt a kiss beside her lips. "Are *all* angels named Michael?" she murmured sleepily.

"Just the best of us."

It took her a moment to awake, but suddenly she sat up and bumped her head into his as he sat back on the bed.

"What do you think you're doing?" she hissed at him.

"I came in to wake you up and you were lying there and you looked so very beautiful and—" His eyes were wide. "Emily, I think I've just given in to temptation."

He looked so shocked that she couldn't keep from laughing. It was too early in the morning to be angry. "Wasn't there another angel who did that? And didn't he get thrown out of you-know-where?"

"Emily, this is no laughing matter. I'm not supposed to give into temptation. I . . . I could get into trouble."

In spite of herself, Emily was pleased at the look of horror on his face and his words. What woman hadn't dreamed of being so sexy she tempted a good-looking man into sin? "Oh well," she said, then sat up and stretched, knowing her nightgown pulled against her breasts when she did.

Michael raised one eyebrow. "I think an evil demon followed you home and right now he has taken possession of your soul. Aren't you a married woman?"

"Engaged," she said quickly. "That's all." Then when she saw that he'd tricked her into nearly renouncing Donald, she threw a pillow at him. "Get out of here! I have to take a shower and get dressed."

His face was serious. "There's no need to throw me out as I've certainly seen you take a shower before. My favorite part is when you rub lotion up and down your legs, and what is that pink thing you smooth across your round little—"

"Out! Get out of here! Now, before I turn you in to the police for being a peeping tom."

Michael stopped by the door. "He was one of mine too. Why don't I tell you about him while you shower?" He had just managed to pull the door closed when another pillow came flying at him. She could hear him laughing as he headed toward the kitchen.

It was while she was in the shower that she began to ask herself what, exactly, she was going to do with this man. As she looked back over the last days, it seemed that she had tried to get rid of him. Or had she? But every time she tried to get away, something—some force—held her back.

I should call Donald and ask him what to do, she thought, but she could easily imagine his wrath. "You're harboring one of the ten-most-wanted criminals in your apartment, Emily? The FBI is searching for this man and you're planning on visiting a haunted house with him? What's that? You say he's an angel and he's been your guardian spirit for centuries? Oh well, in that case I understand."

No, Emily couldn't quite visualize Donald being so understanding. But then, he was right, wasn't he?

On the other hand, what was she supposed to do with this man? Turn him out on the street and have someone turn him in? No doubt there was a huge reward out for him, and anyone would love to have it. But then she couldn't keep on waking up with him kissing her, now could she?

She could almost hear her mother saying, "For once, Emily, make a decision using your head instead of your heart." Taking a stray man to live with her, however temporary, was indeed a decision made with her heart.

But of course she did want to find out anything she could about the old Madison mansion. Was it really haunted, or was it just people's imagination? And if it was haunted, by whom? And what happened to the body of the man Captain Madison had been executed for killing?

She turned off the shower, stepped out and grabbed a towel. But how would a man wanted by the FBI know anything about whether or not there were ghosts in a house? she thought angrily. Only if she believed his story of being an angel would she believe—

She ran a towel roughly over her hair then picked up her hair dryer. Michael Chamberlain was *not* an angel. He merely had some clairvoyant abilities and was quite good at making people believe what he wanted them to.

However, as she put on a little lip gloss, she thought how it would be nice to visit the old Madison mansion with another person. Donald had laughed at her when she'd asked him to go with her and all of her women friends had flatly refused to go. Which was of course her own fault, for having told them what happened when she'd visited the house alone.

Yes, she thought, she'd get him to go with her to the house then she'd figure out how to get rid of him—tonight. She'd come up with something tonight, because she had to go to work tomorrow and he couldn't stay in her apartment alone.

Feeling good that she'd at last made a logical decision, she went into her bedroom and pulled on a pair of jeans and a lightweight sweater. Ordinary clothes, she thought. Except well, maybe, the sweater had shrunk in the wash and was an itty-bit too snug and the jeans had a tear along the bottom curve of her buttocks where she'd caught them on a nail a few years ago. Since then, they'd been shoved to the back of her closet. Donald didn't like her to wear jeans— and certainly not jeans with three-inch-long tears in the seat.

Feeling a bit nervous about her attire and thinking she really should change into something more fitting for her age, she opened the door only to halt in shock. Her tidy kitchen looked as though the refrigerator had exploded. Food was everywhere; cans were half-opened; a carton of eggs was overturned, yolks running down the front of a cabinet. On the stove was a skillet smoking as the contents burned. At the exact moment Emily saw the mess, the smoke alarm went off.

"It looks so easy when you do it," Michael shouted, standing in the middle of the mess and looking at her in astonishment. He glanced up toward the alarm. "Will the police come now?"

Emily ran to the utility closet to get the broom to turn the alarm off.

"Emily, you're so pretty when you're angry," Michael was saying from the passenger-side of the car.

"That's the oldest line in the world," she said, her mouth tight. "And *you* are going to clean up that kitchen."

"Gladly," he said, but he was grinning at her. "Maybe you'll teach me how to cook."

"You won't be here that long. In fact you have to leave tonight."

"Yes of course. Maybe I'll go on a plane. It might be nice to fly in one of these bodies."

"Where would you go?" she said before she thought.

He looked at her, eyes twinkling. "I don't know. Where would *you* like to go?"

She opened her mouth to say Paris, then glanced at him. "*Donald* and I want to go camping in the Rockies."

"Really? That's interesting. I would have thought you were more the art-museum type. I can see you in, uh, Rome. No, wait—in Paris."

Emily didn't make a reply to what he was saying but looked ahead. "There it is," she said, nodding toward the old house on the hill.

Built in 1830, the house was an enormous, rambling place that Emily often thought was reputed to be haunted merely because of its many years of neglect. Nearly every window was broken, and the roof had holes in it here and there. The town owned the place but couldn't afford, and didn't want to bother with, its upkeep.

"Nice house," Michael said, watching her. "But you've always loved big houses, haven't you? Did I tell you about the time you were one of that queen's maids?"

She was *not* going to listen to him or believe him.

"The one with the red hair? Wore a big. . . ." He made a circular motion around his neck.

"A ruff?"

"Lace. Oh, she did love pearls. And you loved her. She was very good to the women who worked for her, if they didn't marry against her will, that is. She thought that if she had to marry her country, so should all the other ladies."

"Elizabeth," Emily said softly, pulling her car to the front of the house. "You're talking about Queen Elizabeth, aren't you?"

"I guess. It's difficult to remember one from the other. I do remember that you liked those houses she lived in."

As she turned off the ignition, she saw that his eyes were sparkling and she knew that he was well aware of how very interested she was in what he was saying. Not that it was possible, but could he have actually *seen* Elizabeth's court? If he had, then maybe he could answer a few questions that had plagued historians for centuries.

"Once again, you're trying to distract me from the matter at hand," she said, leaning back against the seat.

"No, Emily, I'm just—" He didn't finish that sentence and she wondered what he'd meant to say, but she waited and he still didn't finish it.

As she got out of the car, she looked up at the house. There were signs everywhere saying NO TRESPASSING, and there were boards across the broken windows on the ground floor, but they didn't deter her.

When Michael was standing beside her, she tried to become as businesslike as possible. "All I want you to do is walk through the house and use your . . . your abilities to tell me what you feel. Some dreadful things have happened in this house and I think there are probably strong vibrations. I hope you can feel them strong enough to tell me what is in there."

"I see," he said just as seriously. "But am I allowed to *talk* to these vibrations?"

She knew he was making fun of her. "You can run away with them and all of you can live happily ever after for all I care," she said sweetly.

Michael chuckled, then led the way onto the porch. When Emily almost stepped onto a rotten board, he took her elbow and moved her away from it.

From her pocket she took a large key and inserted it into the rusty lock on the front door. "I don't know why anyone bothers locking it, since everyone stays away. Only the local kids get close enough to throw rocks through the windows but, other than that, the place is left alone."

"Afraid of the ghosts, eh?" Michael said. She knew he was laughing at all humans, laughing at their weaknesses and their fears of what they couldn't see.

"Not all of us can be as enlightened as you," she said as she put her shoulder to the door and shoved. "Just because we don't have your powers of perception is no reason to—" She gave a third great heave to the door, but this time Michael reached over her head and placed his hand against the door, and it swung open easily and noiselessly.

Unfortunately, Emily was just preparing for another great shove, so she went tumbling into the entrance hall. She would have fallen flat on her face if Michael hadn't caught her. "You could have warned me," she said, brushing off her side where she'd hit the interior wall. "And why did you let me nearly crush my arm pushing before you did your little magic stunt of opening the door?"

When she looked up at Michael she was stunned at his expression. There was real fear on his face as he slowly turned about the large entrance hall.

"Emily," he said softly, "listen to me and listen very carefully. I want you to leave here and to do it *now.*"

"What's going on?" she asked, looking up at him. If she'd ever seen anyone who could be said to have his hair standing on end, it was Michael.

"Don't ask questions, just *go.*"

"Not until you tell me what's wrong," she said firmly, hands on hips. After all, it was her haunted house, wasn't it?

"This spirit is *very* earthbound, so he has physical power. He means to kill this body." Michael pushed her toward the door.

It took her a moment to understand what he was saying. "You. You're saying that he means to kill *you?*"

He didn't bother to answer as he shoved her through the door. "Only God can destroy a spirit. Bodies are—"

She didn't hear any more because the door that was usually so difficult to open and close slammed shut and cut him off.

Instantly Emily tried to open the door again, but it was locked, and when she tried her key, it wouldn't go inside the lock. "Michael!" she shouted, pounding on the door. "Let me in this instant!" But there was no response from the inside and she could hear nothing. She went to a window and tried to peer between the boards, but she could not so much as see a shadow.

It was then that she heard sounds coming from inside. Her breath caught in her throat as she heard what sounded like something whizzing through the air, then hitting the wooden floor with a sharp *whack!* Frantically, she tried to think what she should do. Call the sheriff—and tell him that a ghost is attacking an angel and he must get here fast and *do* something? Such as? she thought. And if the sheriff did see Michael, wouldn't he notify the FBI?

Emily went back to the door and began pounding on it again, but she had hit it only once when it swung open. Cautiously, with her heart pounding, she stepped into the shadowy hall.

No one was there. In fact, she couldn't hear a sound anywhere in the house. Looking about, she nearly screamed when she almost backed into the swords that were stuck in the entrance hall floor. Exactly where Michael had been standing was what looked to be three cavalry swords, their tips buried two inches into the floor boards. They were still quivering.

Reaching out, she touched the nearest sword. The man who had been hanged for murder had been a captain in the U.S. Cavalry.

Emily didn't think what she was doing—she just shouted, "Michael!" then started running up the stairs to the second floor of the house.

Heedless of whoever or whatever had thrown those swords, Emily went tearing through the house at breakneck speed, throwing open doors to rooms and closets. Years ago she had obtained a copy of the house plans from the architectural firm in Philadelphia, still in business, that had originally designed the house. She had studied them until she could have walked about the house blindfolded.

"Michael, where are you?" she shouted. Her voice echoed off the empty walls, making her feel less alone, less frightened of what she could feel all around her.

It wasn't until she was on the third floor, at the top of the house, that she realized that she was becoming hysterical. Had Michael disappeared as quickly and as easily as he had appeared in her life?

When a strong hand shot out of nowhere and covered her mouth—with an arm wrapping around her midsection so tightly that she could hardly breathe—Emily started kicking and struggling with all her might.

"Ow!" Michael hissed in her ear. "Stop that. Those shoes of yours hurt."

At that she bit his hand; he released her and she whirled on him in a fury. "Where have you been?" she demanded. "I've been searching for you all over this house. You could have answered me and—"

Michael grabbed her hand and started running, pulling her along behind him. "Is there an upstairs? The top of this place? I don't know the word."

"Attic. Yes, there. That room has a staircase hidden in a closet. Captain Madison was very private about his attic."

"Don't mention his name to me," Michael said grimly, still pulling her by the hand as he ran into the bedroom and flung open a door half-hidden by paneling. "Go!" he ordered, half-pushing her upward as he followed close behind her. "Am I right that there's a way out of this room? I can feel that it isn't a closed space."

"Yes," she said. "The captain has a tunnel for escape but I don't know how safe it is after all these years. This house is rotting."

"The mind of that man is rotting," Michael said under his breath as they emerged up the stairs into the attic of the house.

"Oh my," Emily said, looking around. She'd never been up here before. It was full of trunks and old wardrobes and other things that she very much wanted to explore.

"Don't even think about it," Michael said, grabbing her hand again. "Now, where is this exit? We have to get out of this place."

Emily had to concentrate. It was difficult, for against one wall was a glass case full of old books. What was in there? Rare editions? First editions signed by the authors? Maybe even the original manuscript of a classic novel. Maybe—

"Emily!" Michael snapped. "Where is the exit?"

She had to blink a couple of times to bring herself back to the present. "There, I think—under the eaves. But I really don't think it's safe. Maybe we should—" She glanced again at the books with longing.

"Should what? Stay here and be skewered?"

She stood back as he ran his hands along the wall in the eave trying to find a door or an opening. "Found it," he said, then pried it open with his fingertips because he could find no latch. When he reached for Emily, she was within two feet of the glass cabinet and her hand was extended toward the doorknob.

Michael grabbed her, shoved her toward the tiny door, then bent her to her knees. "I'm going first and, so help me, if you stop to look at any material object I'll make you sorry," he said, then disappeared into the darkness behind the little door.

"Alice through the rabbit's hole," she said, taking a deep breath and beginning to crawl.

There were sounds around them. Emily couldn't tell if they were from the creaky old house or other things that she didn't want to think of. "Would you mind telling me what's going on? I thought you were friends with ghosts. Can't you just talk to this man?"

"Put your hand here," he said, reaching out and guiding her. Emily could see nothing at all, not her own body or Michael's, but he didn't seem to distinguish between dark and light. "Good, now, come on. Slowly. Yes, that's right. We'll be out of here soon."

"Would you answer me?" she asked impatiently. She couldn't bear the silence in the darkness; she wanted constant reassurance that he was still with her.

"The spirit in this house wants to kill this body so my spirit will go back where it belongs. I'd prefer not to die until I've found out why I was sent here in the first place."

"I see," she said. His words made her even more frightened, so she tried to replace her fear with anger. "You're an annoying man," she snapped. "Why aren't you afraid?"

"Afraid of what?"

"Death! Everyone is afraid of death."

"Careful there! That board is rotten. Good. You're doing well, Emily. People are afraid of death because they don't know what comes after death. I do. And it's pretty good."

"Someone's trying to kill you and you're talking spiritual philosophy?" she snapped.

"You know of a better time than this to pray?" There was amusement in his voice.

"Actually, no," she said as she felt fear coursing through her. She hated this attic, hated crawling, hated—

"Adrian, where are you?" Michael said rather loudly, as though he meant to distract her from her thoughts.

"Who is Adrian?"

"My boss."

"I thought Archangel Michael was your boss." A cobweb hit her in the face and she started frantically brushing it away, but he turned and gently smoothed the sticky mass from her face.

"No," he said softly, his hands on her face. Emily could feel her fears calming. "Archangel Michael is about two hundred levels above Adrian, and I'm about ten levels below Adrian."

"Oh, I see," she said, but she didn't see. When Michael turned back around and started crawling again, she felt less frantic and much less frightened, but she still didn't want to be in the dark in silence. "What you're describing sounds more like a corporation than Heaven." Before he could respond, she said, "And don't you dare tell me corporations are based on Heaven. That I will *not* believe. *They* are based on the other place."

"Same basic structure. Satan steals ideas."

"What a surprise," she said sarcastically.

He chuckled. "Emily, I'm going to miss you."

"Do you think the person who takes you away will be dead or alive?" she whispered.

Laughing, Michael stepped through an opening, and suddenly there was light. Reaching back, he took her hand. She was at last standing upright, no longer on her knees. And maybe it was seeing light or maybe it was Michael's hand touching hers, but she no longer felt afraid.

"He's here," Michael said. There was relief in his voice.

"Who is?" she asked, and found that she was whispering. If her memory of the house plan was correct, they were now inside a tiny secret room inside the ground floor of Captain Madison's study. The room was smaller than a modern walk-in closet and the door was so hidden that no one in the outside room could see it.

"Adrian is here," Michael said, grinning. "He has no body for this earthly spirit to threaten so there's no need for him to be afraid. Adrian will calm the man and you'll be safe."

She didn't want to think how lightly Michael valued his own life while he seemed to think constantly of hers. "Did you try opening the door?" she asked, reaching past him.

But he caught her hand. "Not yet. It is not time," he said quietly.

There was something strange about his voice, but

Emily was not going to think about it. Better that she make jokes to keep her fear under control. "Great. I'm stuck in a closet with an angel who's in the body of a killer while more angels are outside calming down an angry ghost. That about it?"

"You always were clever, Emily. Clever and beautiful. Emily. . . ."

His voice was so serious that she looked up at him. It was very dark in the closet room, but she could see his outline and she could feel the warmth of his big body so near hers. Her heart was still pounding, but she told herself that that was due to what she had just come through, not to her proximity to him.

"This body and, uh, your body are making me feel things," he said softly. "I want to put my lips on your neck. Kissing your neck seems as necessary to me this moment as breathing. May I?"

"No, of course not," she said even as she turned her head and tipped her chin to allow access to her neck

His lips were on her neck and Emily was sure she'd never felt anything so divine in her life. He was so gentle, yet ardent at the same time. Without thinking of what she was doing, her arms went about his waist and drew his body closer to hers, then she turned her face so his lips could find hers.

But in the next second the door flew open, letting in a flood of light that dazzled Emily's eyes. Turning toward the open door, she saw nothing but an empty room. When she glanced back up at Michael he had turned pale.

"I am up the river without a whip," he muttered.

"Paddle," she said, her voice catching in her throat and her knees feeling strangely weak. She wasn't sure she was going to be able to stand if he removed his arm from around her waist.

But in the next second, Michael dropped both arms from around her and came to attention like a soldier. When she looked at his face, he appeared to be listening to someone. But there was no one in any part of the room that she could see.

After several moments, he turned to her. "Emily, stay here. This isn't going to be pleasant. Adrian has a terrible temper." With that, he closed the door and left her in the dark.

Immediately she could hear Michael's voice on the other side of the door. She couldn't make out the words but there was a tone in his voice she had never heard before, one of quiet reverence and deep respect. And he sounded just like a soldier being dressed down by his superior officer.

Emily began to recover herself, either from Michael's kisses or the ordeal of the attic tunnel—she didn't want to know which. Instead, her curiosity took over. It couldn't be true, of course, but just maybe on the other side of that door, one angel was being bawled out by another and, well, maybe she shouldn't miss it.

Cautiously, she opened the door and saw Michael standing in the middle of the room, head down, nodding.

"It's the body," he was saying softly. "I don't seem to have control over it. Yes, I understand. But she is so beautiful I have difficulty resisting her attraction."

Behind him, Emily smiled. She'd often been told she was cute and pretty in a pleasing way, but the way this man said she was beautiful almost made her believe it.

"But her spirit *is* beautiful!" Michael said fiercely, as though defending her honor, and Emily smiled broader as he paused and listened some more.

"You wouldn't know why I was sent here, would you?" Michael asked the unseen other person.

Emily listened in silence as Michael nodded and murmured, "Mm-hmm, mm-hmm," over and over. After several minutes, he turned his head slightly in Emily's direction and explained. "He's telling me that he doesn't presume to know what is in the head of an archangel, but he doesn't think my mission includes kissing pretty girls in closets."

At this Emily smiled and Michael winked at her, and a moment later he turned and smiled. "You ready to go? This body is hungry."

"But what about—?" she began, but Michael fairly pushed her from the room, out of the house and into the car.

Emily was cleaning the kitchen, scrubbing dried egg from the fronts of the cabinets, while Michael was sitting on a stool at the little bar and thinking.

On the drive back to her apartment he had been mostly silent, but she could tell that he was worried. It had taken some doing to get the cause of his worry out of him.

"I have to find out why I'm here," he'd said. "After what happened today I could be withdrawn before I even find out what I've been sent here to do. I'm much too mortally attracted to you, Emily, and I'm letting that interfere with discovering and executing my objective."

Emily had no answer or advice to give him. He had

seemed to take this morning's terror in a haunted house all in stride, but she was still shaking. Crawling through filthy attics was not her idea of fun. But all that concerned Michael was that he hadn't found out why he was on earth.

"What are you planning to do tomorrow?" he asked as she began to make sandwiches for their late lunch.

"Go to work. Remember that place? It will be chaos by the time I return and I'll have to—"

"I'm going with you."

"No, you're not. And don't even think that you are. You can't be seen."

"Too ugly?" He was trying to make a joke, but the humor didn't extend to his eyes.

"No, too dangerous. You'll be seen."

"And if anyone does see me, what can they do to me? Kill me?"

"I really wish you wouldn't talk so lightly of something so serious."

"The only thing serious about my death would be if it happened before I completed my assignment here—whatever it is."

"You don't think it has to do with what happened at the Madison mansion?" she asked.

"I'm not sure. Could be, but. . . ." His head came up. "I just think that I'll know what it is when I come to it. I'm concerned that. . . ." He looked back down at his hands and didn't seem as though he were going to say any more.

"You're concerned about what?" She tried to sound lighthearted, but she knew that what he was thinking about was serious.

When he looked back up at her, his eyes were soft.

"You see, Emily, the truth is, I'm not a very *good* guardian angel. I tend to play favorites and like and dislike people too much. We're all striving to be like God. He loves everyone. Really. It doesn't matter who they are or what they've done—God loves them."

Michael took a deep breath. "We try to be like Him but, well, I'm not even close. I tend to, well, intervene."

"And how do you do that?"

"I warn my favorites of danger, that sort of thing."

"Like tickling their noses when something dreadful is about to happen?"

"Exactly. I guess if I did the same for all my people, it would be all right. But I can't seem to do the same for each one of them. For example, I have this one spirit who is really bad. Pure, pure selfishness. Evil. He murders, beats people, tortures children."

"But you're supposed to love him."

"Yes, exactly. Adrian treats all *his* clients the same. But I—" He gave her a sheepish look.

"What do *you* do to him?"

Michael grimaced. "Make him get caught. In every lifetime I whisper in someone's ear where he is and they catch him and lock him up. If he escapes I make sure he's caught again. In one lifetime I kept him in prison for twenty years for stealing a spoon because I knew what he'd do if he were free. And when he was released I made him steal a melon and back he went."

"I can see that you're a *terrible* angel," she said, but the laughter was bubbling from inside her.

"It's not funny. God has granted you mortals free will and I am *not* supposed to tamper with it. Adrian would have told me that the man *could* have changed.

But when I put him into prison he didn't have the free choice to try. But, Emily, when you watch a man do nothing but evil for over three hundred years, you think: He is *not* going to change, not ever!"

Emily had no response to his problem. All she could do was say that she thought he was right. But what did she know about being an angel? Not that he was one, of course, she made herself add.

"Mustard or mayonnaise?" she asked.

"What are they?" he asked. Her explanation distracted him.

# Chapter 9

THE NEXT MORNING AS EMILY WAS WALKING TO WORK she thought about how she'd meant to get rid of Michael by this morning, but she hadn't. He had a way of making her forget all her best intentions.

Last night he'd asked her to show him what he'd seen men do with steel and food. It took her a moment to understand what he meant, because at first she imagined swords, and sheep being sacrificed on ancient altars. She was almost disappointed when she figured out that he meant modern grilling. There was a little wooden deck between her apartment and Donald's, so she dragged out charcoal and lighter fluid, then gave him instructions while she went to the store to get steaks. She was fully prepared for the whole building to have burned to the ground by the time she returned, but she was happily surprised to see perfect coals ready and waiting. And Michael was so pleased with himself he was nearly floating. "Want me to float? I can, you know," he said, and she couldn't keep from laughing.

After dinner, he'd wanted to learn to dance like he "used to see her do." This took a bit of time, but she finally figured out he meant a waltz—as he'd seen her do in an Edwardian lifetime. Not that she believed in reincarnation, of course, but she did pick up the moves extraordinarily quickly. As she and Michael spun about the room together, he told her of a ball she'd attended and the silver dress she'd worn, with diamonds in her hair.

"You were the most beautiful woman there," he said, "and no man could take his eyes off you."

"Even my husband?" she teased, but Michael looked away and didn't answer. And she didn't ask, because heaven only knew what had happened to her in a time before modern medicine.

True or not, the stories he spun almost made her see herself in another time and place. She could see the candles, smell the perfume, hear the soft laughter of the other dancers. She could almost feel the corset cutting into her skin and making her waist tiny while the long skirt, heavy with thousands of tiny silver glass beads, twirled about her legs sensuously.

When the music stopped and Michael removed his hand from hers, the vision disappeared, and it was all she could do to keep from flinging herself back into his arms just to have it reappear.

It was Michael who said, "I think we should separate for tonight, Emily. Good night." Then he'd turned away abruptly, leaving her alone under the glaring modern lightbulbs. No more candles, no more bare-shouldered gowns.

But it was when she was locked safely away alone in her bedroom that she gave herself a good talking to. She *had* to get control of herself. "Detachment," she said aloud. Detachment and distance. And maybe tomorrow night a call to Donald, even though he didn't like to be bothered during the week. Except for emergencies. And wasn't this, she thought as she slipped between the sheets, an emergency?

So now—walking to work after having tiptoed out at 5 A.M. while Michael was still asleep—she told herself she was *not* a coward. She left early because she had a lot of work to do, no other reason. And leaving Michael a note in which she *sternly* told him he was *not* to leave the apartment all day, not to allow anyone to see him, was just a common-sense precaution. He knew he couldn't be seen, but it was better to remind him, wasn't it? And a letter showed more force than a conversation, didn't it?

Again, she thought of waltzing with Michael. "Maybe I'll call Donald at lunch," she murmured, then increased her pace.

"And how's your family, Mrs. Shirley?" Emily asked the heavily pregnant woman across the checkout desk of the library.

"They're all well, except the youngest has a cold. And how's Donald?"

"Excellent health. He's—" She broke off as she looked up and saw Michael come walking into the library.

"Emily? Are you all right?" Mrs. Shirley asked. "You look like you've seen a ghost."

"No, just an angel," Michael said, leaning on the counter and looking at the swollen, pregnant and very tired Mrs. Shirley as though she were the sexiest person he'd ever seen.

"Oh my," Mrs. Shirley said, fluttering her lashes. "I don't believe we've met. I'm Susan Shirley and you are—"

Michael lifted her extended hand to his lips and lingeringly kissed knuckles that were permanently reddened from ten years of caring for her growing brood of children. "I'm Michael. . . ." Hesitating, he looked at Emily and she knew he'd forgotten his last name.

"Chamberlain," she snapped, and gave him a look meant to let him know she was going to kill him for appearing in public.

But he ignored her and looked back at Mrs. Shirley. "Yes, of course—Chamberlain. I'm Emily's cousin. On her mother's side. And I'm staying with her."

"Why, Emily, you should have told us," Mrs. Shirley said, making no effort to remove her hand from Michael's.

Emily was choking too hard to be able to speak. Cousin? *Staying* with her?!

"Emily, honey," Michael said, "are you all right? Can I get you something to drink?"

As Mrs. Shirley looked from one to the other, she gave a little smile, and Emily knew that her life, as she knew it, was now over. Within three hours all of Greenbriar would know that her "cousin" was *staying* with her.

"Tell me, Mr. Chamberlain, are you married?"

"Yes!" Emily spat out, the word catching in her throat so hard she started coughing.

Michael reached across the desk and thumped her on the back, but after one thump his hand motion turned into a caress.

"Separated," Michael said, smiling at Mrs. Shirley. "Alas, a divorce is underway."

Emily, still coughing, jerked away from Michael's hand on her back, but when he left his arm draped across the counter she gave it a good, hard stamp that said his due date was in two weeks.

Michael didn't take his eyes off Mrs. Shirley but he withdrew his arm while Emily finally finished coughing.

"Well, Emily," Mrs. Shirley said, "I better get back to the house before the kids destroy it. I must say that it's been a surprise and a delight to meet you, Mr. Chamberlain."

"Michael, please," he said.

"You must come to dinner at my house so my husband and I can get to know you. Or no," she said as though she'd just thought of it, "a divorce can be so lonely—maybe I should introduce you to a few of my women friends."

"I would like that *very* much," Michael fairly purred. "Oh, but you'd better make it soon because those babies are coming early."

"Babies?" she said, puzzled. "Oh no, it's just one. I'm just extraordinarily big and I have two whole months yet."

To Emily's pure disgust and Mrs. Shirley's obvious delight, Michael put his hands on her enormous, hard belly. "Two babies, a boy and a girl, and you have only five weeks left."

"Oh," Mrs. Shirley said, smiling, for all the world looking as though she'd just been blessed by the pope, as she started toward the door. "I do think I'll call my doctor and maybe I'll insist he do another sonogram."

"Yes," Michael said sweetly. "And don't forget your invitation."

"Oh, never fear," she said, backing out the door as though to turn her back on him would make her miss even a second of seeing him.

When she was gone, Michael turned back to Emily, still smiling.

"You are insane!" she hissed, keeping her voice low so the other people in the library couldn't hear her. "Do you know what you've *done?*"

"I wanted to see your library in this dimension," he said cheerfully.

She took a deep breath and started to count to ten, but she only got to three before he leaned across the desk so that she was almost nose-to-nose with him. "Mrs. Shirley will tell every woman in town about you and within twenty-four hours the FBI will be here!"

"Actually," Michael said calmly, "I don't think that's true. I was talking to someone this morning and—"

"Dead or alive?" she snapped.

"Alive."

She narrowed her eyes at him. "With or without a body?"

Michael gave her a one-sided grin. "Without. She

said there are twenty women to every man in this town and—"

"She? She who?"

"The spirit who told me this is a woman. Are you jealous?"

"Not in the least. I just want to know where you met this woman and if she is haunting *my* apartment."

"No, she stays at The Duck's . . . er, ah, Donald's. She told me that there are so few men in this town that I'm safer here than anywhere else on the planet. Even the women who have men are without them most of the time. She said I'm certainly safe from anyone telling something that will get me thrown out of here."

Emily wasn't going to comment on this distorted view of her beloved town. And besides, a patron, Anne Helmer, noticed them and decided she just *had* to check out her books at that moment. Michael opened his mouth to speak to the woman but Emily gave him such a fierce look that he turned away and became intensely interested in a poster announcing Nancy Pickard's latest mystery.

When Anne was gone, Emily turned back to Michael, her voice lowered. "What was a *woman* doing in Donald's apartment?"

"I don't know. It seemed rude to ask."

"Great. Etiquette for ghosts," she murmured, her lips tight.

"Emily, are you angry with me about something?"

She was not going to answer what she was sure he knew was a redundant question, nor was she going to allow him to sidetrack her. "What do you want here?"

"I thought I might look over the documents you have on the house we went to yesterday and since Lillian said this is the town's center—"

*"Who* is Lillian?" she asked so loudly Hattie and Sarah Somerville looked up from the true-crime novels they were reading. Quieter, she said, "No, don't tell me, she's the bodiless spirit who lives in Donald's apartment, right?" She gave Michael a false smile. "Since he's not there all week maybe she should pay rent."

"She has no pockets to hold cash, and it might cause problems if she tried to open a bank account. You know how you mortals are about spirits."

"Stop laughing at me. And what do you mean she has no pockets?"

"I wouldn't dare laugh at you and Lillian left this world when she was taking a bath so. . . ." He shrugged, then his eyes lit up. "Maybe you'd like to give her a job here in the library. She could certainly make people bring their books back on time and she'd be company for those two men sitting over—"

"Stop it! I do *not* want to hear any more of your stories about . . . about naked ghosts. And I certainly don't want to hear about any ghosts in *my* library."

"Sure? They're awfully nice men. Except that I think one of them may have murdered—"

"One more word and I'll throw you out of here," she hissed as she glanced sideways at the Misses Somerville. They were trying so hard to hear that their bodies were leaning at forty-five-degree angles toward Emily.

Michael was grinning. "So where do you keep this research?"

"Why don't you go back to *my* apartment," she said pointedly, "and I'll bring all of it home with me?"

"Not a chance. I want to stay near you until I find out what evil surrounds you."

"You mean, other than you and your bodiless spirits, that is?"

"Emily, Emily, I'd almost think you *were* angry with me. You better smile, because people are beginning to wonder what you and I are whispering about so intimately."

She suddenly thought that it would be better for him to stay near her than to be out of her sight. At least this way she'd know where he was and what he was doing. Besides, she was making *no* progress in getting him out of here. "All right, go sit over there and I'll bring out what I have so you can look through it."

"Thanks, but I'll take that corner table. The men want something to do and they can help me look."

Emily glared at him. "All right, but if one of them starts moving pages or whatever and frightens my patrons I'll. . . ." What could she do to punish ghosts? She gave Michael a fake little smile. "I'll tell Adrian on all of you." She was quite pleased to see the color leave Michael's face.

"You catch on too fast," he said, but as he turned away, he winked at her. And, later, when she dumped a foot-high stack of papers on the table in front of her, he whispered, "They want to meet Lillian." Then he wiggled his eyebrows in such a way that Emily had to turn away to keep from laughing. The thought of two dirty-old-men ghosts, bored from spending heaven only knows how long sitting around in a library, wanting to meet a naked-lady ghost, was almost too much for her. It took her a moment to recover enough to be able to say, "When you finish with that, I have more." Unfortunately, her voice did not come out sounding as stern as she wanted it to.

# Chapter 10

$F$RIDAY NIGHT, EMILY THOUGHT AS SHE LEANED BACK against the tub and closed her eyes. Of course, everything that she'd done this week had been wrong, but still, she had to admit that it had been the most interesting week of her life. Not as good as if she'd spent the time with Donald, she reminded herself, and yet it had been extraordinary.

When Michael appeared in the library on Tuesday, she'd been terrified that he'd be recognized. She imagined him lying in a pool of blood on the pavement, FBI and Mafia men standing over him with tommy guns. Or whatever kind of guns they had nowadays, she thought. But after a very nervous afternoon and no hit men appearing, she began to relax.

Well, sort of relax. The truth was, she hadn't had so

much as two minutes' peace since Susan Shirley had left the library and started spreading the word that an eligible almost-bachelor was sitting in the library.

Greenbriar was a commuter town and all week there were few men around. Most of them were like Donald and had apartments in the city where they stayed during the week, coming home on Friday nights with briefcases loaded with work.

"It's a war town, is what it is," Irene had said. "The men go off to war every Monday morning and they come back on the weekend shell-shocked."

Emily didn't think Greenbriar was that bad, but sometimes there did seem to be an air of man-hunger on the wind.

So as soon as the word passed that an adult, heterosexual male was in town he became the attraction of the year.

And oh did Michael love it, Emily thought with some disgust as she ran a sponge over her left leg. He loved every minute of the attention, whether it was from lonely women or children who rarely saw their fathers.

By the end of that first day, Michael quit trying to read the mass of research that Emily had given him— which she suspected was no sacrifice—and had given his attention to the people of Greenbriar. By lunchtime he'd left the pile of papers and moved to the pretty corner of the library where Emily had set up the children's section. There were chairs and big floor cushions and a thick carpet that she had spent three months pleading a nearby dealer to donate.

As Emily stamped book after book after book— since all of Greenbriar wanted a reason to be there—

Michael set up what seemed to be a repair shop in her library. It had started innocently enough when the head fell off the doll belonging to a child who was standing beside her mother, who was welcoming Michael to town. The mother, divorced and raising her daughter alone, didn't notice the child's big, tear-filled eyes as she looked down at her headless doll. But Michael noticed. Kneeling, he took the two pieces of the doll and put them back together.

The mother was nervously talking, saying nothing, but trying to make a good impression, while Michael had eyes only for the child.

"Do you know any stories?" the little girl whispered, looking into Michael's big dark eyes.

"I know lots of stories about angels," he said softly, "and more than anything, I'd like to tell you a few of them."

The child nodded and held up her hand for Michael to take, then followed him into the children's corner. The child's mother blinked a few times, then she turned to Emily and asked if it would be all right if she left her daughter there while she ran a few errands.

"I . . . ," Emily began. It wasn't her policy for the library to be used as a daycare center, but then she glanced at Michael and the child; they were both sitting on the floor engrossed in some story he was telling. Emily said that of course the child could stay.

After that, there was no holding back. Children from all over town appeared with broken toys and ears eager to hear whatever Michael would tell them.

At three o'clock Emily called her part-time assistant and asked if she could come in to work, as she was desperately needed. Gidrah was so shocked by this request that she said not a word and was there so quickly that Emily was afraid to ask how fast she'd driven.

"Lord a'mercy," Gidrah said, her big brown eyes wide as she took in the busy library in a glance. "Who is he?"

Gidrah was a foot taller than Emily and outweighed her by a hundred pounds, and she was the most generous person Emily had ever met. Gidrah lived on the edge of town with a husband who showed up only now and then, and with two teenage sons who did little but eat and watch TV all day. She told Emily that coming to work was her greatest joy in life.

"My cousin," Emily said over the heads of three women who were lined up at the counter waiting for her to stamp their books. "Could you man the desk while I find books for people?"

"Sure thing," Gidrah said, her eyes still wide and still staring at the top of Michael's head where it could just be seen over the children's. "He the Pied Piper?"

"An angel," Emily said without thinking, then gave Gidrah a look and shrugged before she disappeared into the stacks. And once she was no longer chained to the checkout desk, she was like all the other women who packed the library: She was dying to hear what stories Michael was telling.

With her arms full of books, Emily halted on the outskirts of the group and listened. She didn't know what she'd expected of Michael's stories. Probably religious overtones, or at the very least, Bible stories, she thought. But he was telling them about American history. Except that he was telling them about the

American Revolutionary War from the standpoint of someone who had *been* there.

And he could answer all the questions the children asked. "What did they eat?" "How did they go to the bathroom?" "Did their daddies work in the city?" "Did they like video games?"

Nothing stumped Michael, and without thinking Emily found herself creeping forward because she had a question or two that she'd like to ask. But when Michael looked up at her and winked, she remembered her job and took the books to the waiting patrons.

Gidrah was stamping books as fast as she could get them open. "I think you better close the window because those papers of yours are blowing all over the table," she said, nodding toward the far corner where Emily's research on the Madison tragedy was stacked.

To Emily's absolute horror, she saw that her pages were being turned over one by one, just as though a couple of invisible people were reading them. As she watched, a thick file folder was moved from the stack and put on the table, then the cover lifted.

Trying not to run and draw attention to herself, she nevertheless tripped over two chairs as she made her way to the back. "Stop it!" she hissed to the table. "You're going to scare my patrons." Immediately the papers stopped moving.

She should have felt good about stopping them, she told herself. But, instead, she felt like she had just denied two patrons the right to use the library. Just because these two patrons had no bodies, she had no right to halt them, did she?

"Damn, damn, double-damn," she muttered, then

pulled a big corkboard screen from the corner and moved it around the table. "Go on," she said in disgust. "But if anybody walks by here, you stop moving the papers, you understand me?"

Emily wasn't sure but she thought that as she turned away she distinctly heard a man's voice say, "Thank you." She threw up her hands. "Great. I am now helping ghosts to overcome their boredom."

Gidrah nodded toward the screen. "Who were you talkin' to?"

"Myself," Emily answered. "I have my Madison research back there and I don't want anyone touching it." She moved away before Gidrah could ask why she didn't put the papers back in the office. And what was she to answer—that she'd prefer that those two dead men, one of whom might be a murderer, stay out of her office?

So now it was Friday and for four days the library had been a madhouse. At first the women had come to meet Michael, their eyes full of hope for a wild romance and a commitment. At least that's what Emily saw in their eyes. But as the days passed, things had changed.

"Suffer the little children to come unto me," Gidrah had said on Wednesday afternoon as she looked at Michael, laughing with the children and showing them a game from the fifteenth century. "That's what he reminds me of, what it says in the Bible. He wants the children to come to him. Just like Jesus."

"I think Michael is a different level," Emily said tightly as she carried another stack of books to the checkout counter.

"Level?" Gidrah said, then smiled. "I do believe

that you're jealous, Emily. And I find that rather odd seein' as how you're engaged to marry Donald. By the way, how is he? How does he like your livin' with that gorgeous hunk of muscle and black hair?"

As Emily put the books on the counter, she didn't say a word.

"Well, well," Gidrah said. "If the color of your face is anything to judge by, I'd say that Mr. TV-man doesn't know about this, ah, cousin. Tell me again, exactly how is he related to you?"

Emily wondered how she could have ever liked Gidrah's sense of humor. "On my mother's side," she said sweetly. "We have the same grandmother."

"Oh," Gidrah said as she rapidly stamped three books. "Is this the same grandmother who used to go to school with *my* grandmother? The one who married that man from Tulsa and had only one daughter who was your mother? *That* grandmother?"

"I *hate* small towns," Emily muttered as she disappeared into the stacks.

It was only at night that she spent any time with Michael, and that was only because they acted like fugitives and escaped. On Tuesday, as soon as she'd closed the library, there were women waiting with hot casseroles. "I thought that since you worked all day and had a guest you could use a little help in the kitchen," a woman said, and Emily had no idea who she was. But there was a white line on her ring finger that showed that a wedding ring had recently been removed.

"Thank you, but—" Emily began, but Michael was already taking the dish and smiling in delight at the woman.

"And here's my name, address and telephone number," she said. "So you can return the dish."

Since the casserole was in a throwaway aluminum baking dish, Emily gave her a terse smile. "Of course," she murmured. "How kind of you." She looked at Michael. "Shall we go?"

As they walked back to the apartment, four cars, with only women in them, slowed down and reminded Michael of some social invitation he had accepted. When they got to the apartment there were seventeen notes stuck between the door and the frame. "For you," Emily said, as she shoved all of them at Michael.

Once inside, she went to her bedroom with no intention of coming out ever again. She didn't know what she was so angry about, but angry she was. When Michael opened her bedroom door without knocking, she started to tell him that this was *her* private territory, but instead, to her horror, she burst into tears.

Immediately, Michael sat down beside her on the bed and pulled her into his arms. "It's all right," he soothed. "No one is going to come after me."

"It's not that," she said, wiping her tears on the back of her hand. "It's—" Actually, she had no idea what was wrong with her, but it had something to do with Michael no longer being her private, secret property, and she did not, under any circumstances, want to look into *that*.

"Let's take the food and escape into the woods," Michael said, his arm still around her. "I want to be with just you and I want you to tell me everything you did today and I'll tell you about the children."

"And those women," she said, sounding like a little girl.

"You know, Emily, not one of them has as good a heart as you have. Not one of them has your purity of spirit or generosity. Why, some of them were downright . . . what's that word for those fish you mortals think about so much?"

She started to say porpoises but she knew he meant sharks. "Predators?"

"Exactly. They didn't like me or want to get to know me; they just want a male."

If he'd told her that she was the most beautiful woman in town, as most men would have done, she wouldn't have believed him. But he said things about her heart, how he saw the inside of her.

Before she could say a word, there was a knock on the door and she looked up with a grimace.

"You get on your jeans, the ones with a hole in the seat, and I'll go get some more food, then we'll escape," he said as he headed for the front door. "Alfred and Ephrim told me some things today, and tomorrow they want paper and pencils so they can make notes."

Emily opened her mouth to ask who Alfred and Ephrim were, but she knew. "They can't let anyone see them writing," she called after him. Then as she realized what she'd said, she laughed. Weren't people supposed to be afraid of ghosts? She got up and went to her closet to get her torn jeans.

# Chapter 11

By THE TIME THEY GOT AWAY, AFTER EMILY HAD handed the telephone to Michael at least a dozen times, and she'd listened to him accept every invitation extended, it was nearly dark outside. "It's too late to go now," she said, her mouth in a thin line of disgust. Of course she knew she was sulking over a missed picnic, something that shouldn't have bothered her at all. After all, she usually spent most of the week alone. And, truthfully, she even spent a lot of weekends alone, since Donald had to stay in the city if he was covering a breaking news story.

But Michael put down the telephone, picked up the picnic basket, grabbed her hand and led her out the door, the phone ringing behind them. "Not afraid of the dark, are you?" he teased, leading her down the stairs so fast it's a wonder she didn't fall.

"Not anymore," she answered, laughing. "Not after today. Not after I've bawled out ghosts and told them to behave. And when did you have time to talk to them? Every time I looked up you were busy telling stories to the children."

"Ephrim came over and told me a story while I put little Jeremiah's wagon back together. I just told it to the children."

They had reached the edge of the woods and Emily hesitated. Being a sane and sensible creature, she didn't usually go into dense woods at night.

"Come on," Michael said, pulling on her hand. "The wood sprites will show us the way."

"Oh, of course," she muttered, tripping along behind him. "Whatever was I thinking? Wood sprites. Ephrim wasn't the one who . . . ah, uh . . ."

"Murdered his wife, chopped her up and hid her body parts in a trunk?"

"What?" she asked softly and stopped right where she was. Wood sprites or no, stories of chopped-up wives told in a dark forest were too much.

Halting, Michael grinned at her and she could see his white teeth in what little light there was left. "No, Ephrim didn't kill anyone. He was accused and executed but he vowed to stay on earth until the killer was found."

"Oh. And did he? Find the killer, I mean?"

"Guess not since he's still here. I do wish you mortals would stop making those deathbed vows. They cause so many problems. Just look at poor Ephrim," he said, pulling on her hand and she started walking again.

"Yes, poor thing. He's bored to death. Or, maybe

that's not the right comparison. How long ago was his wife murdered?"

Michael stopped for a moment and seemed to be listening to something or, knowing him, to someone. *Wonder what wood sprites sound like?* she thought, then he pulled her hand and led her into what seemed to be impenetrable brush. But there was a path there and it led to a clearing near a little spring. Even in the dark it was a place of incredible beauty.

"You like it?"

"It's beautiful," she whispered, looking up at the trees that seemed to form a cathedral ceiling.

Opening the picnic basket, Michael took out a bottle of wine. "The sprites are naughty creatures," he said as he poured her a full glass. "They only allow mortals to come to this spot when the woman is fertile. According to them, half the first babies in town have been made right here."

Laughing, Emily took the wine.

"You asked me a question, what was it?" Michael asked as he rummaged in the basket, brushing her hands away when she tried to help.

"Mmmm, I don't know," she said, stretching out her legs on the grass and listening to the water. Maybe it was her imagination, but this spot did seem to be very romantic.

"Emily," Michael said softly, "don't lean back on your arms like that, and do you have something to tie your hair up with?"

For a moment she couldn't help herself, but she stretched and then tossed her hair just a bit. Michael's tone made her feel like an irresistible temptress.

"Get out!" Michael shouted, waving his arms. "Out! All of you!"

His harsh, loud voice broke the spell and Emily sat up abruptly. "What was that all about?"

"Wicked creatures. They said they could—"

"Could what?"

"Shield us from Adrian's eyes," Michael said, looking down at the cheese he was cutting. "And that you are fertile now," he said softly.

"Oh," Emily said, eyes wide. She couldn't think of anything else to say.

"Now, about Ephrim," Michael said in a business-like tone.

"Yes," she answered, taking the plate he handed her. "The man who didn't dismember his wife." Maybe thinking about murder would take her mind off the atmosphere of this secluded, sweet-smelling little nest and make her think of what she and Michael were supposed to think of.

"Yes," he said. "Ephrim." Michael sounded as though he were having difficulty remembering who Ephrim was. "Oh yes. He told me that a few years ago he'd met a man who knew Captain Madison."

"A few years ago? But Captain Madison died a hundred years ago so how—oh, I see. Dead men. Ghosts. Tell me—do they have parties and a regular social life?"

She was making a joke, but Michael didn't take it as such. "No, not usually. The truth is, Emily, that spirits who stay on this earth after their bodies die are not really very happy individuals. Most of them don't even know they don't have bodies. And it's usually something tragic that keeps them here on earth."

Emily blinked at him. It was sometimes odd to be with a person who had no idea that ghosts were something to be feared. But then, even Michael had feared Captain Madison. "So, anyway, what did Ephrim's friend have to say about that dreadful man?"

"That's just it," Michael said, refilling her glass with wine. "He said that you couldn't hope to meet a nicer man than Captain Madison. He was generous to a fault and the men on his ships loved him so much they would have willingly died for him."

"This is the man whose spirit threw swords at you at the Madison house? *That* Captain Madison?"

"The very same. I like this. What is it?" he asked, holding up a bowl full of food.

"I have no idea; it's too dark to see. Besides, she's in love with you, not me. But her hair is not naturally that color."

Even in the dark, she could see Michael's grin. "You can't see what's in the bowl, but you can see the bowl enough to know who sent it?"

Emily didn't bother to answer him. "So if Captain Madison is such a nice man, why is he still haunting his house? And why was he hanged for murder in the first place? I think your ghost's memory is faulty."

"Ephrim said that the people who knew the captain couldn't believe he'd ever killed anyone. According to what he heard the girl the captain married was in the family way and the baby's father had left town."

"Ah. . . ." Emily said, licking powdered sugar off her fingers from the cookie she'd just eaten. "That would make sense. Maybe the old captain fell in love with his young bride and when her lover came back years later, the captain murdered him. Love can make even nice people do awful things."

"Really?" Michael said, one eyebrow lifted. "I wouldn't know about that since I've seen little in this world."

"Okay, Methuselah, I know you're an old man but—"

"Methuselah? Did I tell you that he was one of mine?"

Emily grabbed a handful of grass and threw it at him. "Can you be serious for even a minute? How are we going to find out why you're here if we never work on it?"

He kept his eyes on his plate, which he was refilling for the third time. "I thought I was some slap man and I killed people for a living, so what do you mean 'why I'm here'?"

"Hit man, not slap man. And you may not be an angel, but you're definitely not a murderer. And," her head came up, "do you think that maybe Captain Madison was executed wrongly and that's why he's so angry? And why he refuses to leave this earth? Maybe you were sent here to find out the truth so his spirit can be set free."

Michael had his mouth full of what looked to be Jell-O salad. He really did have the palate of a nine-year-old, she thought. "Maybe he was hanged for something he didn't do—we see a lot of that in my business—but what does that have to do with you, Emily? Captain Madison isn't one of mine, you are. I was sent here for something to do with *you*."

"If I solve this mystery and write about it and it

makes bestseller lists, that could make me rich. Rich is about me."

"Somehow, I don't think so."

"Too mortal, right?"

"Definitely. What is this?"

"Cherry pie. You really shouldn't eat meat loaf, Jell-O and pie all at the same time. So what *does* Captain Madison have to do with me other than that I've been researching him for four years? And what does Captain Madison have to do with you?"

"I'm beginning to think we are howling at the wrong moon."

Emily had to think a bit to figure that one out. "Barking up the wrong tree," she said. "So I take it you don't think Captain Madison has anything to do with why you were sent here."

She had to wait while he ate what looked to be a quarter of a pie in one bite. "Emily, I am truly puzzled by everything. I've spent nearly a week with you and maybe my perceptions have lost a lot in the move from there to here, but I really can't see much evil around you. Oh, there are several women who are jealous of you but—"

"Me? Why in the world would anyone be jealous of me?"

"Let's see. Where should I begin? You are young and pretty and smart and you make things happen. People like you, trust you and want to be near you. You receive rewards and honors and you have a boyfriend. You—"

"Okay, I get the message," she said, embarrassed, but pleased. "So no one is secretly thinking about killing me?" she said, smiling, meaning it as a joke, but Michael was serious.

"No. No one I've seen yet, but there's always tomorrow. Am I right in thinking that tomorrow you don't go to the library?"

"No, Gidrah runs the place on Saturdays." She didn't say that it would probably be empty if he weren't there.

"Could we walk around town tomorrow? I want to go into every store, see all the houses. There has to be some danger somewhere. I'm just not sensing it."

"All right. You can meet Irene tomorrow. She's my best friend and she works in the city during the week. She's a glamorous personal assistant to some madly famous attorney and she always has marvelous stories to tell."

"You've always liked her," Michael said under his breath.

"Past lives?" she asked, trying to sound as though she didn't believe him, or if she did, she didn't care, but she would have loved to hear how she and Irene knew each other.

But he didn't say anything about Irene. "You ready to go?" he asked as he began to shove things back into the basket. "This wine has made me sleepy."

Emily wasn't sure what had happened, but she knew something had changed his good mood. On the way back to her apartment he didn't say anything, just held her hand and led her through the darkness as easily as though it were bright day. Once she heard him mutter, "Shut up," then she was almost sure she heard a chorus of giggles and the fluttering of wings.

When they got back to the apartment the light on

her answering machine was flashing, but Emily couldn't bear to hear yet another woman inviting Michael to some party or movie or whatever. As for him, he went to the shower and when he returned with a towel around his waist he told her he was going to bed.

"Is it something I've done?" she asked softly as he walked past her.

"What could you have done? You haven't done anything bad in centuries," he answered before sauntering toward the living room couch. But when Emily kept standing there, he said over his shoulder, "Emily, dearest, go to bed. And be sure to lock your door. In fact, bolt it so I can*not* get in."

"Oh," she said, smiling, then happily went to her bedroom. She closed the door, but she didn't lock it, and she certainly didn't bolt it.

# Chapter 12

YOU *ARE* GOING TO GO," EMILY SAID, HER VOICE ANGRY and disbelieving at the same time. "*You* are going out to a pool hall with those men, drinking to all hours of the night and doing heaven knows what else. And those men know who you are!"

Michael was calmly shaving, his shirt off, wearing only his trousers, his hair still damp from his shower; he didn't bother to look at Emily or respond to her anger.

"Are you going to answer me?" she demanded.

"They have no idea who I am. Not who I actually am," he said, wiping the rest of the soap from his face, then inspecting himself for cuts. He wasn't used to handling a razor blade.

"They know who the world thinks you are and that's the same thing."

"Do you know where that brown shirt is?" Michael asked, looking through Emily's closet. "Or maybe I should wear the green one."

"Wear one that goes well with blood," she muttered, leaning against the doorjamb, her arms tight across her chest.

As Michael went past her, the brown shirt in his hands, he kissed her cheek. "I had a good time today, too, and I'll miss you tonight, too."

"I won't miss you," she said. "That's an absurd idea. I've spent so much time with you over the last week that I'm looking forward to time alone. I have several books I want to read."

Michael didn't respond but the little smile he was wearing said everything. Damn him, she thought, but they had had a wonderful day together. She had loved showing him her tiny town and introducing him to people. Most of the men were home for the weekend and he'd stopped by each house and chatted so easily with the people that it seemed that he'd lived in Greenbriar all his life.

And everywhere they went people liked him. They were invited inside houses for tea and coffee and lemonade. As they sat on the porch of the Keller house, Emily said, "Someday I'd like to have a house like this. I want a big porch and a green lawn and a swing set."

"Not me," Michael said, making her look at him in surprise. Then she turned away. What did it matter to her what he did or did not like?

"I'd like to have the Madison house. I'm used to big spaces and that's a big house. And I'd want at least six children."

"Your poor wife," Emily said, watching him.

"I don't think anyone would pity *my* wife," he said under his breath in such a way that little chills ran up Emily's spine.

The next minute Mrs. Keller brought out lemonade and cake and nothing more was said of what either of them would want if things were different.

Irene wasn't home from the city yet, if she was going to come, so they didn't get to meet her. And only one bad thing happened. At the Brandons' house, Mr. Brandon, a lawyer, stared at Michael and said, "Didn't I see you on TV?"

Emily was suddenly too frightened to say a word, but Michael smiled and said, "My picture was shown, yes."

Mr. Brandon was obviously searching his brain for what he remembered. "Weren't you accused of being a Mafia hit man, then dragged to jail by the FBI? And weren't you shot?"

"I was," Michael said cheerfully. "Shot to death. But Emily found me, used a pair of pliers to pull the bullet out of my head and I've been her faithful slave ever since."

Emily was sure she was going to faint but Mr. Brandon, after an initial moment of shock, started laughing, slapped Michael on the back and invited him to spend that evening out with the boys at the local pool-hall-cum-beer-joint. And that's where Michael was getting dressed to go now.

And Emily wasn't invited to go with him.

"So, how do I look?"

Much, much too good, Emily thought but would

rather her hair fall out than tell him so. "Fine," she said stiffly, "and I hope you have a lovely evening."

Michael just laughed, kissed her cheek again, then ran out the door—and Emily was left alone for the first time in days.

With Michael gone, the apartment seemed too big, too empty and altogether unwelcoming. "This is absurd," she muttered, as she folded and hung up his clothes that he always left strewn where they lay. She was used to spending the days alone, and even most weekends, so why did she think she needed a man she hardly knew to entertain her?

With new resolve, she pulled a novel from a stack that had been sitting there untouched for a whole week and tried to focus her mind enough to read. When that didn't happen, she cleaned out the refrigerator. Then she vacuumed the entire apartment and made a casserole—which she froze because there wasn't room for it in the refrigerator what with all that the women of Greenbriar had brought for Michael. After that she changed the sheets on her bed and put them into the tiny stack washing machine in the kitchen. Then she ironed the new shirts she and Michael had bought for him that morning.

By then it was 1:00 A.M., yet there was no sign of Michael's return. She looked up the number of the pool hall in the phone book but managed to prevent herself from calling. He was an angel, so what could happen to him?

But of course he wasn't an angel, she told herself. He was just . . . just . . . well, she didn't know what he was exactly, except that he was helpless. She'd had to show him how to tie his shoelaces because he couldn't figure out how to make a bow.

At 2:30 A.M., she heard a car pull up by the stairs. Frantically, she ran around the apartment and turned off the lights, then ran to her bedroom, planning to pretend to be asleep and therefore unaware whether he was or was not there.

But a dead person couldn't have slept through Michael's entry into her apartment. He was singing off-key to something about his heart being broken by a two-timin' woman, and he crashed over every chair, table and bookcase in the room.

Emily got out of bed, turned on the dining room light and glared at him as Michael grinned back at her. "You're drunk," she said tightly.

"That I am and look at this, Emily my love." From his pocket, he took out a wad of dollar bills that even across the room looked beer-stained. "I won this."

She dropped her arms and her jaw. "You were gambling?" she whispered. And when he nodded, she said, "What would Adrian say?"

"Sod Adrian," Michael said, grinning. "That's my new curse word. I heard lots of them tonight. Want to hear more?"

"No, thank you."

"What makes a word good or bad?" he asked seriously as he pulled wadded-up money from every pocket. "And why is a word bad in one country and not in another? And why are you so very pretty?"

Losing her prim look, Emily shook her head. "You are going to have a beauty of a hangover in the morning so you'd better get to bed and get what rest you can." Walking toward him, she put her arm around his waist to help him walk to her bedroom. It was no use trying to get him to the couch because she was sure he'd fall off.

Companionably, Michael put his arm around her shoulders. "We had pizza, Emily. You didn't tell me about pizza. And we watched . . . ah. . . ." He made a gesture of throwing that almost sent him sprawling.

"Football."

"Right. Football. And we saw two men hitting each other."

"Boxing," she said, pushing him to sit on the bed, then she knelt to take off his shoes. "And how did you win all that money? By looking ahead and seeing who was going to win the matches?"

He had his hand on her shoulder to steady himself. "That was the oddest thing, Emily. I knew who was going to win every game. I even knew what punch was coming when, but it didn't matter. And the second time we watched the match on . . . on. . . ."

"Videotape."

"Yes, on video, everyone else in the place knew what was coming, but no one cared. We still liked it just as much the second and even the third time. Isn't that odd?"

"You have just stated one of the great mysteries of all time, something that puzzles every woman on this earth. If you find out the answer, do tell me. Now lift up."

Obligingly, Michael half stood so Emily could help him remove his trousers. "I'll do that, Emily," he said with great solemnity. "I'll do anything you want. There were lots of women there but none of them had a spirit like yours. Yours is so clean and shining, yet so warm and loving at the same time."

When Emily had removed his shirt, she pushed him back onto the bed and pulled the light covers over him. "It's late and you should go to sleep now."

But as she reached to turn off the light, he caught her wrist. "Emily, I have never had a better time in my life than I've had with you this last week. I have enjoyed every minute of your company. I would give my life to protect you from any harm."

She pulled her wrist from his grasp, turned out the light, then, sitting on the edge of the bed, she looked at him for a moment. His eyes were closed and she thought he had gone to sleep so she reached out and touched his forehead, then smoothed back the hair at his temples. When he left would he take away her memory of him?

He looked so sweet lying there, his eyes closed, only the moonlight from the window illuminating his dark, handsome features. Feeling like a mother with her child, she bent forward to kiss his forehead.

But Michael twisted and pulled her lips to his, and he proved that kissing was instinct. His hand sliding to the back of her neck, he turned her head so it was slanted to his, then he opened his mouth over hers and kissed her deeply and thoroughly, his lips covering hers as though he meant to devour her.

For Emily, all thought was impossible as she felt his big, strong body through the sheets, felt his thighs against hers, felt the strength and the heat of him.

"Emily," he said as he pulled away from her mouth and his lips descended onto her neck.

Somehow, Emily managed to retain her sanity. Or

at least retained a sense of who she was, who he was and where she should be, which was *not* cavorting in bed with this man she had known such a short time.

With great effort and the use of some strength, she pushed against his chest and freed herself. "No," she managed to say, but her voice was weak.

Michael didn't try to pull her back to him, but the look in his eyes was almost enough to break her resolve. There was such yearning in his look, such longing, that she almost fell against him.

But, somehow, she got to her feet. "I better let you get some sleep," she said in a voice that broke in the middle. She cleared her throat. "I'll see you in the morning."

Before he could say a word, before she had to look at those eyes of his for one more second, she turned and fled the room.

The sun hadn't been up very long when Emily was sitting on the railing of the little deck outside her apartment, sipping a cup of tea. She'd left the door open in case she heard anything from Michael, but it was unlikely that after the night he'd spent he'd rouse before noon. Besides, she was glad for this time alone as she needed to think about what was happening between her and this man she hardly knew.

Maybe he didn't know it (or maybe he did with his powers of perception) but last night she had made a fool of herself. What did it matter to her if this man went out with other people? What was it her business if he showed himself around town? Or if every single woman and half the married ones in town courted him?

Actually, none of it was her business. What was her business was—

Suddenly she heard a shout from inside the apartment, followed by a crash, then what sounded like a body hitting the floor.

"What are you—" came a man's voice.

"Just who the hell are you? And what are you doing here?" another voice shouted in return.

Outside, Emily's eyes widened until they were the size of oranges, for she knew exactly what was happening. "Donald," she gasped, dropping her mug of tea as she started running.

In the bedroom, a nearly nude Michael was on the floor, looking up at Donald, who was glaring down at him with clenched fists. From what Emily could see Donald was about to attack.

With a motion that could only be described as a leap, she put herself between the two men, standing protectively over Michael, who, from the look of him, was learning the definition of "hangover." "Donald," she said in her sweetest, most pleading voice, "let's go into the living room and I can explain everything."

"Get out of my way, Emily," Donald said through clenched teeth. "I'm going to kill him."

Michael put his hand to his head. "I think this body may die of its own accord," he whispered.

"Please, Donald," Emily said, her hand on his arm. "Let's go in the other room and I will explain."

It took Donald a moment to control his anger enough that he could focus on Emily. "You want me to leave him alone *here?* In your bedroom?"

"It's where my clothes are," Michael said, his voice

innocent, but Emily glared at him as she knew very well that he meant to push Donald's anger.

Donald made a lunge for Michael, who was trying to untangle himself from the covers that were wound about him, but Emily threw her body onto Donald's, her hands pressing into his chest. "Please," she begged. She could feel his heart pounding under her hands.

By the time Donald was able to hear Emily, Michael had freed himself and was standing behind her and that was when she felt some of the rigidity leave Donald's body. Donald may be angry, but he was no fool, for Michael was a great deal larger than he was. For all that Donald was as beautiful as any model, he was short, and even hours in the gym couldn't put the bulk on him that Michael naturally carried. Besides, Michael's dark hair and eyes and the stubble of black whiskers now on his chin and jaws made him look like the underworld gangster that he was accused of being.

"Come on," Emily urged, pushing Donald away from Michael and toward the living room.

With reluctance, Donald allowed himself to be pushed from the room. As Emily shut the door she glared at Michael, standing there in the early morning light in just his tiny undershorts. "Get dressed," she hissed. "And don't come out until I tell you you can."

Smiling, obviously not upset at all, Michael winked at her just before she firmly closed the door.

"Everything," Donald said as soon as she was in the living room. "I want to know every word of why that . . . that. . . ." Abruptly, he looked at her, his face a reflection of the horror he was feeling. "He's the man on the news, isn't he?" Donald said, his voice so low she could hardly hear him. In the next instant, he had the telephone in his hand.

"What are you doing?" she gasped.

"What you should have done a week ago. I'm calling the FBI. We'll tell them that he held you hostage and I'll back you up. I'll say—What the hell are you doing?" He half shouted the last because Emily had unplugged the phone from the wall.

"You can't call anyone," she said. "You have to listen to me and let me explain."

"You are going to explain why it's all right for you to harbor a man who is on the FBI's most-wanted list? No, don't tell me. Let me guess. He's told you some cock-and-bull story about how he's innocent and he's been framed and no one understands him and—"

"No, no, no!" she said, then tried to calm herself enough that she could come up with a great whopping lie that would make Donald believe she should hide a wanted man.

Donald had his arms folded across his chest. "All right, Emily, I'm listening. But wait, before you start telling me what I'm sure is going to be the most fantastic story I've ever heard, I want to know why you didn't think to get him out of your bed before I got here."

Trying to calm herself, she sat down. "I didn't know you were coming," she said honestly, her mind fully occupied with making up a story to explain Michael's presence in her apartment. A story other than the truth, that is.

Donald didn't say a word but got up and went to her answering machine and pushed the play button. "Hi, honey, really sorry I won't be there on Friday but, as I'm sure you've seen on the news, the assassination attempt is taking all my time. I should be back Saturday night. Love ya." The next message was also from Donald. "Sorry, muffin, but I'm not going to be able to make it tonight. I haven't slept in two days, but I'll be there early Sunday for sure. Why don't you snuggle in bed and wait for me? I'll make it worth your while."

There was a third message on the machine, a woman's voice. "Emily, dear, this is Julia Waters and I just called to invite Michael to dinner on Sunday night. I do hope he can come. Oh, and if you're not busy, we'd love to have you, too."

During the last message, Donald looked at Emily in disbelief. "Other people in town know about him?" he asked, aghast. "They have seen him? Seen you with this criminal? Do you know the penalties for harboring such a man as him?"

"He's not who he seems to be," Emily said softly, still unable to think of a reason to give Donald for why she was helping Michael. Now Donald was standing, while she was sitting, and he was towering over her. Maybe he seemed small next to Michael, but to her he seemed the size of a building.

"You didn't play these messages, did you?" Donald asked quietly. "That's why *he* was in your bed, wasn't it? Or maybe you spent the night in bed with him and you didn't care whether I found him with you or not."

"No!" she said sharply, her head coming up. "He came home drunk last night so I put him to bed in my room. I slept on the couch. We are *not* lovers."

"And how am I supposed to believe that? You've lied to me about everything else, so why not that?"

Emily knew she should stand up to him. As Irene kept telling her, she was too often a doormat, but she felt guilty because, well, she had completely forgotten Donald over the last few days. Yesterday, oddly enough, not one person had asked about him. Turning her head to the side, she glanced toward the bedroom door. She wouldn't put it past Michael to have performed some sort of black magic to keep her from thinking of Donald, keep other people from mentioning him. Did Michael have the ability to do that?

"Well," Donald said, pulling her attention back to him. "I'm waiting."

"I'm trying to help him find out the truth," she managed to say. "He's innocent."

"Of course he is," Donald said. "There isn't a guilty man in prison."

Emily did seem to have a bit of a spine because she glared up at him. "If that's the way you're going to listen, I'm not going to tell you anything."

With an elaborate gesture worthy of the worst ham actor, Donald took a seat across from her. "Forgive me for my anger," he said, "but I have been standing outside a hospital for two days trying to find out if the mayor of the city was alive or not. But then, you wouldn't know about that, would you? No, of course not. You and. . . ." He sneered toward the closed bedroom door. "The two of you have been too busy socializing with all of Greenbriar to hear about the mayor. So now, will you tell me why this man is *living* in your apartment? Why do you refer to it as 'home' as though it were *his* home?"

Emily wanted to ask if the mayor was all right, but she couldn't as that would confirm Donald's worst thoughts. And with a glance about her apartment, it was easy to see why Donald guessed that Michael had been living there for days. His freshly ironed shirts were hanging on the knob to the linen closet; a pair of his shoes were in front of the couch; on the table near the door were three worn *Sports Illustrated*s, plus the contents from his pockets.

"We are researching to find out who the real culprit is," she said weakly, looking down at her hands. When Donald didn't say anything, she looked up at him. His face was so full of rage that it made shivers run down her spine. "Like I help you find out things," she said. "You've always told me that I'm good at research so I . . . I'm helping him find out who the real criminal is."

"Are you in love with him?" Donald asked coldly.

"No, of course not," she said quickly. "He's just a . . . a, well, a friend."

"You don't usually allow friends to live with you."

Suddenly, Emily had the oddest thought: Why doesn't he leave? Wouldn't most men who found another man living with their fiancée throw a fit and *leave?* "And you believe him?" Donald asked into the silence. "You believe whatever lie he's concocted and in return you feed him, give him a place to live and even introduce him around town? Is that right?"

"It's not what it seems," she said softly. "He. . . ." She raised her head. "He's lost his memory and doesn't know anything. Actually, he's aphasic."

"He's what?"

"Aphasic. He's lost certain parts of his memory, like what foods he likes and how to buy clothes and how to get a job and an apartment."

Donald's look was making her slow down.

"He knows nothing," she said, giving Donald what she hoped was a conciliatory smile. "Really, the man can't figure out buttons without help."

Donald didn't bother answering her but stood, picked up his jacket from across a chair, then looked down at her. "Emily, one thing a journalist learns is to sniff out lies, and right now, all you're telling me is one lie after another. I don't know what's going on here. For all I know, he may be blackmailing you, or threatening you with bodily harm, but if you don't let me help you, I can't."

When he started putting on his jacket, Emily jumped up from the chair. "Donald, I'm sorry, really I am. I'm trying to explain something that I don't understand myself. If you'll just bear with me I—"

"You'll what?" he said, glaring down at her. "Make up your mind between us? Decide whether you want me, someone you've known for years, or whether you want him, a known criminal you've known for a week? Is that what I'm supposed to bear with?"

"I . . . I don't know," she said. "I don't seem to understand anything right now. My life is so confused."

"Well, let me make it easy for you. It's either him or me," he said softly, then walked out the door.

# Chapter 13

Two minutes after Donald left, Michael walked out of the bedroom. He had on a pair of trousers and a shirt that was hanging out and unbuttoned. From the look of him, he now understood what demon rum meant.

"Not a word," Emily said in warning, not looking at him. "I don't want to hear a word from you. I just want you to pack your bags and get out. Now."

Michael sat down on a chair across from her. "I don't have any bags. Unless you mean the kind we get groceries in."

She gave him a quick, malevolent look, meaning to show him that she hated him. But there were circles under his eyes and his face seemed to be longer than it usually was. "Good," she said. "I'm glad you feel rotten. You deserve it. You are *ruining* my life."

Michael ran his hands over his face. "If it weren't for me, you wouldn't have a life," he said softly.

"And what is that supposed to mean? I had a perfectly good life until you arrived and I will once again as soon as you leave."

"You can lie to anyone except me. You were as lonely as anyone on this planet until I showed up. Is there anything I can do for this man's head? And this stomach hurts too."

With as much haughtiness as she could muster, she stood. "I want you out of here within the hour." Then, still trying to keep control of herself, she went out onto the deck and sat down on a chair and waited, her hands across her chest.

She didn't know how long she sat there but she heard the shower running, then there was a quiet time when she knew that Michael was shaving. She was not, under any circumstances, going to think about what he had said about her loneliness or how her life was going to be after he moved out.

After a while, she heard him in the kitchen, then moments later, he came onto the deck, took the chair next to her and put something on the little table that stood between them. She wasn't going to look at him or whatever he had put down.

"I brought you tea," he said softly. "With milk the way you like it and some of those buttery things we got yesterday. What do you call them?"

"Croissants," she said, her mouth rigid. "Are you packed?"

"I'm not leaving."

At that she turned to glare at him. He was clean now and his jaws looked almost raw from his shave, but his eyes held not only pain from the hangover but some sadness that she did not want to acknowledge.

"If you don't leave, I'm going to turn you over to the police."

"No you aren't," he said smoothly as he picked up his mug and began to sip his tea. "Emily, I know you don't want to admit to yourself who or what I am, but that doesn't change me. I'm an angel. No . . . I'm *your* angel and I know what you want better than you do. Right now you're confused. You seem to want both of us, me and that man, and you can't make up your mind which of us you want more."

At his words of truth, some of the fight went out of her. "If you aren't an angel, you're a criminal. Either way, you aren't the man I . . . I need."

"I know that," he said softly, then looked at her with eyes so full of pain that she looked away. "I know that more than you do. Once I find out what evil is around you, I'll be taken away. For all I know, you won't even remember me." Pausing, he took a sip of his tea. "But now I've found the evil."

"So tell me, I'm dying to hear. Was it gambling, whiskey or men punching each other in the face?"

"It's Donald."

At that Emily's bad mood broke and she started to laugh. "This is your best one yet. At least Donald has a reason to be angry since I'm engaged to him, but you and your jealousy are the stupidest—"

"He brought it with him."

"Oh right," she said, glaring at him. "Have it in his back pocket, did he? Or maybe he carries evil in his briefcase."

"I didn't say your beloved Donald *is* evil, I said that

it came with him. The evil has something to do with him. It's through him that the bomb was put under your car."

"Might I remind you that the bomb had to do with *you.*"

"No it didn't. I told you that at the time. There was some way that the men who put the bomb under your car knew where you were and they thought it was a good time to get rid of you. They knew the FBI came to see you so they thought that would take the fire off of them."

"Heat. Take the heat off," she said, frowning. "You're not making sense. It's not as though I'm royalty and my whereabouts are reported in the Court Circular. I'm not even on TV like Donald is so how—" Emily looked up. "The broadcast Donald did. I almost forgot it in all this turmoil. Donald gave me an Angel."

"He did *what?!*" Michael's mouth was a tight line and the force of his question obviously made pain shoot through his head.

"Could you stop being jealous for even ten seconds? The TV station where Donald works awarded me an Angel. It's a statue they give out every Saturday to someone in the state who's done some public service. I was on the TV just before the story about you, and Donald told where the convention was where I received the award. I was staying a few miles away but it would have been easy to find out where I was."

"Wait a minute," she said, narrowing her eyes at him. "You're trying to distract me. This isn't about any car bomb, this is about you, me and the man I love. I've done something horrible to him. I can't imagine how I'd feel if I returned from work and found that he had another woman *living* with him. But that's what I've done to Donald."

"If we don't find out who's trying to kill you, you won't have any future with any man."

"I think it's time we turn this over to the police," she said, but she refused to look at him. What did the FBI do to a man on their most-wanted list? But that wasn't her problem. If he was what he said he was, that wouldn't be a problem to him either.

"You're right," he said and she knew he was answering her thought. "I'll be safe. But won't they do something to you if they know you lied to them when you told them you didn't know where I was?"

"Great," she said, throwing her hands into the air. "I'm a fugitive as much as you are. Or, I guess, in this case, even more than you are since you can sprout wings and fly away." She was trying to be as nasty as she could.

But Michael didn't pay any attention to her venom. "Emily, I think your only hope is to find out why I'm here, fix it, then I'm sure I'll be recalled. And once I'm recalled I'll be out of your life for all eternity."

"Recalled," she said softly.

"Sure. As you well know, this body is already dead."

In spite of herself, she looked at him. Now that she was calming down, she didn't like to think of never seeing him again.

"You like this body, don't you?" he asked and his voice was husky.

Emily snapped out of her reverie. "No, I do not. I like Donald's body. Understand that? *Donald's* body. In fact I like everything about him."

Michael looked away from her, across the deck to the trees of the woods and there was a tiny smile on his lips that infuriated her. "You'd miss me dreadfully if I left." Before she could say another word, he looked at her and grinned. "Emily, love, when you tell me to get out and the words come from your heart, I'll be out of here in a minute, but now you don't want me to go. In fact, you rather like having made ol'-what's-his-name jealous."

"I hate you."

"Yes, I can feel your hatred," he said, chuckling.

Emily turned to him. "Look, this is serious."

"No, it's not. In fact that man wants you more now than he ever has before. He's always thought of you as Emily-who-waits so it's not bad to rake him up."

"Shake him up," she said, then took her mug of tea and sipped it. It had grown cold but she didn't notice. What Michael was telling her was like something out of a self-help book. How to Entice Your Man, or something like that. Emily had never been one for trying to make a man jealous. But it was a tactic that Irene used often. But then, when a woman looked like Irene she could afford to risk losing a man while she toyed with his temper and his love. As for Emily—

"I don't like what you're thinking," Michael said with anger in his voice. "Look, can we just stick to business? Can't you, for once, be firm with that boyfriend of yours and tell him this is what you're going to do? Tell him that you *are* going to help me find some information and if he doesn't like it he can . . . can. . . ." He gave her a look of puzzlement. "What is it the men say? Something about leaping into a lake?"

"If he doesn't like it he can take a flying leap. Or he can jump into a lake."

"Perfect. Can we have something to eat now? Something soft, something I don't have to chew."

In spite of herself, she smiled. "I really do think you're from the devil."

"Pleeease don't let Adrian hear you say that. This head couldn't stand his yelling at me."

She gave him a lopsided grin. "Tell me, will you get bawled out if you cause permanent damage between Donald and me?"

For a moment Michael looked as though he was going to deny that, but then he grinned. "Emily, love, you are too clever by half. I don't know many of the rules of this mortal life but I know I'm not to interfere. I know that from experience."

"Oh? And how did you learn that? Did someone find out you were sending one of your poor mortals to prison before he even did anything bad?"

When Michael gave her a ducked-head, sheepish look, she laughed. "Come on and I'll bake you some Jell-O."

"That sounds good," he said and had no idea why she was laughing at him.

# Chapter 14

EMILY JAMMED ANOTHER PILE OF PAPERS INTO THE
trash and when half of them slid across the floor
because the bin was full, she angrily grabbed the lot
and managed to get two paper cuts in the same finger.

"Damn, damn and double-damn!" she muttered,
sucking on her finger as she sat down heavily on her
office chair. There were three black plastic bags full of
old brochures, yellowed papers and out-of-date pam-
phlets that Emily had been meaning to throw out for
years, but she'd never found the time or the energy.

But as she glanced out the window toward the
setting sun, she gave a grimace and looked about for
something else to clean or discard or organize. She'd
been in the library all day, using one of her precious
days off to do work she hated. But today she needed
something to take her mind off what was going on in

her real life. A life that included two men who seemed determined to drive her mad.

After Donald had left her apartment that morning, she'd tried to call him but he hadn't answered his phone. Knowing how important calls were to him, his not answering showed how truly upset he was. She went to his apartment but her knock was met with silence. And when she saw that his car was gone, she knew he'd returned to the city.

Michael was no help. He was obnoxiously pleased that Donald was gone and Emily was free to spend her day with him.

But, suddenly, Emily didn't want to spend her Sunday with either man. Instead she wanted time alone—and something that would keep her busy while she tried to decide what to do.

So now, after hours of work cleaning out old files and discarding papers, she was exhausted, and she wasn't any closer to reaching a decision now than she ever had been.

Donald was the love of her life, of course, she thought. It was just that Donald was always so *busy*. And always away. There were times when she was so lonely she talked to the characters on TV. She dreamed of a normal life of breakfast together and being able to plan a weekend without worry that the man in her life would be called away to an emergency.

But she guessed many women lived as she did; many women had doctors and firemen for husbands, men who were often gone.

But, oh, it had been nice being with Michael! He was so attentive, so. . . . So *not* hers, she reminded herself. What did she really know of him? On one hand he was a wanted criminal, on the other he was the kindest, gentlest man she'd ever met. He was—

"So what have you done with my husband?"

Blinking, Emily looked up to see a tall, dark-haired woman glaring at her. She was a beautiful woman, with that kind of perfect makeup you saw only on foreign soap operas, and she wore a red suit that Emily thought must have been sewn onto her generous curves.

"Are you deaf?" the woman said. It was then that Emily saw the gun the woman was holding.

"I—" Emily began but had no idea what to say. Small-town librarians weren't usually confronted by guns pointed at their heads.

"Mike!" the woman spat at Emily, stepping closer and extending her arm so the gun was nearer to her face. "Where is Mike?" she half shouted as though she really believed Emily were deaf.

"At home," Emily said softly, the words catching in her throat.

"*Your* home?" The woman looked Emily up and down, a sneer curving her perfectly lined lips.

Incongruously, Emily thought that if all the lipstick she'd ever worn in her life were combined, it wouldn't equal what was now on this woman's lips.

"You make a change from his usual bimbos," the woman said. "But then Mike likes to experiment." For a moment the woman took her eyes off Emily to look around the room. "You never know a man, do you? Mike's always liked the wild side of life, gambling, killing, lots of blood and money. You know the sort."

Emily gave a weak smile. "We don't get too many people like that in Greenbriar."

For a moment the woman hesitated, then she smiled. "You're not like the others, are you?" With a sigh the woman sat down on the only other chair in Emily's office and began to rub her left ankle. Her rather large feet were encased in red sandals with heels so high Emily had only seen their duplicate in a book with the title *Fetishes*.

"So you wanna tell me about you and Mike?"

For all that the woman seemed to be relaxing, she never let go of her grip on the gun, and when Emily nervously knocked a pile of papers to the floor, the woman instantly pointed the gun again.

"I, ah, I hit him with my car," Emily managed to say, even though her throat was horribly dry.

"And afterward he conned you," the woman said. "What'd he do, tell you he was gonna go to the police if you didn't do what he said?"

"Yes," Emily said, her eyes wide in surprise. "That's exactly what he said."

"Mmm, I wasn't sure it was him but now I am. So what con story did he use on you? He's innocent, of course, but he always has a long list of things he is, like a typewriter salesman. That was my favorite. He got lots of sympathy for that one. Every woman with a computer felt sorry for him. What was his line to get to live with you?"

"He says he's an angel," Emily heard herself saying.

"Bloody hell," the woman said under her breath. "That's a new one. Did you fall for it?"

"Pretty much," Emily answered, giving the woman a tentative smile.

For several long moments the woman looked at Emily, her perfectly made-up eyes narrowed. "My father always said schooling was wasted on girls. Guess he was right, if you've read all these books and still believe a killer like Mike is an angel." She leaned forward. "So how did he explain his missin' wings? Or did he grow some?" This last seemed to amuse her a great deal and she laughed hard, showing what had to be artificially white and unnaturally perfect teeth.

"Real angels don't have wings," Emily said and was amazed at her own calmness. But then, what else could happen to her? In the last few days she'd encountered ghosts, angels and a bomb. "Are you planning to kill me?" she asked.

"No." The woman seemed offended that Emily would think such a thing of her. "I just want you to take me to Mike so I can turn him over to the cops."

"But he's your husband," Emily said.

"You ever live with a man who was nectar to every female under the age of ninety? Even little girls like him."

"They run to him and sit on his lap," Emily murmured.

"Right. Well, it got to me seein' all the twenty-five-year-olds running to him, so to speak. It wasn't the losers he killed, the world didn't need the likes of them anyway, but I sure minded all those *girls!*"

"Then he *is* a hit man? The FBI didn't seem to be sure."

"Of course he is and they know it. Who do you think killed him? Or rather, tried to. I can tell you that I was shocked when I heard he was still alive. So, you ready to go?"

Emily was caught off guard by the woman's abrupt change of subject. "Go?"

"Yeah. Let's go get Mike and get this over with."

"Over with?" Even to Emily she sounded like a broken tape recorder, just repeating what she heard.

"Look, honey, let's get real. Who do you think turned him in in the first place? I got sick of him and his women so I told a few people where he was and they were real grateful, if you know what I mean."

Emily knew the woman had turned her husband in for money and now she wanted Emily to lead her to Michael so she could turn him in again. Would she be given a second reward?

The woman misinterpreted Emily's hesitation. "Look, maybe we can share this reward. You lead me to him and if I can take him with no trouble, I'll give you twenty percent."

"Take him?"

"Yeah, as in kill him," the woman said as though Emily were a simpleton. "You wanta get rid of him, don't you?" She narrowed her eyes and her hand tightened on the gun. "Or have you fallen for him? Maybe you really do believe he's an angel."

"No . . . I . . ." A degree in library science didn't prepare one for dealing with angry wives with guns. And it didn't prepare one for making life and death decisions.

"Whose side are you on, anyway?"

"Yours," Emily answered immediately while she tried to think of something to divert this woman. Could she persuade her to meet her somewhere neutral?

"I think you better go with me. He at that house of yours?"

"No, I think he went out with the boys. He likes football and video replays."

For a second the woman stared at Emily as though she'd lost her mind. "Mike? Like football? Like the boys?" The woman abruptly stood, her hand firmly on the gun as she pointed it toward Emily's head. "All right I get it now. You're a plain little librarian and you like the excitement of harboring a killer. It'll probably be the only exciting thing that ever happens in your life."

"Of all the presumptuous things I've ever heard," Emily said angrily, also rising, "that is the worst! Where do you get off thinking you know anything about *my* life? Just because I live in a small town doesn't mean—"

"Were you ladies looking for me?"

They both turned to see Michael standing in the doorway, his hair rumpled as though he'd just been roused from sleep.

"She has a gun!" Emily screamed as she made a leap toward the woman.

But the gun went off before Emily could do anything and Michael was directly in the line of fire. She landed in a heap on the floor at the woman's feet, then turned to look up at Michael as he reeled backward toward the doorway. For a moment he put his hand to his shoulder and Emily was sure he'd been hit, but the next moment he was standing upright and walking toward the woman.

"I don't think there's any need for such violence," he said softly, advancing toward her.

"So what new act is this, Mike? Trying to impress the little girl? She's not your usual type, is she? Or are you preying on innocents now that every bimbo in the country has been to bed with you?"

Michael kept walking toward the woman, his hand outstretched. "I think you should give me the gun," he said softy. "I don't want you or Emily to be hurt."

"I'll give you hurt," she said, then lifted the gun slightly as she tried to pull the trigger. But Michael was too fast for her. Even as she watched from her place on the floor, Emily didn't see him move. One minute he was standing on the far side of her office and the next he was in front of the woman and the gun was in his hand, not hers.

"You bastard!" she shouted, then lunged at him. He caught her in his arms and held her tightly as she attacked him with her fists and her pointed shoes and her teeth.

"Get out of here, Emily," Michael said as the woman grabbed his hair then sank her teeth into his shoulder.

Emily could tell that Michael was in pain and she looked about for something to hit the woman with so she'd stop her attack, but she saw nothing.

"Go!" Michael ordered. "Now!"

Emily didn't hesitate again as she ran from the office into the dark library, then out the front door and into the night. As the cool air hit her she calmed down enough to think, What now? She couldn't very well leave that woman with Michael, but then she couldn't call the police either, could she?

Before she could make a decision, the heavy door to the library burst open and the woman ran outside, past Emily without so much as a glance in her direction. Emily plastered herself against the wall, hoping the woman wouldn't see her. She thought the woman no longer had the gun but she wasn't sure.

It wasn't until Emily rounded the corner that indignation overcame her. The woman was carrying Emily's handbag! Visions of credit cards and keys and the pillbox her father had given her danced before her eyes. Without thought, Emily started running after the woman.

As Emily rounded the corner and saw that the woman was heading straight for Emily's car and her keys were already in her hand, Emily shouted, "You're not stealing *my* car," then made a giant leap toward the woman.

Later, Emily couldn't remember clearly what happened next as everything seemed to happen at once. She leaped just as Michael appeared out of nowhere, grabbed her and threw her backward toward the building. Emily hit the outside wall of the library with a force that almost knocked her unconscious. Dazed, she looked up in time to see Michael running after the woman as she opened the car door and got inside.

But just as Michael reached the car, it seemed that the sky lit up and the world exploded. Emily put her arm over her eyes to protect them from the blast and turned her head toward the wall.

In the next second she was on her feet and trying to run toward the blazing inferno that had once been her car. The last she had seen of Michael he'd had his hand on the car door.

But Emily couldn't get within ten feet of the blaze.

There was the smell of gasoline and the fire was leaping high, up toward the trees. After several attempts to get near the burning car, she stepped back, her hand over her eyes, feeling her skin scorch from the heat.

"Michael," she managed to whisper as she stepped back.

But as she reached the relative coolness of the library wall, her eyes barely adjusting to the brightness before her, she saw something move inside the fire.

"Oh my God," she whispered, feeling sick. "One of them is still alive." She could not imagine the kind of agony a body must be going through to be alive inside such heat.

But as she looked there seemed to be a column of light, a different kind of light from the red of the fire. The light she saw was golden and it looked as though it weighed a great deal, almost as though it were made of pure gold.

With fascination, Emily watched the golden light with eyes wide open, and saw that it was growing. It went from just a thin column of light to larger, until it was the size of a human body. When the light was about six feet tall, she saw it move again, and it was moving toward her! She backed up against the wall, putting her hands up as though to protect herself.

The golden column of light moved away from the burning car and when it was no more than a few feet from her, the light began to fall away, like the shell from an egg, and she could see Michael inside the light. Fascinated, she watched the light move down until Michael was standing before her, not a mark on his body, his clothes intact, not so much as a scorch mark on him.

It was all too much for Emily, and she felt the blood drain from her as she began to faint. She was conscious just long enough to know that she didn't hit the ground, for Michael's strong arms caught her.

# Chapter 15

SHE AWOKE IN A FRENZY OF TERROR AND WOULD HAVE started running if arms hadn't held her back.

"Be calm, Emily," said a voice that had become familiar to her and, as she always did when Michael touched her, she quieted.

"What happened?" she said as dreadful images filled her head and made her cling to Michael.

She was across his lap, his arms cradling her, her head against his chest where she could feel his heart beating rapidly.

"Emily," he said softly, "I was so worried about you. I was so frightened." His voice was so low she felt it more than heard him. "I was told that you were in danger but I was afraid I wouldn't reach you in time." He pulled her closer to him, so her mouth was against his neck. "I thought she might kill you. I wouldn't want to hold your lifeless body," he whispered, then moved her so he could look at her face.

He didn't have to tell her where they were for she knew. It was the tiny grove of trees that was sheltered and secluded and protected by the wood sprites—the place where they allowed no woman who was not fertile.

"But you were the one in danger," she said, looking up at him, feeling the skin of his neck so very near her lips.

"No, I was never in danger. Now I realize I cannot be harmed until it is time for me to go. And I can't go until I know that you're safe."

As he held her and his energy calmed her more, she began to remember what she had seen. "You were killed, weren't you? You were blown up by the explosion."

"This body was, yes. But such a small thing cannot hurt a spirit."

As conscious thought began to return to her, she pushed away so she could look at him. "You really are an . . ." She couldn't seem to say the word.

"An angel. Yes, Emily, I am. I have never lied to you. I was sent here to protect you and to find out the problem that surrounds you. I have always told you the truth."

She kept staring at him as he held her in his arms. "You were shot to death but you lived. Then you were blown into a thousand pieces but you lived through it."

"Yes," he said quietly. "This body is only borrowed and it is protected as long as I need it."

"You're not real," she said and could feel panic

rising in her throat. "You're not a human being. You're a . . . a monster. Like a werewolf or something else horrible. You're—"

She broke off because Michael kissed her. And he kissed her with all the passion that had been stored inside him for days, for years.

And Emily responded in kind. She flung her arms about his neck and lost herself in his kiss, opening her mouth under his and giving herself to him.

"I am all too real," he said against her lips. "I am more real than anyone else you've ever known and I've loved you for centuries, Emily. For hundreds of years I have watched you throw away your kindness and love, your very goodness on men who weren't worthy of the sight of you, while I have loved you every minute. I have wanted to know what it would feel like to hold you in my arms, to kiss your neck," he said as his lips trailed hotly down her neck. "To kiss your eyes," he said as his lips moved over her closed eyelids. "Your hair, your cheeks, your nose."

"Oh, Emily, I love you," he said, pulling her close to him, so close she could hardly breathe. "I want you so much. I want you near me all the time. I have been your—"

She didn't want to hear another word he had to say. If he were going to be polite and *ask* her if he could make love to her, she might have the good sense to say no. She didn't want good sense now, she wanted this man's kisses and his hands and his skin against hers.

She put her mouth on his, then opened her lips and let his tongue slide into her mouth. And after that there were no more words as his hands seemed to know what to do and how to do it. Expertly, he slid his hand under the loose tail of her baggy sweater, then his hand moved over the bare skin of her back to find her bra strap and undo it in one quick motion.

When his hand moved to her breasts and his thumb touched her nipple, she thought her heart might stop. His hand closed over her breast and began to caress her in a way that no man ever before had.

Emily's experience in lovemaking was limited. The truth was that Donald had been her only partner and what she knew of sex she knew from him. In her own eyes, she had had a wonderful sex life, but Michael showed her differently.

For one thing, he took his time. He removed her clothing with gentleness and wonder. The way he looked at Emily made her feel beautiful, as though she were unique of all the women on earth.

"I have never seen anything on earth or in Heaven as beautiful as you, Emily," he said when she was lying nude in his arms. "There is no angel to equal your beauty."

He kissed her body and caressed her until she was reaching for him, wanting him to take her.

And when he did, it was with a tenderness that she had not known could exist. She could feel his love for her, feel his spirit touching hers as he caressed her and held her.

Time, she thought, as he made love to her. Michael made her feel as though they had all eternity to touch each other, to look at each other and to experience love at its best. And he made their lovemaking seem magical, as though he had the knowledge of the ages at his disposal—which he did.

As the night wore on, they made love in every way she'd ever dreamed of, and every movement with Michael was sensuous and loving. He made her feel that she was the most desirable woman in the world and that his only goal in life was to please her.

"I love you, Emily," he said again and again as he touched her in ways that she'd never dreamed of being touched. "I have watched you for years," he murmured once, "and I hope I know what you like." Closing her eyes, Emily imagined lovers in perfumed silk shirts, with feather beds beneath them.

Reading her mind, Michael said, laughing, "I can give you feathers," then Emily had the vision of great white wings surrounding them. They were encompassing and protective, but at the same time so very, very sexy. She was being made love to by an angel!

Giggling, Emily buried her face in the feathers, then laughingly bit one. "Ow!" Michael said, so she bit again and the two of them went rolling about on the sweet-smelling grass.

"What about *them?*" she asked, nodding her head toward the canopy of trees overhead. Michael knew she didn't mean the trees, that she meant she wanted to see the wood sprites. Smiling, he rolled with her until she was on top of him, her bare legs against his white wings that were spread out on the ground, his naked body between her legs.

Suddenly, the woods about them were transformed from being just an ordinary wood into a kingdom of magical beings. For just a flash of a second, she saw a tall, handsome, thin man floating in the air and smiling at her. He was surrounded by at least a dozen lovely young women—all thin, all draped in gauzy silks—and they were all smiling at her impishly as they hovered about in the soft, warm, evening air.

"Oh my," Emily said in awe when the vision had disappeared as quickly as it had come. "Is that what you see all the time?"

"Mmmm," he said, obviously not interested in the wood sprites that danced about them. "Emily, have you ever made love in a tree?"

"Let me think," she said, seeming to ponder the idea. "There was that time on the railroad tracks, but a tree? No, I don't think so. But maybe I should reread my diary to make sure."

"Ha!" Michael said then scooped her into his arms and they were, well . . . if not actually flying, they were floating.

"Wings?" she said, looking down at the ground which was now some distance beneath them.

"Might as well get some use from the things. As it is they're a bloody great nuisance. They're hot, heavy and they itch."

Emily clung to him as they traveled upward. "But oh so divinely beautiful," she said, kissing his mouth softly.

"Then they're worth it," he answered, smiling back at her. "They're worth any amount of discomfort to see you smile at me like that."

"You seem to have all my smiles," she said, clinging to him.

"I just want them for eternity, that's all."

"And how long is eternity?"

"Until I stop loving you, which will be never."

Emily put her head back and let him kiss her neck. "I so love it when you do that."

"And what about this? And this?"

Emily didn't have the strength to answer—at least not in words.

# Chapter 16

WHEN EMILY AWOKE, IT WAS FULL DAYLIGHT AND SHE was alone in the little glade. And she was stark naked. It was romantic to be nude at night when a beautiful man was making love to you, but to wake up in full sunlight, alone with no clothes on, just made her feel embarrassed.

"Michael?" she whispered, but received no reply, so her embarrassment increased. What if some school-children, playing hookey, had come upon her?

Quickly, she grabbed her clothes from where they'd been tossed into the bushes and pulled them on. So much for angels, she thought with disgust. An angel didn't just turn over and go to sleep, he flew away into never-never land.

Now that it was daylight, the sane and sensible Emily was back and she was trying not to remember what had happened last night. Or what she thought had happened. There couldn't have been wings and wood sprites, couldn't have been. . . . Well, the truth was, she was an engaged woman and there just couldn't have been another man.

It was while she was pulling her sweater over her head that she finally remembered what had happened last night. The woman with the gun! The car explosion! Had she really left the scene of a crime?

She was still pulling her sweater down as she started running toward the library. Had anyone found the car yet?

She was some distance from the library when she saw the red lights and heard the noise of many voices. Obviously, the car had been found. Emily slowed her pace and kept herself hidden in the trees, thinking that it was better to find out what was going on before bursting onto the scene. When she was close enough, she saw two fire engines, half a dozen police cars and two big news vans with satellite dishes on top. There was general chaos and confusion as what seemed to be a hundred people ran about and tripped over each other.

At the edge of the forest was a pile of firemen's coats, great heavy things that would cover a person twice Emily's size. Cautiously, she picked up one of the coats, put it on and then put on a helmet that pretty much covered her face.

Cautiously, she walked into the midst of the mayhem and went to a man who was fiddling with what looked to be a sound machine for one of the news vans. "What's going on?" she asked.

The man didn't look at her but kept turning knobs. "Where have you been that you haven't heard?"

"I spent the night cavorting with angels and wood sprites and just woke up."

The man gave a half-smile in her direction then turned more knobs. "The local librarian was blown up in her car."

"W-what?"

"Emily Todd, librarian, blown up," he said. "Seems she was leading a double life. Librarian by day, criminal by night."

"Criminal?!"

The man gave Emily a sharp glance but she pulled the helmet closer down over her face so he couldn't see her. "Yeah. She was living with the FBI's most wanted criminal. There's rumors that she had something to do with the mob. She used to spend a lot of time in the mountains and they think she was taking goods to mobsters on the lam. She seems to be a real piece of work because she had the whole town believing she was taking books to underprivileged kids. She was even given some awards for it, but here she was working for the mob."

Emily could only stare at his profile as he turned knobs and then listened to earphones.

"It was Donald who broke the story," the man continued.

"Donald?" Emily managed to whisper through a throat closed to the point of pain.

"Yeah, you know, Mr. News? Surely you've heard of him. He broke the Johnson case a couple of years back." The man paused as he finally seemed to have adjusted the knobs to his satisfaction. "So now it looks like he's broken the Todd case. You know, I wonder if she's any relation to Mary Todd Lincoln? That woman was crazy too. Hey! Maybe I oughtta tell Donald and he can look into it. Listen, help yourself to coffee and doughnuts. Nobody's looking."

Emily was too stunned to move, much less eat anything. She just stood there staring at the control panel as though it were of great fascination. So now it seemed that she was dead. And it was a good thing too since she was a thoroughly evil person who helped mobsters escape the law.

"This can't be," she said to herself. "I'll just have to tell the truth and get this sorted out." With resolve, she reached up to remove her helmet but then she saw the men who had come to her hotel room that night. FBI, she thought. If she went to them she'd have to tell the truth, that she had harbored a man thought to be a criminal. And that she had lied to them. And last night that man's wife had been blown up in Emily's car and instead of reporting it to the police, Emily had run away into the woods and made love with a man who was not her fiancé.

"Worse and worse," she muttered.

"What is?" asked a woman standing near her. "This mess or life in general?"

"This mess," Emily said, ducking her head so her face couldn't be seen. "I just arrived here, so what makes everyone think it's Miss Todd in the car?" She thought the "Miss" made her seem a bit more respectable than what the sound man had insinuated.

"It was her car and her handbag was blown free. Of

course it's not positive yet as there wasn't much left of the body but Donald identified her as his former fiancée."

"How could he do that?"

The woman shrugged. "I don't know but he certainly seems to know it's her, and it may be the biggest story of his career. Seems that Miss Emily Jane Todd was into some heavy dirt. There's talk of drugs and money laundering and who knows what else? Lord! And to think that Donald almost married someone like that! Just goes to show you that even with years of dealing with criminals you can still be bamboozled. Hey! Are you okay? You ought to get something to eat. Fighting that fire must have been hard work."

Emily tried to breathe but it wasn't easy. Under the heavy coat she was sweating profusely. It was as though she were seeing her own future and what would have happened to her if she had been the one to start the engine of her own car. If she had, she would be dead now and her name would have been ruined forever. All her years of trying to do right and to give more than she received would have gone down the drain. Instead, everyone would remember her as involved with the Mafia. As someone who harbored criminals, as someone who lied to the FBI.

When she swayed on her feet and felt as though she were going to faint, she caught herself. She would not collapse now! she told herself. If she were to fall to the ground in a stupor at the injustice of what she had just heard, she'd never recover. She'd be hauled off to FBI headquarters and probably be locked up and never heard from again.

No, instead she had to think and to plan. Alone, she thought with some bitterness. So much for angels, she thought angrily. Where was her guardian angel when she needed him? Was he practicing using his wings and that's why he had left her alone to figure out what to do?

Turning, she saw that the woman had a notebook sticking out of her pocket. Heavens, she was probably a reporter. One wrong word and Emily would find herself in prison.

Emily glanced at the woman from under the helmet just enough that her blushing cheek could be seen. A blush of rage instead of the shy embarrassment that she hoped the woman took the red for. "Could I impose on you for something? You wouldn't know Donald Stewart very well, would you? I mean, are you high enough on the ladder to be able to get me his autograph?"

"Of course I am," the woman snapped so Emily knew that she had probably never spoken to Donald in her life.

"Then could you get it for me? Could you get him to make it out to 'Muffin'? That way when my sister sees that it has my nickname on it, she'll think that Mr. Stewart and I might have been . . . well, you know, acquainted."

"Muffin?" the woman said in disgust and Emily could see that she already regretted saying that she would get the autograph. With a grimace, she told Emily not to move, that she'd be back in a moment with the autograph.

"I wouldn't move for the world," Emily said honestly, then stood rooted where she was as the woman made her way through the crowd toward Donald, who Emily could see was sitting on a chair having his face made up in preparation for appearing on camera.

As Emily watched the back of Donald's head, she knew that he'd received her message and knew what it meant. Twisting about in his chair, he looked at her, saw her tiny form dwarfed by the huge fireman's coat. Emily raised her hand in greeting and in seconds, Donald was beside her, her upper arm locked in his grip as he half dragged her into the shade of the trees.

"Just what do you think you're doing here?" he demanded when they were alone.

Emily pulled away from his grasp. "What is that supposed to mean? Aren't you glad that I'm not dead?"

"Of course I am," he snapped, not sounding glad at all. "It's just such a shock, that's all. We all thought that . . ."

"That you had the story of a lifetime, is what," she said bitterly, then her bravado left her; she could feel tears gathering. "Donald, I thought you loved me."

"I did. I mean, I do, but, Emily, really, you must admit that you've treated me pretty badly these last weeks. You were *living* with another man."

"Not in the way you mean," she said, trying to find something in the pockets of the coat to wipe her nose with, but the pockets were so low down that she could reach only the top of them. "You've said horrible things about me and you know they aren't true. You know that I was only helping Michael because I'm the world's softest touch."

Donald shrugged. "It was a story."

For a moment his callousness stunned her then her

mouth tightened into a thin line. "You knew very well that wasn't me in that car, didn't you?"

Donald didn't answer but glared at her. "Better you were dead than run off with that . . . that . . ."

"You did all that for revenge, didn't you? You decided to blacken my name, make a big story of it, then what, a few days from now I'd turn up alive and a retraction would be printed on page twenty-three of some local newspaper? Is that what you planned?"

"It's what you deserved," Donald said tightly. "How dare you hurt my reputation and my entire career with that killer? Really, Emily, how could you do something like that to me?"

"I didn't do it *to you*. I took him in because he's a nice man and he needed help. It had nothing to do with you."

"Anything you do has to do with me. It has to do with my future. I chose you because you were loyal and I was sure you'd never give me any trouble. How could you betray me like this?"

"Me?" she gasped, then calmed herself. "Donald, why did you ask me to marry you? And before you make up a lie, might I remind you that all I have to do is walk out there and tell those people I'm alive and you'll look like a fool on national TV. It is national, isn't it? I assume you got that out of this."

"Yeah, it's national. And it's my big break."

"So answer me. Why did you ask me to marry you? Truthfully, Donald, you're so beautiful, so why didn't you want one of those long-legged beauties who's always hanging around you?"

Reaching out, Donald took her hands in his. "Because I wanted a woman who pays attention to *me*. I

Jude Deveraux

don't want one who throws tantrums and expects me to soothe away her tears with roses and diamonds. No, I want someone like you, Emily, someone who has eyes only for me, who's at home when I call her. I want a wife who can be a mother, who's content to stay home and raise the kids. Deliver me from those spoiled women who expect a man to wait on her and tell her she's beautiful ten times a day. When a man wants a future like I want, he doesn't need a wife who's sneaking around in motels. No, I want a motherly type. Pretty but not gorgeous. Smart but not an intellectual. Amusing but not a great wit. Someone I can rely on. Like you, Emily."

Still holding her hands, his face full of his honesty, he bent forward and kissed her on the nose. "Emily, love, I know how sensible you are and I know you will be about that dreadful man, that escaped criminal. I know you're going to give him up because I've asked you to. I need a woman who is willing to help me and . . ."

His eyes lit up and he smiled in a conspiratorial way. "I'm going to reward you for helping me. How about setting a wedding date a year from today?"

For a moment Emily could only blink at him. His idea of a reward was marriage to him.

Suddenly, it all became clear to Emily and she understood why a handsome, famous man such as Donald would ask a plain, boring, practical woman like her to marry him. "It was always your career, wasn't it? You never loved me in the least, did you?"

"Emily, it wasn't like that. I have loved you. Really, I did."

"You loved me as long as I was no trouble, but the

minute I did something that could hinder your precious career you were ready to throw me to the wolves." She glared at him. "On *national* TV!"

"Emily," he said and the way he said it made her know that she had some power over him, but she didn't know what it was.

But then she saw everything. If she were to walk out of the woods now and show herself, Donald would look like an enormous fool. Nationally. If she was going to save herself she'd better do it now. "I know I've always been the epitome of acquiescence." She'd be damned if she was going to call herself a doormat. "But, so help me, Donald, if you don't straighten this out, I will. The woman who was blown up is Michael's wife."

For a moment Donald looked blank, as though he couldn't remember who Michael was. "Chamberlain? You mean his wife found him? When the FBI couldn't? I know I said that she'd find him first but I didn't think I'd be so right on."

"Spare me your self-congratulations. She found him and was planning to kill him. And why not since she was the one who turned him in to the FBI in the first place? But here's a scoop for you: *I* was the one targeted by whoever put the bomb under the car, not Michael or his wife."

"You?" Donald said in surprise, then his lips curved into a smile. "Who in the world would want to kill *you?*"

Without a word, Emily turned on her heel and started toward the news vans, but Donald caught her arm.

"All right, I apologize. He's made you feel this way,

hasn't he? What happened to the nice Emily I cared so much about?"

"Car bombs. Gun threats. Pulling bullets out of skulls. Ghosts. You name it and I've been through it. What are you going to do with this information?"

"That Chamberlain's wife was blown up?"

Emily stared at him.

"Okay, I'll think of something and I'll clear your name."

"You better or I'll make sure yours is so dirty that you'll never be elected to any office."

"You are *not* the Emily I have always known."

"Good. I want you to make it clear that I'm an innocent victim in all this and that no one knows where I am. But I don't want a manhunt out for me."

"How about if I say you're in protective custody?"

"Just so my name is cleared," she said, then removed the heavy coat and helmet and handed them to him.

As she turned away to head deeper into the forest, he said, "Emily, who *is* trying to kill you and why would they want to?"

"All of Heaven is working to answer that question," Emily said over her shoulder and kept walking.

"But what about the wedding?" Donald called after her.

She looked back at him and gave him her sweetest smile. "How can you marry me, Donald? I'm dead, remember?"

# Chapter 17

So much for bravado, Emily thought once she was in the woods and hidden from the newspeople. Now what should she do? Part of her wanted to run back to Donald, throw herself on him and beg his forgiveness. "Standing up for yourself is a lonely business," she said aloud, then sat down on a rotten stump and hoped for some divine inspiration to tell her what to do.

"Looking for me?" asked a familiar voice, but Emily refused to look up at Michael. He had deserted her when she most needed him so why be nice to him now?

Seeming oblivious to Emily's anger, Michael stretched out on the grass at her feet so she turned the other way so she wouldn't be looking at him. "I didn't leave you, you know. You had to make your own decisions about your boyfriend and I had to stay out of it. I'm not allowed to interfere."

For a moment Emily looked into space, then, slowly, anger began to run through her. "Interfere?" she said, her teeth clenched. "That's all you know how to do. You have taken my perfectly sane, happy life and turned it into something out of a horror novel. A woman held a gun to my head, then minutes later I saw her blown up. I've had not one but two bombs planted in my car—a car I no longer have, I might add. Then of course there're all the women leaving casseroles on my doorstep. And now the man I love is . . ."

Michael handed her a handkerchief and she blew her nose. Damn it all anyway, but her anger was turning into tears, and she was afraid they were tears of self-pity.

"Where did you get this?" she asked, looking at the big linen square. There was an "M" embroidered in the corner.

"Madison. We've made our peace as long as I promise not to publish what really happened when he was alive."

Emily still refused to look at him or to take the bait he was dangling before her. She wasn't going to give him the satisfaction of asking what really happened with Captain Madison.

"It's a shame the way your mortal history can get twisted about. Everyone thinks that Captain Madison was horrible for marrying that young woman but really . . ." Michael gave a great sigh. "But I guess you're too upset over Donald to want to hear anything about Captain Madison."

Emily had to bite her tongue to keep from asking but she wasn't going to allow him to distract her. "This is all a joke to you, isn't it? My life is in shatters because of you but all you can do is make jokes."

"All right, no more jokes. You want truth, then the truth is that your life was a mess before I showed up. As always, you choose dreadful men to fall in love with. Your Donald? He chose you because he thought you were too boring to ever give him any trouble. He saw that the way you looked at him was akin to worship and he knew you'd run a tidy house, put on hundreds of dinner parties and basically work yourself to the bone for him. Yet you'd ask for little or nothing in return. On his side he could do what he's been doing forever, and that's have affairs with every woman he can get into bed with him, which, considering his job and looks, is a considerable number."

Pausing, he looked at her. "You want more?"

"I didn't want that much," she said under her breath. "I just wanted . . ."

"To live in a dream. All mortals do. None of you want to know the truth. Emily, I know you're angry at me right now but if you had married him, your life would have been miserable."

She glared at him. "You're my guardian angel so why didn't you fix it? Isn't that what you guys are supposed to do?"

Michael took a while before he answered and she could tell that he was choosing his words carefully. "An angel can't interfere on earth unless given permission to do so by God. Oh, an angel can find a mortal the occasional parking space." He paused to smile at this idea. "But an angel can't end a life or prolong a life without God's permission.

"And an angel can*not* interfere in love! Big taboo, that one. Guardian angels are sickened to see those in their charge marry wife beaters and child molesters. But they are forbidden to prevent love from going where it wants to go because, you see, God loves love."

Michael paused to see if she'd stop him but at her silence, he continued. "However, angels can make things happen to allow a person to see the truth about the one they love. But, unfortunately, it's true that love is blind and rarely does anyone actually see the truth even when it's presented to them. Fathers used to prevent daughters from marrying horrible men but today love has even vanquished fathers.

"Love is the *only* thing on earth stronger than evil. It is stronger than money and sex and all sin. Whenever anyone truly loves someone else, God gets stronger. God is brought to earth by the pull of love."

Again he paused to look at her. "You didn't love Donald and you never would have. You shouldn't settle for what you can get, Emily, because you deserve the best."

At that she stood, hands on hips, and glared down at him. "You know, lectures like that make me crazy. Everyone these days spouts holier-than-thou statements about the wonderful man a woman deserves but what I want to know is, Where is this man? Where do they grow these fabulous men who are kind, considerate and worth a woman's love? Where's the man like my father who came home from work on time and whose whole life revolved around his family? I only seem to find men who think I'm boring and angels who make love to me then leave without a backward glance."

Instantly, Michael was on his feet and reaching out his hand to her, but she didn't take it. He moved to stand in front of her but she looked away. "Last night I was wrong," he said softly. "If it will make you feel any better I've spent the morning being bawled out by Adrian. It seems that I committed a serious breach of ethics and I'm going to be . . ." He took a deep breath. "Demoted. When I get back I get sent down a level. I'll have . . ."

When he spoke his voice seemed to catch in his throat. "I'll have new clients, new people to look after."

"Then you won't be *my* guardian angel," Emily said, her eyes glittering angrily.

"No," he said softly. "I won't be watching over you."

"Good! Then I can choose my own lovers, my own friends, my own everyone and everything without your interference."

"Yes," Michael said. "You'll go through life without me."

Emily cocked her head at him. "So why are you still here? You got bawled out, told you've done a really bad job of everything, so why weren't you recalled?"

Michael shrugged. "I have no idea. Adrian has tried to get through to Archangel Michael but . . ."

"He was put on hold?" Damn! she thought. She hadn't meant to make a joke.

But Michael didn't smile. "In Heaven, being put on hold could mean waiting for centuries."

Emily wanted to bite her tongue to keep from laughing but she couldn't. "You are the worst possible angel," she said, but there was no animosity in her voice because finally, after all the ugly happenings of the morning, last night was beginning to come back to her. "Did Adrian say anything about . . ."

"Last night?" Michael asked and he had such a cocky grin that Emily had to turn away. "A bit. In fact he said more than a bit. He said, well, days' worth. He had to expand earth time to fit it all in. While you were telling Donald what you thought of him, I was being yelled at for what on earth time would be about ten and a half days."

"My goodness. Adrian seems to like to talk."

"He seems to like to talk to *me* anyway." Michael raised his head. "Speaking of which, did you find out anything?"

"Find out anything about what?"

"About who's trying to kill you? Did your former lover have any ideas about who was after you?"

"Well, we didn't really have time to discuss that. He was—" She looked away.

Michael took her chin in his hands, then tilted her head up to look into her eyes. "What was that skunk trying to do to you?"

"I don't want to talk about it," she said, moving away from him. "I just want to go home and—"

"Your home is no longer safe. When Donald corrects his mistake the men who put the bombs in your car will know you're still alive. They may know already. I'm feeling that your apartment isn't safe."

"But where am I supposed to live? How do I go to work? How do I—?"

Michael put his arms around her and held her close to him; she could feel his heart beating against her cheek.

"I don't want to touch you," she whispered. "You're not real. You're not going to stay here. I just lost one man I loved and I can't bear to lose another one. It's not fair!"

"That's just what Adrian said," Michael told her, holding her close, stroking her hair. "He didn't care what I did to myself but what I had done to you was beyond the rules. You see, once a woman falls in love with an angel, no mortal man can live up to him."

"What?!" Emily sputtered, pulling away to glare at him. "You think *you* are so good that a one-night stand with *you* will ruin me for all men for all time? You are the most unangelic person I have ever met. You're vain, conceited, and you know nothing whatever so you are a bloody great nuisance. I could adopt six children who'd be less trouble than you are. You can't even—Would you mind telling me what you're laughing at?"

"I'm glad to see you're back to yourself," he said, laughing, then he took her arm companionably in his. "I think we should find out who's trying to kill you, don't you? You know, Emily, I was thinking that if you did find out maybe you could write a book about whatever has led up to this and maybe you could sell it. I do feel that I owe you a story because Captain Madison swore some dreadful curses if his story was published."

"I guess I could write, but how do we find out who's trying to kill me?"

"You didn't believe me but I told you that Donald was the source of the problem."

"More of a problem than you know," she muttered.

Michael grinned enough to split his face. "Had some trouble, did you?"

"I thought you knew everything."

"I just know that you two had a difference of opinion. Want to tell me every tiny detail?"

"No, not a word. But what were you telling me about Donald being the source of evil?"

"Do you know where he lives?"

"I assume you mean in the city. Yes, I do. You aren't planning to go there, are you? I know that I can't go because—" she broke off.

Michael looked at her in curiosity. "Why can't you go there?"

"Because now I'm a wanted criminal. If someone recognizes me from the broadcast they'll turn me in. But what does that matter since I'm already dead?"

"Come on, Em, cheer up. You're dead and I'm an angel. Things have to get better."

She didn't laugh at his joke. "I want to clear my name and my reputation." As she said this, she gave him a look out of the corner of her eye.

"Go ahead and turn me in," he said with a smile as he read her mind. "They can't hurt me and I can assure you that I'll be back as soon as Heaven can get me to you. Face it, Emily, you and I are together until this mystery is solved. I'm on a mission from God."

"All right then, what do I do first? I want my life back. I'm tired of bombs and the FBI and of angels. And I am especially sick of ghosts. I want *normal!*"

"You have just hurt the feelings of some very nice

people," he said, eyes twinkling, then at Emily's look, he sobered. "All right, no more jokes. All I know is that the source of the evil is your beloved Donald, the one who has sold you for a river."

"Sold me *up* a river."

"Whatever. You must get into his apartment, not the one here in Greenbriar but the other one, the one where he keeps the wom—" He broke off at Emily's look. "Where he keeps his trophies and awards for his honest journalism reporting."

Emily gave him a look of warning, which Michael ignored.

"How can we get to his other living place?"

"Bus, car, train, helicopter. We could walk if we want to take a few days. But everything costs money and my purse was blown up in that car. With that poor woman." She said the last with sadness and horror.

"The one who turned her husband in for the ransom? The one who tried to kill him a second time for a second reward? That woman? Let's go on a train. One of my clients used to own a lot of trains."

"Don't tell me, one of the robber barons."

Michael began to pull her along, so she started walking. "He didn't really steal but he made people do what he wanted them to. You want me to tell you about the pearl necklace he bought his wife?"

Emily wanted to be told that she could go home, take a hot shower and find out that none of this ever actually happened.

"Elk up, Emily. Soon we'll find out what's caused all this and you'll get rid of me and you can have your life back." Before she could tell him that the correct word was "buck," he said, "I'll make you a promise. I swear here and now that I'll find the perfect man for you. I'll find him then direct you to him."

"I thought you weren't going to be my guardian angel anymore. I thought you got demoted."

"I did, but not for a hundred years yet. I have to finish what I've started, don't I? And I have to train someone else and I have to learn a new job. All that takes time."

In spite of herself, Emily laughed. "A hundred years." They had reached the edge of the woods and before them was the southern road out of Greenbriar. "So how do we get to the train station?" she asked with a grimace. "It's at least twenty-five miles and when we get there how do we pay for the tickets?"

"I'll think of something. Trust me."

Oddly enough, in spite of all that had gone wrong in her life since she'd met him, she did trust him.

# Chapter 18

$A$s of this moment it isn't clear whether Miss Todd had anything to do with the grisly murder of this morning but until she's found and questioned, no one knows for sure. So that's it for today. Donald Stewart signing off."

Emily turned away from the TV in the store only to see another bank of televisions, each with her photo on prominent display. "So much for Donald's honor versus his career," she muttered. She should have carried out her threat to expose him. With her jaw set, she left the store and went back to the street.

"I don't know what these are but they're good," Michael said as he handed her a greasy bag and a tall drink in a paper cup.

"Tacos," she said, looking inside, then shaking her head at him. She still hadn't recovered from this morning when Michael had made a man in a long black limousine stop and offer them a lift into the city. They'd had a very pleasant ride and when they got out, the man had given Michael a thick wad of cash.

"How did you get a limo to come through Greenbriar?" Emily asked in awe.

"Witchcraft," he said, grinning. "Black magic."

"You'd better be quiet or Adrian will hear you."

"You know, I think maybe Adrian is a bit jealous. I bet Archangel Michael has never asked *him* to do anything. And I further bet that if I pull this off I might not be demoted after all. I wonder if Adrian is worried that I'll be put a level above him."

Emily shook her head in disgust. "Angels are not supposed to be jealous nor are they supposed to be ambitious."

"And mortals are supposed to live in peace and harmony. Now, I want you to wait here while I get us something to eat," he said, "then we're going to your Duck's apartment."

For once, Emily didn't protest the name Michael was using. So now she was devouring one greasy taco after another as Michael propelled her down the street. She wasn't overly anxious to get to Donald's apartment. After all, what might they find? Evidence of his unfaithfulness? Truth was that Emily hoped Donald was remembering every sweet moment they had spent together and was dying to get her back. Fat chance! she thought as they approached Donald's apartment building.

"I guess it's no use telling you that the doorman

won't let us go up without Donald's permission," she said then nodded at Michael's smug smile.

Sure enough, the doorman acted as though Michael was a long lost friend and minutes later they were in the elevator and Michael was looking a bit green.

"Too fast, too high," he muttered as they stepped off onto the twenty-sixth floor.

Emily knew where Donald kept a key hidden inside the fire hose behind the emergency door but Michael put his hand on the knob and it opened.

"I like your place better," Michael said, looking about at the glass and chrome and black leather apartment. There were mirrors everywhere, floor to ceiling.

"All right, you've seen everything, so let's go," Emily said, feeling distinctly uncomfortable in this apartment she'd so seldom been in before.

"It's here," Michael said softly.

Emily, thinking he said, "He's here," was halfway out the door before Michael could catch her sleeve.

"Coward. He's not here," he said, as always, reading her mind. "At least I don't think so. Shall we look in the bedroom? Maybe there are some leftover blonds."

"Very funny. I hope Adrian demotes you to where you actually belong."

"Then I could see all the men from your past lives," he shot back. "Would you like me to tell you about the life you dedicated to the gambler? You spent forty-some years believing he was going to change."

"Would you find whatever it is you think is here and leave me and all my lives alone?"

"I can't," he said, walking about the room. "At

least I can't leave you alone for another hundred years. Tell me, Emily, what sort of man did you have in mind to spend your life with?"

"Smart, funny, devoted to me. A slave to me, actually. And rich so he can take me to Paris."

"I thought you wanted to go on a river. Rafting, was it?" Suddenly, he drew in his breath as he reached a tall cabinet against the wall opposite the door. "It's in here."

In spite of her good sense, Emily stood absolutely still. What was inside the cabinet? Evil demons? Ghosts? Something or someone who would jump out and could never be forced back inside?

When Michael opened the door to the cabinet, Emily's heart nearly stopped, her hand flew to her throat and she gave a sharp gasp. But there were only books inside the cabinet, row after row of leather-bound books.

"They don't look very evil to me," Emily said, annoyed with her reaction. "Those are Donald's broadcast scripts. I know because I found the book-binder for him."

Tentatively, as though he might burn his hand, Michael reached up and took out a book, then opened it. As Emily said, inside were the working scripts of Donald's broadcasts. In spite of the elegant, expensive leather binding, the scripts were marked on, the cheap paper bent and torn. Closing the book, Michael put it back into place then ran his hands over the rows of books.

"What are you doing?" Emily asked impatiently. "You're not going to tell me that books can be haunted, are you?"

Turning, he looked at her and his face was serious. "What have you had to do with these. . . ."

"Scripts," she said, tired of his jealousy. "They are just scripts of the longer broadcasts that Donald has done. There is nothing sinister about them."

"What did you have to do with them?"

"Me?" she began, then stopped. "I helped in the research, that's all. They were Donald's ideas and I—" She broke off because he was looking at her as though he knew she was lying.

"All right, it gets lonely in Greenbriar during the week so I read a lot. And maybe now and then I come up with an idea for a story for Donald to do. Then maybe I do a little research. It's nothing anyone couldn't do. I use interlibrary loan and the Internet. Stop looking at me like that! I do *not* tap into files that I shouldn't or do anything illegal or even unethical. I just help Donald, that's all."

"No wonder he asked you to marry him," Michael said under his breath.

"And just what is that supposed to mean?"

"Emily, you were his whole career. How many of these stories were chosen by you, researched by you, then written by you?"

"A few," she said. That Donald was a lying, betraying jerk didn't mean she was. The credits on the news shows had shown that Donald had written and researched them; Emily's name never appeared on any of the scripts. And that's the way she wanted it, she'd told herself often. Some of the stories he had done were quite controversial and. . . .

She looked up at Michael. "Perhaps I stepped on a few toes and someone found out it was me, not

Donald, who had found out what I did. Is that what you think?"

"Exactly."

For a moment Emily's head whirled with memories of all the stories she had "helped" Donald with. In fact, that's how they'd met. Emily had repeatedly written to Donald begging him to come to her library to speak to a group of teenagers about broadcasting careers, but all she'd received were form letters saying his schedule wouldn't permit him to come. Emily had racked her brain to find a way to entice him to her library, then she remembered something she'd read about endangered species, and she remembered something the wife of a big-time building contractor had said in jest, then she remembered something she'd heard on TV. When she put it all together it made a rather good story, so she wrote it up and sent it to Donald.

Two weeks later Donald came to Greenbriar, met Emily and talked to the students, and ended up renting an apartment and making the tiny town his weekend home. And Donald had investigated what Emily had written, found it all to be true, so he'd done an exclusive on the evening news. In the end, the building contractor had been stopped in the middle of the job and Emily had heard that he'd lost millions in future contracts. But Donald had won an award for the story and he'd celebrated by buying champagne and roses for Emily and taking her virginity.

"Why are you looking so strange?" Michael said. "How many of these stories have given someone a reason to hate you?"

Emily gave a weak smile. "I'd think they'd hate Donald. He read them and he received the awards."

"Contrary to your opinion of him, it doesn't take much of a brain to realize that Donald is an idiot. He's a pretty face and he reads rather well. No one who had spent half an hour around him would believe that he discovered these stories. Kill Donald and what do you achieve? Nothing. A person needs to kill the source, which is you."

"Oh," Emily said as she sat down hard on one of Donald's black couches. "I never thought of it that way. I encouraged Donald to allow me to remain anonymous. I never wanted the limelight. I just wanted to see that justice was done."

Michael smiled at her. "I like that you never change. You have always been a lover of justice. A couple of times you've even given your life for justice."

"Is this one of those lives?" she asked timidly.

"Not if I have anything to do with it. Now, let's get busy. I think we need to look for a case that isn't finished. Do you remember which ones those would be?"

"Does that include the men who are getting out on parole soon?"

For a moment Michael just blinked at her. "When I asked you what evil surrounded you, why didn't you think of all these reports you had done?"

"I didn't think anyone knew about my connection to them. Donald always said I was his secret weapon."

"Donald wanted to take all the credit for himself," Michael said with a grimace. "All right, what's done is done. How do we start going over these? If we take them one by one I can feel which have evil attached to them."

"Why not just pick up the bound scripts?"

"Too diluted. There's bad energy there but it's too weak. I need the source. Where is your original research?"

"On computer disk," she answered, being purposefully vague.

Michael glared at her.

"All right. Everything is on Donald's portable computer. He didn't want to leave anything with me because. . . ." Breaking off, Emily looked at Michael.

"You don't have to tell me, I know. He didn't want anyone to accidentally find out that you had done all the work and he had done nothing."

"That's not exactly what he said, but maybe it's the truth."

"So where is his computer?"

"You can't look into a person's private files. It's illegal and unethical and, besides, I have no idea. I would imagine it's with him or at his office."

"I doubt that he'd leave it at the office. He wouldn't want anyone snooping. Shall we look around here?"

Emily knew better than to tell Michael that they couldn't stay there to go searching through Donald's private effects because she well knew that Michael would do whatever he wanted to do. "Bedroom?" she said. "Or would you rather take the living room first?"

# Chapter 19

"HAPPY NOW?" EMILY ASKED. "WE'VE COMMITTED grand theft as well as breaking and entering, but we have nothing. So, are you terribly happy?"

"Not in the least," Michael answered, ignoring her sarcasm. "There is something wrong here but I don't know what it is."

"What's wrong is that Donald will probably be coming home any minute and he's going to call the police and have both of us sent to jail. You may be able to fly out but if someone kills me in jail I'll stay dead."

"A common problem with mortals," Michael said without looking up from the book of scripts.

It was now after 6:00 P.M. and, as Emily said, they had found nothing. Not that the day hadn't been interesting. They had found Donald's personal computer and with its seven hundred bytes of disk space, all Emily's research had easily fit onto it. The problem was that Donald had a password to protect all his files and Emily had no idea what the word was. After she'd explained to Michael what was needed, he'd said, "Lillian will know what it is. She makes your duck's life her business."

"Shall we call her?" Emily asked, reminding him that Lillian was a naked lady with no body. "Or do we conduct a séance?"

"I'll ask Henry to go for me. I'd go myself but I have to drag this body around and it takes too long."

"I hate to hear who Henry is."

"He lives here."

"Of course. Why did I even wonder?" After that Emily didn't ask too many questions as Michael spent the next hour poring over more of the bound volumes, page by page. And later, he cocked his head to one side as he seemed to listen to someone—or something—then he informed her that the password was "Mr. News."

"Not very original, is he?" Michael asked, refraining from remarking on Donald's vanity in using such a password.

And Emily bit her tongue to keep from asking how one ghost transferred information to another. How did they travel? The whole thing made her feel creepy to know that there was an invisible world around her world that, until recently, had seemed so solid.

But even if she'd wanted to, Emily couldn't have said anything because, abruptly, Michael said, "We have to go. Now."

"He's coming, isn't he?"

Once again, Michael seemed to be listening to someone. "Yes," he said softly, then gave Emily a long look. "We must go this instant."

There was something in his manner that made her hesitate. "Is it more bad spirits? Are they after you?"

Michael didn't answer as he shut the lid of the computer (making alarms go off because he hadn't exited properly) tucked it under his arm, then began to push Emily out the front door of the apartment.

But they were too late, for coming down the hall toward the apartment was Donald, his arm around a beautiful blond who Emily was sure didn't have a brain in her head. It would be much too unfair for her to have brains and legs like that, Emily thought as she stood rooted to where she was and stared.

But Michael reacted. Grabbing Emily, he shoved her against a wall and began kissing her with passion. Within seconds, her thoughts were on Michael only; Donald was forgotten.

When Michael broke away, Emily stared up at him, her eyes full of stars.

"They're gone now," Michael said, still hiding Emily from view with his big body.

"Who?" she whispered, then remembered when Michael smiled down at her smugly.

"Get away from me!" she said, pushing at him.

"But I thought you liked for me—" The look she gave him made him break off, but he was still grinning. "Let's go," he said and, taking her hand, he began to run with Emily trailing behind him.

When they reached the street, she was out of breath. "He's going to know who took his computer," she said, panting. "He knows that I know where the key is hidden."

"Do you think your Donald doesn't know who is trying to kill you and why?"

"I refuse to believe that," Emily said firmly. "For all that Donald may be a bit vain, I can't believe that he actually knows about . . . about murder. He doesn't want me dead."

"Not unless your death gets him the biggest story he's ever had in his life," Michael answered, then put up his hand and yelled, "Taxi!" One stopped immediately.

"Where are we going?" she asked once they were inside.

"There's only one place that's safe for us," he said as he settled Donald's computer on his lap.

"Oh no, not there," Emily said, groaning. "Not the Madison house."

"I thought you liked the place."

"I did. I do, but—" She broke off because he was smiling at her. "Drop dead." She knew too well that he was reading her mind and that her fear was for him and the way the angry spirit in that house had treated him. She was not going to fall for him, she told herself. She could not; would not. "Yes, of course," she said after a while, her voice as cold as she could make it. "Evil is your business, not mine. But I do know that taking a taxi all the way back to Greenbriar is too expensive. And it would draw too much attention."

"Sure," he said, grinning. "We'll take a train. Did I tell you—"

"Yes!" she snapped, then turned to look out the window. "You told me everything."

"I like this stuff," Michael said. "What is it again?"

"Gin. You shouldn't be drinking it. I'm sure it's against God's laws."

"Excess in all things is against God's law. You want to tell me what you're so angry about?"

They were sitting on the floor of the Madison house, or rather on a double layer of thick oriental carpets that Emily was sure were worth a fortune. There was a fire blazing in a fireplace that probably hadn't been cleaned in a hundred years, and to the side were the remnants of a meal of Moroccan chicken and chocolate mousse. She had to give it to Michael that he had quickly adjusted to the comforts of human life and he had certainly learned a lot about food in a short time. Now Emily sometimes found herself asking him how to do things.

"A golden sovereign," he said, making her look at him in puzzlement. But she looked away quickly because he looked too handsome in the firelight. The darkness of the house seemed to enclose them and make them cozy and safe.

"I beg your pardon," she mumbled as she demurely sipped her diet cola. She was staying away from anything alcoholic.

"I think you people say, 'A penny for your thoughts.' Well, I'm offering more. I offer you all the gold buried in the foundation of this house."

For a moment she looked at him with eyes wide with curiosity, but then she looked away. "Nothing," she said, not allowing herself to ask about any gold. "I'm just tired."

"Emily, you can lie to anyone else, but not to me. What's wrong?"

"You can read minds so you tell me," she snapped.

"Your life has been shattered and you don't know how you're going to put it back together," he said softly.

He was so perfectly right that when she tried to speak, she couldn't. She wanted to be brave. She wanted to be strong and tell herself that everything would be all right, but she couldn't. Before she knew it was happening, tears began to run down her cheeks.

"Emily," Michael whispered and when he tried to pull her into his arms, she fought him, but he held her firmly and didn't let her pull away.

"It wasn't fair of you!" she said against his chest, then used her fist to hit him. He didn't flinch as he held her, her face pushed into the soft wool of his sweater. "I was happy. Maybe Donald is a jerk and maybe I would have been miserable as his wife and maybe he wanted me for the wrong reasons but I didn't know any of that. I was *happy*. Do you understand that?"

"Yes, of course," he said, holding her and stroking her hair. "You have always been happy with them at first."

"Stop it!" she half-yelled, then tried to push away from him. He held her firmly. "I don't want to hear about the past or the future. I just wanted what I had *now*."

"But I ruined it," he said softly. "Once again I ruined your life."

"Have you done it often?" she asked sarcastically, beginning to lean against him, no longer attempting to pull away. What a hideous few days she'd had!

"Emily." His voice was very low when he spoke and she felt it as much as heard it. "I have done horrible things to you."

At that she pulled away enough to look up at him. His eyes were very dark and he was staring into the fire, but his arms were tight around her.

"I. . . ." He hesitated.

"What did you do?"

Michael took a deep breath. "I have not just ruined your life now, I have ruined your last two lives."

Emily did pull away so she could see his eyes. "Tell me what you did," she said firmly.

He paused before he spoke and she could tell that he didn't want to tell her what he was about to say. "I deserve a demotion. I deserve whatever fate Adrian gives me for what I have done to you. You see, Emily, you are so very good."

"Yes, yes," she said impatiently. "I'm so good my fiancé is out with someone else."

"That's just it. These men here on earth do not appreciate you. They see only what is on the surface of a woman. They see that you are lovely to look at, but they don't look deeper to see that inside you are beautiful beyond compare. These human men do not seem to care at all for a woman's spirit. If a good spirit is encased in a fat body or has a plain face, the men do not want her."

"But, if I were gorgeous like that woman we saw with Donald . . ." she said sadly.

"No, you are beautiful, but you do not decorate

yourself as she does—that woman we saw with your . . . your. . . ."

"Ex," she supplied, sighing.

"Yes, with your ex."

"So you still haven't told me what you did to me in the past."

"You were the same then as you are now."

"Plain and practical?"

"No! You were trusting and easily led. Your heart is so loving that you. . . ."

"I what?"

Michael sighed. "You believe anything a good looking man tells you, that's what. There are few to equal you on earth, Emily," he said with disgust. "In life after life I have watched you throw away your goodness on alcoholics, on ne'er-do-wells who feed off of you. Do you have any idea what it was like for me to have to stand by and watch you and your two children nearly freeze to death one winter because your odious husband drank away the children's food money? You took in washing, Emily. Your soft hands. . . ." Pausing, he lifted her hand and kissed first the palm then the back of her hand, then each finger, one by one.

"So what did you do?" she asked softly.

"I directed you to a lady who needed sewing done. At least sewing was easier than washing and she—"

"No, I mean, what did you do to me in the last two lives?"

"Oh."

When he said no more, she put her head back on his shoulder. "Go on, you can tell me."

He took a deep breath and it was a while before he

spoke. "In your last lifetime, when you wore the silver dress, I chose that dress for you. I knew you'd look good in silver. You asked how your husband liked you in it. Emily, I . . . I didn't let you marry. Every time a man came along and you thought of marrying him, I'd tickle your nose so you'd get away from him. For the last two lifetimes I've not let you marry or have children. For two lifetimes you've died a virgin."

Emily pulled away from him and for a moment she was speechless, then she gaped at him. "What kind of angel are you? How could you do such a thing to someone under your protection? I don't think you were *sent* to earth, I think you were *cast out.*"

"Emily, please, you have to try to understand. After that washing life I made sure you had a rich, strong father, but even he couldn't prevent you from falling for a wastrel of a man. All that man wanted was your inheritance and he would have spent every penny you had and left you as a washerwoman. I couldn't bear to see it happen to you again."

"So you made my nose itch and left me a virgin. Just out of curiosity, how did you prevent the man from carrying me away? I assume he fought for my father's money."

"He, uh, well, he was caught in an embarrassing situation and had to marry someone else's daughter."

"And you saw to it that he was caught."

"Yes."

For a while Emily sat still in his arms, not moving, not knowing whether to believe him or not, but it all, somehow, made sense. All her life she'd had a feeling that she would never, ever, never get married, that no man was going to want her. When she was a girl she used to cry over pictures of babies and when her mother asked her what was wrong, Emily had said that she knew she'd never have any children.

"You did this to me for two lifetimes?"

"Yes," Michael said, his voice heavy. "I know it was wrong of me. I shouldn't have done it. In the end your life was almost as bad as it would have been if you had married the rotter."

"Let me take a guess. I lived the life of a recluse, surrounded by books and maybe a cat or two. Once a month I put on a literary tea for elderly ladies so we could discuss the latest bestseller. And I never had young friends because I couldn't bear to see their children and hear of their happy home lives."

Michael didn't speak for a while, but when he did, it was a barely audible, "Yes."

"I can see that. It's the life I have most feared, what I used to dream would happen to me. And you did that to me *twice?*"

"I thought that everything went wrong the first time because I didn't know what I was doing. But I thought I'd get it right the second time. I thought I'd find a wonderful, caring man for you then I'd nudge you both into the right direction and for once you'd have a happy life on earth."

"I think I can guess this one too. You never found a man worthy of me."

"Exactly. Who can live up to your goodness?"

Very slowly, Emily moved away from him and when he looked at her he was startled to see anger in her eyes.

"You bastard!" she said softly, but there was power

in her voice. "I'm not some . . . some *angel,*" she spat at him. "I'm a flesh-and-blood woman, not someone to be worshiped but to be loved. I don't want to be put in a museum and looked at because I'm—ha, ha—'good.' I want to live and experience all that life has to offer. I bet I was happier when I was a washerwoman than I was when I was rich and had ladies' meetings."

"Yes, you were," he said in wonder. "And I never could understand that. I saw to it that you had everything. You had—"

"I had *nothing!* Do you hear me? I had absolutely nothing whatever. I had—" Suddenly it was all too much for her and she couldn't continue. "You'll never understand. Never. Donald gave me—"

"I *know* what he gave you!" Michael half-shouted. "For all that I'm an angel, right now, in this body, I'm first of all a *man.* Do you think it's easy for me to see you like this and not touch you? I had one night with you and now I must pay for it for all eternity. But it was worth it. Yes, holding you was worth all the punishment in the world."

For a moment Emily stared at him, then she fell into his arms. "Michael, I can't love you. I can't. You're not real. You'll disappear."

Michael held her as though to let her go would end his life. "I know," he whispered. "It's the same with me. How can I love a mortal? How can I return home and watch you life after life with . . . with. . . ." He took a deep breath, then held her at arm's length. "What if I take away all memory of me?"

"You can't do that," she said, looking into his eyes. "You've told me enough that I understand that not even God can erase love. Maybe I won't remember why I feel so empty but I'll always know that there's something missing. Am I right?"

He took a moment before answering. "Yes. You cannot forget love, whether it's love for a human or love for God."

"I don't miss Donald, but I miss you when you so much as go into another room. I was angry at you for leaving me alone after we made love."

"I know. I didn't want to leave but I was . . . taken. My spirit and my body were moved elsewhere."

She put her head against his shoulder. "We shouldn't have done what we did and I've tried hard to forget it ever happened, but I can't. I'm afraid, afraid of being alone after you leave."

"Emily, you will never be alone, you never have been, never will be."

She looked up at him. "It won't be the same if you don't have a body."

"I know. I'll be able to see you but you'll be unable to see or hear me. And you may be unable to remember me at all." For a moment he held her, then he pulled away to look into her eyes. "All right, Emily, my love, we have two choices. One is that we can cry in our soup or—"

"Beer. Cry in our beer."

"Good. I like beer more than soup," he answered then grinned at the smile he got from her. "Anyway, we can cry over what is going to happen to us, because, make no mistake about it, we *are* going to be separated. Or we can live for the moment and try our best even though we know that tomorrow may bring bad news."

"I see," Emily said, pulling away from him. "By that I take it you mean that we should spend every minute you have on earth making love and being with each other."

"Exactly," he said brightly, smiling in delight. "Precisely."

"You *are* a man, aren't you? Angel or not, you are definitely a *man!*" She spat the last word at him as though it were something vile and loathsome.

Michael looked at her in bewilderment. "Your thoughts are too confused for me to read."

"You poor thing," she said, moving away from him. "I am one hundred percent on Adrian's side. You are indeed the *worst* angel in Heaven. I don't even know how you got to be an angel. You tell me that I'm bad at choosing men, but even I can see through what *you* are trying to do."

Michael's face was a study in confusion as he was obviously trying to figure out what she was talking about. "What have I done?"

"You got me away from Donald just for your own purposes, didn't you? And you let me rot without male attention for two lifetimes, also for your own selfish purposes, didn't you?"

"I, uh, well, maybe I was a bit selfish, but I was trying to protect you."

"Oh? And are you trying to protect me now when you're being so damned *nice* to me?"

"I wasn't trying to do anything bad," he said in confusion. "I—"

"That's just it, isn't it? You come here and you're nice to someone who you *know* is the world's worst judge of men, then you're so blasted nice to me that I fall head-over-heels in love with you and then what? I ask you, then what?"

"I. . . ." Michael scratched his head. "I don't seem to follow your logic."

"Well, good! I'm sick of being told what I am by you men. Sick of it! Do you hear me? Sick!"

"So what do you want me to do?"

"Find me a man, of course. I don't want to live alone. I want a house in the country and I want at least three children. You're an angel and you can see into people's hearts so you find me a man before you leave."

"But we have to find out who's trying to kill you."

"I see. You have the time to do that but not to do something good for me, is that it?"

"Emily, I seem to have lost my intelligence. I can't figure out why you're angry at me. I am thoroughly confused."

"It's very simple. You came to earth and ruined the life *I* chose. Maybe in your eyes it wasn't a good life but it *was* a life. But, now, thanks to you, I have nothing. I am two-thirds in love with an angel who is going to leave this earth and may or may not take away my memory of him when he goes, and I live in a tiny commuter town where I see very few men and meet even fewer. Being a small-town librarian doesn't open a lot of doors, does it?"

Emily almost felt sorry for Michael as his handsome face became a glower of concentration as he thought about what she was saying. But Emily was tired of being told she was a doormat, tired of what seemed to be centuries of falling in love with the wrong man. She had no doubt that she was in love with Michael and she didn't want to examine that too closely, but, by golly, sometimes a person needed to be selfish! Maybe it was wonderful that an angel had come to earth to save her life, but what kind of life was it going to be if she spent the rest of it alive but pining away for some man who she might not even remember?

"Well?" Emily said and was surprised by the strength in her voice. Her mother had taught her to be nice at all times, but right now being selfish felt amazingly good. She was going to use an angel for her own selfish purposes. "Can you find a good man for me or not?"

"I guess so," he said quietly. "What did you have in mind?"

"Apparently I usually prefer drunkards and men who marry me to give dinner parties, remember? So why ask me what I want? I want a man who will treat me well, one I can have children with, one of those men you read about, a man a woman can trust, one she can rely on."

"I see. Those are more difficult to come by in the present day and age. There's too much temptation in this world to—"

"Then when you're back home you'll just have to watch out after me, won't you? I mean, that *is* your job, isn't it?"

Emily could see that that's not what he had in mind, and truthfully, it's not what she wanted either. But what she was wanting more with each day was a lifetime spent with Michael. Not with someone like him but with him. Where else was she going to find a man so awed by life? A man who looked on a football game as one of the wonders of the world? Where else was she—?

She made herself stop thinking. She was not going to get to live with Michael and if she wanted to stay sane then she'd better get that idea out of her mind. As her friend Irene said, "The only antidote to a man is another man, preferably one who is younger and better looking."

"All right," Emily said firmly, trying to sound businesslike, "do we have a deal?"

"A deal?"

She'd never heard anyone sound so dejected. "This is an example of, I scratch your back, you scratch mine."

"Ah, at last something I like," Michael said in such a lascivious way that Emily had to turn away to hide a smile.

She turned back. "No, not like that. From now on we're business partners, nothing more. No more hanky-panky. That way you won't get bawled out by Adrian and demoted even lower, and I'll get a man and some kids out of all this. Sound good?"

"Sounds scientific," Michael said glumly. "And I don't mind what Adrian says. He's just jea—"

"Deal?" Emily said, holding out her hand to shake. "By the way, I don't think I like skinny men. They have no zest for life."

"Right," Michael said, shaking her hand.

"Now that that's settled, shall we get some sleep? Tomorrow we have to start going through those files and you have to start finding me a lifetime partner." With a smile, Emily went to the other side of the room to the mattress Michael had dragged down from the attic earlier. It was musty, as were the old quilts on top of it, but she was so tired that she knew she could sleep anywhere.

As she settled down, she smiled into the darkness. For the first time since she ran into Michael she felt that her life was going to begin, not finish as she'd seen in the last days. They needed to find who was trying to kill her, then Michael would find her a husband, someone nice, someone she could have children with, someone. . . .

She drifted off to sleep with a smile on her face.

But Michael did not sleep. He knew that Emily had no idea of the difficulty of what she requested. He knew that he had no "good" men among those he looked after. At least not good enough for Emily. So he'd have to contact some other angels and see who they had. Then, of course, the man had to be of suitable age and size. And wouldn't it be nice if he lived near Emily?

Michael tried not to think of what he was doing, tried his best to dampen down his feeling that he wanted no other man to touch "his" Emily. "Mortality is for mortals," Adrian had said. "Leave it to them to make their own mistakes, to wallow in their own bad karma." Adrian had meant that Michael was not to put himself on an earthly plane where he felt possessive of this mortal woman. Adrian wanted Michael to remember that he was an angel and above such lowly feelings.

But Michael didn't feel very angelic. In fact, maybe if the truth were known, he had never felt very angelic about Emily. For right now what he wanted most in the world was to climb into bed with her and make love to her.

But he didn't do that. Instead, he settled the earthly body that was housing his spirit onto the second mattress then pulled his spirit out of the body. "Astral projection," it was called on earth. Then, in spirit form, he went to Heaven and began to confer with other angels about what man could make his Emily happy.

When his spirit returned in the morning, his body was rested, albeit a bit stiff from not having moved all night, and Michael had some names and some places and a plan. Also, he had a heavy heart. Even Adrian hadn't lectured him when he'd seen how miserable Michael was. The other angels couldn't understand what Michael was upset about, but they could feel his pain and they sympathized.

For a moment, before his spirit reentered the body, Michael hovered over Emily, watching her sleep, and he vowed that he'd do the best job that he could. He'd try to make up for the loneliness he'd caused her in the past and maybe, if he were clever enough, he'd change Emily's luck with men in the future.

Swooping down, he kissed her cheek: it was an angel kiss, given often, but rarely felt. However, Emily stirred in her sleep and Michael moved away. He must not let her see what he was feeling. To burden her with his feelings of jealousy and regret, even to pile his love on her, was not fair. As she'd said, he was going to leave and he had no right to take her heart with him. From now on, he was going to do the job he was supposed to do and keep his feelings to himself. Yes, he thought, smiling. For once he was going to do the job an angel should do. He was going to give and give and give, with no hope of receiving anything in return.

"But Lord," he whispered as he slid back into the earthly body, "don't let her do that thing with her hair over her left ear. I can only take so much."

# Chapter 20

TWO DAYS, EMILY THOUGHT AS SHE OPENED YET ANOTH-
er big trunk in the attic of the Madison house. For two
days Michael had paid *no* attention to her. Instead, he
had become as obsessed with the computer as any
nerd on earth. That he was doing just what Emily had
wanted didn't help matters, but she had grown used to
his undivided attention and she now knew that she
was, well, rather more than fond of having a gorgeous
man concerned about her every thought and action.

But that seemed to be over. Ever since the night
when Emily had asked Michael to get her a man, he
had been different. The next morning, against Emily's
protests, he had walked into town and returned an
hour later in a truck with a young man from the
phone company. Had Emily not already seen what
Michael could do she would have been amazed when

this man—free of charge of course—ran a line from the nearest pole and installed both telephone lines and electricity in the old house. Michael could run both the computer and the modem in case he decided to tap into the Internet.

Michael also brought back several bags of groceries and when Emily offered to cook breakfast, figuring she would somehow use the ancient stove in the kitchen, Michael declined, saying he had work to do. When she volunteered to help him plug into the Internet, he told her that Alfred was there to help him and why didn't she find something else to do? He'd call her when he found what he was looking for.

Blinking at him, astonished at this turn of events, Emily backed away.

"There are keys to every lock in the house hidden under a tread in the main stairs. It's the third or fourth one," Michael said, looking at the computer screen. She could tell that he was also listening to someone she couldn't see because he was murmuring "Yes" and "No" now and then. Also, there were several mutterings of, "I don't understand," as he touched the keypad.

"Third one," he called after her. "The captain says it's the third tread. And he says that you can snoop all you like, that there's nothing anywhere that tells the truth."

Feeling as though she were a child who had been dismissed and told to go occupy herself, Emily went in search of the keys. Sure enough there were several bunches of keys hidden under the third tread, which had been cleverly fastened down so, only if you knew it would open, could you move it.

"Did it meself," came a voice clearly in her head.

"I have to talk to angels," she said aloud, "but I draw the line at ghosts. Go haunt someone else."

Emily was sure that she heard laughter but it faded away so maybe the captain—or whoever it was—had decided to leave her alone. Muttering to herself that all men were, basically, slime, she headed straight for the attics. If she was going to go exploring she knew exactly what she wanted to explore.

But now she had spent two days in the extensive attics and even though what she had seen and discovered had been wildly interesting, she was still more than annoyed at Michael. How could he turn on and off a person so easily? They had spent nearly every minute together since she'd hit him with her car but now he had his nose in that computer and he didn't have the time of day for her. He didn't so much as eat meals with her. He didn't look up when she came into the room and made no attempt to speak to her when she was near him.

Last evening she had tried to talk to him. "Any luck?"

"Depends on what you call luck," he said, never raising his eyes from the computer screen.

"Have you found any evil?"

"Lots. That's the problem. There is nothing but evil inside this computer. Every one of these stories deals with horrible men and women doing horrible things. It is nearly impossible to find out which evil relates to you, especially since you wrote all of this, therefore all of it relates to you."

"Maybe I could help," she said with more eagerness than she wanted to let him see.

"No," he said blithely. "Alfred and I are fine. You go and look in your attics. The captain says there's some treasure up there but he could just mean something sentimental to him. On the other hand, he was a rich man."

Again, Emily felt that she'd been dismissed to the children's playground. "Found any men for me?" she asked. "I want someone very handsome. And virile. Remember, I want half a dozen kids."

"I found three men for you days ago. Well, hours ago, anyway."

"Oh," Emily said, feeling a bit let down.

Michael glanced at her over the computer screen. "That's what you wanted, isn't it? Have you changed your mind?"

"Of course not. What choice do I have? You're going to leave soon and you sent Donald away so I must take one of these men."

"You could remain single. Or you could marry a man of your own choosing."

"No, thank you. You've made me see how bad I am at that." She glared at the top of his head. "I always choose inappropriate men. Look at Donald. Look at what else I've involved myself with." She meant him, that he was as bad as all the other men she'd chosen over the centuries.

Michael didn't bother to look up. "But then, you didn't choose me, did you, Emily? I chose you. Now, run along and see if you can find the treasure. The captain says it's rubies; his wife loved rubies."

For a moment Emily thought about sitting down on a mattress and not moving, anything to keep from obeying his autocratic dismissal, but, in the end, rubies won out. As she started up the stairs again she was sure she heard laughter and knew very well that it was the captain showing his amusement that she had chosen sparkling stones over revenge. "Your wife probably committed suicide to get away from you," she said under her breath, then immediately wished she hadn't because she could feel the spirit vanish. Instead of being surrounded by warm laughter she felt nothing but emptiness near her.

"Great," she said. "I have offended a ghost and an angel. Who's next? Maybe God should let me at the devil. With my luck I'd make him so angry he'd go into a sulk and never speak to the world again."

With heavy feet, she made her way up to the attic and now she'd spent two days there going through old trunks and looking at the edition numbers in the hundreds of books there. She hadn't found any rubies but she had found some wonderful furniture and books and a set of china that was beautiful.

It was on the afternoon of the second day that she sat on a round-top trunk and surveyed what was in front of her. She had to give it to the captain that he'd been strong enough to keep vandals away from these treasures all these years. Emily knew a couple of antique dealers who'd give a great deal to see what she was seeing now. And if Emily knew anything it was that there were some real treasures up here.

"Wonder how much it's all worth?" she said aloud, but instead of thinking of money, she thought how nice that wing chair with the eagle-headed arms would look downstairs in the living room. There was a huge trunk full of curtains and Emily wondered if they could be relined and reused. Wouldn't the red ones look divine in the dining room? She could almost see the dining room at Christmas, red candles everywhere, those dishes she'd found in a huge wooden crate on the table and heavy silver flatware glowing in the candlelight. And—"

Suddenly, it was as though the whole house began to vibrate. At first she thought it was the beginning of an earthquake but as she looked at the walls and the contents of the room, they were still. It was just the air that was vibrating. It was as though an electrical current was coursing through the air of the room and she could feel it.

"Angels and ghosts," she said aloud and knew that Michael had at last found the evil he was looking for. Without even dusting herself off, she started running for the stairs, but Michael was already there.

"I found it," he said, holding up the computer and she could see that there was a picture on the screen. "It wasn't in the printed matter but in the photographs. I didn't know you could have pictures on these things. I didn't know—"

He broke off as he looked about the attic. Glancing backward, Emily saw what he did. Every trunk, wardrobe, crate, box had been opened and the contents were now standing about.

"The captain said you were a damn good rummager but I had no idea . . ."

Emily narrowed her eyes at him. "You want to show me the photo and stop commenting on what is none of your business?"

"Want to know where the rubies are?"

Emily had to bite her tongue to keep from shouting, "Yes!" He had been cool to her for days now so she could be cool in return. "If the captain wants to tell me he may, but it doesn't matter as I'd just have to turn them over to the city because it owns this house."

"Ah, yes, of course," Michael said. "And you wouldn't want to have the fun of finding them, would you?"

"Could you refrain from making fun of me long enough to tell me what it is that you found? And, by the way, is someone moving those curtains over there?"

"Albert!" Michael said sharply. "You'll frighten Emily. Look at this," he said, handing the computer to her. "One of those men is responsible for trying to kill you. Who are they and what do they have to do with you? What have you done to one of them?"

After a look of disgust at him, she turned toward the photo. There were three men wearing beat-up old fishing gear, laughing into the camera, holding up four fish hardly bigger than pet goldfish.

"I've never seen any of them in my life. Where did the picture come from?"

"The computer," Michael said as though she'd just asked a very stupid question.

"Who put it in the computer and why?"

For a moment Michael listened then he told her that Donald had manned all the pictures into the computer.

"Scanned," Emily said automatically. "So you're saying this is just one of many photos he has on disk?"

"Yes. There are at least fifty of them. No, Alfred says there are seventy-one photos and only a few of them have captions so he doesn't know who the people are."

"I would imagine Donald knows who everyone is in those photos," Emily said.

"Shall we call him?" Michael asked with a smile.

"He might be a bit, ah, perturbed that we took his computer," she answered, smiling back at Michael. The minute their eyes met, he looked away and his friendly manner was once again cool.

She took a deep breath. She was not going to ask him why he'd turned against her or what was wrong with him, or the worst one, what she had done wrong. If he wanted to sulk, let him. And the sooner they found out why he was here, the sooner he could leave and the sooner she could have a life.

"Nice-looking men," she said, studying the photo. "Wonder if they're married?"

"One of them is trying to kill you but the other two might be available. We just have to sort out who is who."

"I have an idea. Why don't I meet all three of them and the one I fall madly in love with will surely be the killer."

Michael had to override his coolness to laugh at that, and in spite of his good intentions, he warmed up. "All right, we have work to do. Tomorrow night there is a big party in the city and we're going to go. There're going to be two men there for you to meet; it's all been arranged. Now I need to know who these men are so they can be there too. Once I meet them I'll know which one is trying to harm you."

"Will you know why?"

"I doubt it but I can make him tell us."

"Then what do you do? How do you stop him from going ahead and killing me? You can't murder him first, can you? You can't make him have a heart attack, can you?"

At that Michael looked aghast. "God decides when people live and die. Angels do not," he said stiffly, as though she'd insulted his code of ethics.

"But, really, what can you do if you find out this is the man?"

For a moment Michael looked bewildered. Obviously he hadn't thought of that. "I don't know. If I meet him I can go right to his guardian and find the answers to a lot of things. But to do it the other way, to take the photo home and try to find who guards this man could take years."

"Could you condense it into earth time and make it a couple of hours here?"

Michael narrowed his eyes at her. "You want me to spend *years* working when you could make a few calls and find out what we need to know?"

Emily had the pleasure of giving a little shrug, as though to say, It's all the same to me.

"Now, is there someone besides Donald who'd know who these men are?"

"What makes you think I would know such a person? After all, I'm not smart enough to be told the truth about Captain Madison's life so how could a dummy like me know about three men fishing?"

"Emily!" Michael said through clenched teeth. "This is no time to play your female games. This is serious! One of these men is trying to kill you and we need to stop him. I feel sure that you know someone who can help us. I need to get the men to this party and we need to Raphael you and—"

"Irene," Emily said quickly, "and what does that mean? That you need to Raphael me?"

In answer, Michael looked at her as though she should know the answer to that without his having to explain. "Call Irene and tell her we're coming and that—"

"A makeover! That's what you mean, isn't it?" Anger began to surge through Emily as she realized what he'd meant by "Raphael her." When Michael had first been in her apartment he had watched TV and when he saw an ad for the *Sally Jessy Raphael* show he'd thought it was about angels. With great amusement, Emily had watched Michael as he sat through an hour of agonizing stories which were all solved by a better haircut. For hours afterward he had asked questions about what makeup means to a woman.

"Don't they see the spirits of the women?" he asked. "Why does it matter what they smear on their eyes? Or what color their hair is? I cannot understand this."

But now he seemed to understand perfectly, Emily thought, if he was planning to do a makeover on *her!* So much for his declarations of her being beautiful just as she is, she thought.

"Give me the telephone," she said, glaring at him.

"Emily, I didn't mean that I think you're not—" Not finishing his sentence, he straightened his shoulders and started down the stairs. "You'd better call her soon. We have a lot to do."

Following him, Emily hoped that he could read every thought that went through her mind.

In minutes she had Irene on the phone, for she had her friend's most private number, the line she always answered no matter what.

"Emily?" Irene said in astonishment. "Where the hell are you? Do you know that the FBI has been here looking for you? And that egomaniac you planned to marry has called me three times. What in the world have you *done?!*"

"You wouldn't believe me if I told you. Look, I need your help."

"Anything, sugar. I'm so glad to see you break out of that stranglehold Mr. News," she said the name with great contempt, "had on you that I'll do anything you want. John could help. I can get him to do anything."

John was Irene's boss and Emily happened to know that Irene was having an affair with him.

"Do you know of a big party that's to be held in the city in the next few weeks? Not a private party but something big."

"You mean the Ragtime Ball?"

"Probably. Can you get me into it? Actually, I need two tickets."

"You are kidding, aren't you? I'm not even invited to that thing. You have to submit a net-worth statement to get invited. And since when have you wanted to do something like that? I had no idea that rubbing elbows with the rich and snobbish was your dream."

"It's not. I just need to meet some men."

There was a pause on Irene's end. "At last. Emily, you have made my whole week."

"No, really, I need to meet some specific men, not just any men. Look, I have a big favor to ask you.

Would you look at a photo of three men and tell me if you know them or not. I very much need to know who they are. I can e-mail it to you."

"Sure. I'll do my best. If they're local I'll know them or I can find someone who does. Send the photo now and I'll call you back. Give me your number."

Michael put his hand on Emily's arm and shook his head. She was not to give the telephone number to anyone—if their illegal line had a number, that is.

"I'll send the photo then call you back."

"Wise move, honey. I wouldn't put it past the FBI to have tapped my lines. Don't tell anyone where you are until this thing is settled. By the way, what happened to that man they said you were protecting, that hit man?"

"Oh," Emily said lightly, "he's long gone. Haven't seen him for days."

"Right. Gotcha," Irene said then hung up.

Emily sent the photo through the wires, waited a few minutes then called Irene back.

"You do know how to play big, don't you, honey? Whatever are you mixed up in?"

"Do you know them?"

"I can't believe that you don't know them. But then they don't usually allow themselves to be photographed. I think they're afraid of someone using their pictures to practice voodoo on, and, believe me, there are lots of people who'd like to stick pins in these men."

"Irene!"

"Okay. The man on the left is Charles Wentworth. He owns most of the banks in the state. The man in the middle is Statler Mortman. He owns land. Like maybe entire states' worth of land. And the guy on the right uses both of them. He gets money from Wentworth, land from Mortman and builds things. Big, ugly things that sometimes fall down on people. You know, Emily, a newspaper would pay a lot for a copy of this photo. Where'd you get it?"

"From Donald."

"Oh my, then it *was* you who stole his computer. He said it was but no one believed him, especially since he'd earlier told people that you were dead. His credibility is plummeting by the minute. Another station has already challenged every word that he's reported. Did you know that they think the woman in your car was Chamberlain's wife?"

"Really? And what makes them say that?"

"Beats me. Autopsy, I guess."

"But how did they find enough of her to autopsy?"

"Oh, hang on, John's buzzing me."

While Emily was on hold, she was looking at the computer screen at the three handsome men and wondering what these men had to do with her. She'd done many stories for Donald but she hadn't worked on any about men this powerful and this rich.

The phone clicked back on as Irene released the hold button and when she spoke her voice sounded odd. It was barely a whisper. "Emily, dearest, you are not going to believe this. John just told me that he and his wife could not attend the Ragtime Ball and he offered me their tickets."

For just a moment, Emily glanced at Michael, knowing that he had somehow made this happen. She didn't like that he'd done this. For all he knew the

Ragtime Ball was the highlight of John's life and of his poor downtrodden wife.

"John says he was never so glad to get out of anything in his life. He says his wife is dragging him off to visit her relatives."

"Irene, may I have the tickets?"

"Of course. Somehow I don't think these tickets would have been available if you hadn't wanted them. Now why do I feel like that, Emily?"

"I have no idea. There's something else, Irene. I'll be bringing a friend into the city and we need a place to stay."

Irene hesitated. "Ah, this isn't a man, is it? About six feet, dark curly hair?"

"What about your phone lines?"

"Do you think that a man in John's position would allow his lines to be bugged? You can tell me anything."

Emily set her mouth in a grim line. "Then I'll tell you the worst of it. I need a makeover. You know, the kind on TV. I need to be made to look as unlike myself as possible."

"That shouldn't be too difficult since wearing lipstick is an alien experience to you. So who's the man you're trying to catch?"

"The truth is that my guardian angel has come to earth, he's promised to find the perfect man for me and he's told me that I'm to meet this man at the Ragtime Ball. So you can see why I want to look my best. I'll need hair, makeup and a dress."

"Guardian angel, huh? Boy, Emily, when you go off the deep end, you sure do fall."

"Yes, but, unfortunately, I fall too hard and too often."

"Better than not falling at all," Irene said. "Look, honey, I'll expect you tonight or early tomorrow. And I'll make appointments for you for all-day tomorrow; the ball is tomorrow night. I'll say one thing for you, when you do move, you don't let any dust settle on you."

"Necessity," she said as she hung up the phone, then said to Michael, "Oh no, I forgot to ask about the dress. I can't borrow anything of Irene's; she's a foot taller than I am."

"Let me take care of the dress," Michael said, but he didn't meet her eyes. "What's the name of that store you like that's in that place?"

Emily was not going to give him the satisfaction of knowing that she understood him. "I have no idea what you mean," she said haughtily.

Looking at her over the computer screen, he lifted one eyebrow.

"Neiman Marcus in Dallas, Texas," she said with her lips tensed.

Michael didn't look up from the computer screen but there was a tiny smile about his lips. "You always know what I want when I want it and you always understand me," he said softly. "Whether I'm in a body or not you understand me."

Emily wanted to shout that she didn't understand him now and hadn't been able to figure him out for the last two days, but she said nothing. Instead, she mumbled about returning upstairs and when Michael made no protest, she went back to the attics.

For a moment Michael watched her back as she left

the room and it took all his strength to stay where he was. "I owe her this," he said aloud to himself then made himself remember her last two lonely lives, lives that he had caused to be unhappy. "I'm not going to do it again," he said, then picked up the phone and, with Alfred's help, got the number to the main store in Dallas.

Thirty minutes later he put down the phone, smiling. With the help of a lovely saleswoman, Michael had ordered a dress that he was assured was to "die for." "I certainly hope not," he'd said and the woman had laughed. When he was told the dress cost over ten thousand dollars, he glanced at the computer screen and by this time Alfred had come up with a credit card number and an address, which Michael read over the line. Credit was approved instantly. He didn't know and didn't ask, but a month later, a fabulously wealthy man received a bill for his wife's shopping which included a charge for a dress, shoes and matching coat. The man's secretary paid the bill without so much as blinking.

With the dress on its way, Michael went back to the computer. Maybe he could yet find out why someone was trying to kill his Emily. "Correction," he told himself. Not *his* Emily. Emily was soon going to belong to a man he had been assured was kind, thoughtful, a good companion, intelligent, had a great sense of humor and—

Michael refused to remember what else his fellow angel had said about the man who was going to be at the ball tomorrow night.

"Alfred," Michael said without looking up from the computer screen, "tell the Captain I want his wife's rubies." He listened for a moment. "Yes, the whole set, with the bracelet and earrings, and, no, he's not going to get them back. I'm going to give them to Emily."

He turned back to the computer and tried to give it his full attention.

# Chapter 21

"IF I DIDN'T LOVE YOU I'D HATE YOU," IRENE SAID AS SHE looked at Emily in the deep-red dress. For something so expensive, the dress was deceptively simple. It appeared to be merely a sheath of red silk satin, but because of the way it was cut and the way the inside was engineered, it pushed Emily's ample bosom up until it was nearly spilling over the top.

"You don't think it's too much?"

"You or the dress?"

"Both I guess," Emily said apprehensively as she tried to push some of her flesh under the silk.

"Darling, do you have any idea how much women pay to get boobs like yours?"

Emily let out a sound that was very much like a giggle.

"I tell you, that boyfriend of yours certainly has taste."

"He's not—"

"Yeah," Irene said, "you told me. He's not your boyfriend. Yeah and I'm a natural blond. What's he doing with that computer anyway?"

"Trying to find out who wants me dead," Emily said, for she'd told her friend the truth. In fact, she'd told her friend the entire truth, but her friend didn't realize it. Irene had laughed a lot when she'd heard a second time that Michael was Emily's guardian angel.

Emily and Irene were an odd choice for friends as they could hardly be greater opposites. Irene was all glamor: her idea of roughing it was to wear only two-inch heels. Emily, on the other hand, didn't own a pair of high heels.

But they had been friends from the instant Irene had walked into the Greenbriar Library and asked about renting a place in town. Much to her horror, Irene had been told by her physician, who knew Irene's true age, something that no one else (including the passport office) did, that she either had to calm down her burning-the-candle-at-both-ends lifestyle or be prepared to pay the price for too much hard-lived fun. Reluctantly and with a great deal of protestation, Irene had rented a tiny house in the absurdly quiet town of Greenbriar. But to her amazement, she had grown to love the place. She'd met Emily the first day; they'd had lunch together at the local diner and had been friends ever since.

"We're no competition to each other," Irene had said. "You're not trying to get my job and heaven knows I don't want yours. Or your boyfriend," she said, referring to Donald. "You don't envy me and I don't envy you. It's that simple."

Whatever the truth was, together it seemed they could find a solution to almost any problem. Emily could see what Irene needed to do in her big city life and Irene always had some exciting advice for Emily to liven up her life. Their only disagreement had been over Donald. Irene hated the man, thought he wanted Emily for his own selfish purposes and often told her so.

When Irene had met Michael she'd liked him instantly. "An angel, huh? With eyes like those, I think he's more likely from the devil."

"He's not for me," Emily had said stiffly. "So don't get your hopes up. He's going to leave."

"I see. San Quentin? Is that where they put hit men nowadays? Or will they try to kill him again?"

It was obvious that Irene thought Emily had again been conned. She liked Michael but she wasn't about to believe that he was an angel.

But now, as Emily stood in Irene's living room wearing her fabulously expensive dress, her hair now a deep red and piled on top of her head, Irene stepped back to admire her friend. Physically, she and Emily were also opposites. Irene was nearly six feet while Emily was barely five. Irene had broad, square shoulders and a figure that was made for clothes. She looked elegant in whatever she put on. Emily, with her bosomy, curvy figure, looked matronly or slutty, depending on what she wore.

But in the red dress she had on now, she looked sexy and elegant and, well, rich.

"You look like your daddy races horses, your broth-

er plays polo and your mother heads charity commit-
tees," Irene said, smiling.

"It's not too much?" she asked again. "You don't
think there's too much of me showing?"

"Not at all. What do you think, Michael?" Irene
asked him. He was standing to one side of the room
and in his tuxedo, he was dazzlingly handsome, but
Emily tried hard not to look at him. She had to keep
her vow to find an appropriate man, one who wasn't
going to, literally, fly away at any moment.

"I think it looks bare," he said, scowling.

"All you men think that," Irene said, smiling. "At
least the possessive ones of you do. Think she'll
attract the attention of the three men in the photo?"

"I'm sure they are interested only in a woman of
means."

"Then they won't want me," Emily said. "I feel like
the small-town librarian wearing borrowed clothes."

"Like Cinderella must have felt," Irene said, laughing, then looked at Michael curiously as he took
something from his pocket.

"Perhaps this will help your self-confidence," he
said as he fastened a necklace about her ivory neck.
There was a band of rubies set in gold that hugged the
base of her neck and several perfect, large, drop-
shaped rubies dripped from the band.

"And these," Michael said as he handed Emily the
matching earrings. Rubies the size of pigeon's eggs
dangled from small, round rubies set in gold. "And
this," he said, adding to her hand a bracelet that was
three rows of round rubies.

"The captain's," she whispered. "His wife's rubies."

"Those are real, aren't they?" Irene said in a whisper of reverence that such jewels deserved. She recovered before Emily did. "If those don't make you change your mind about looking like boring Miss Emily Jane Todd, then nothing on earth will."

"Emily is anything but boring," Michael said and for a moment he looked at Emily with eyes so hot that the rubies seemed to be made of fire. Quickly, he turned away as he went to get her coat.

"Oh my," Irene said. "It's been a long time since a man looked at me like that. And you said he wasn't interested in you in 'that' way? Is that what you said, Emily?"

"I told you, he's going to leave."

"Wait for him," Irene said into her ear. "Wait for him for all eternity is my advice to you."

"Try till the end of time," she muttered, then walked toward Michael where he was holding out her coat. It was white satin, lined with the same red of her dress and shoes. Emily knew immediately that Michael had been right: the rubies had done the trick. As they left Irene's apartment, Emily felt as though she were the most devastatingly beautiful woman on earth. In the limo that Michael had arranged to take them to the ball (she didn't ask how he'd paid for it), she didn't pay one bit of attention to his orders. She didn't hear him tell her that she was to leave everything to him and that she was to stay away from the three men.

"I can read their minds," Michael said. "I'll know which man it is and I'll come up with some way to stop this."

"Only if you know *why* the man wants to kill me,"

she muttered. Wouldn't it make sense if *she* tried to find out? Wouldn't it be interesting if she could charm him with her—she nearly giggled again—charm him with her rubies and her cleavage?

"Emily, I don't like what you're thinking," Michael said seriously. "I see an image of an absurdly large man in your mind. What has he got to do with this?"

Emily gave a little smile and looked out the window. She had been thinking about the latest Schwarzenegger spy movie. Didn't women in spy movies wear red satin and rubies the size of pigeon's eggs?

"I think we should go back to Irene's. I don't think we should go to this party," Michael said then leaned forward to tap the glass that separated them from the driver.

But Emily put her hand on his arm and smiled at her. To her delight, Michael glanced down at her cleavage, turned a bit pale then said no more.

Emily had never felt so powerful in her life.

She looked over at Michael. How could she think of any man other than him, she asked herself, glancing at him again out of the corner of her eyes. He was fabulously handsome in his tuxedo and he had done so many kind things for her. When he'd first said he was going to "Raphael" her, she had been insulted, but now, feeling the way she did, she could only thank him. It was amazing how much difference the right clothes and a few jewels could make to a woman. Not to mention two hours spent on her makeup and another four hours on her hair that was no longer exactly her natural color. "We'll just make it look as though it were kissed by the sun," the hairdresser had said. It had taken many hours to look this "natural" and Emily was sure it was worth it.

"You look nice," she said, smiling at him.

"And you are beautiful," he replied and the way he said it made her feel even better.

What an unselfish man he is, she thought, to do this thing for her. He had said that he loved her yet here he was, introducing her to other men. He had gone to a lot of trouble to find a man for her and he had taken more time and effort to make sure she was attractive to the man. Emily was more used to men like Donald who mumbled thanks when you handed them a stack of papers that represented three weeks' work.

"I really appreciate all you're doing for me," she said softly. "There aren't many men who'd be this unselfish."

Michael smiled at her. "I'm your guardian angel, remember? Taking care of you is my job."

"So what's he like?"

"Who?"

"The man I'm supposed to meet."

"Kind, thoughtful, a very good man. Does a lot of good works. He's in line for a promotion to a higher level in his next life. He really does dedicate himself to good, just as you do."

Emily leaned back against the leather of the seats of the plush car and smiled. For a moment she envisioned a future with a man who was concerned with his home and his family, as she was. "Thank you," she murmured. "It's kind of you to do this for me. I really appreciate it," she said, her voice full of emotion.

It was thirty minutes later that her warm fuzzy feelings toward Michael changed.

"You lowlife, slimy . . ." She couldn't think of anything bad enough to call him. And the words she did think of, she wouldn't say aloud but she dearly hoped he was reading her mind, and to make sure, she sent him some pointed thoughts.

"Emily, honey, he really is a nice man. He—"

"Don't you even *speak* to me," she hissed, then smiled at a woman wearing a slinky black dress who looked at them curiously. She turned back to Michael. "I trusted you. I believed in you!"

"But he is—"

"Don't even say it. He's *good!*" She spat the word at him. She didn't know when in her life she had ever been so angry.

They had arrived at this heavenly party and, at first glance, everything was as Emily had pictured it: there were so many jewels on the women that a single candle could have lit the room and the sparkles would have made enough light. Never had Emily felt as good as she did walking up the steps of that marble building and into that divine ballroom. She hated to relinquish her coat but she did, then took Michael's arm and walked in with the other guests. Everything was perfect and in her beautiful dress and the rubies, she felt as though she belonged.

It wasn't until Michael led them to their table that she grew puzzled. "Their" table was so far from the others that she could barely see the dance floor. Tall palms hid them from the dancers and even from the other guests. It was almost as though they were outside looking in.

"Privacy," Michael said, smiling at her and she'd given a weak smile in return. Maybe it was better to be private when she met the man of her life.

But twenty minutes later she was ready to kill Michael. An elderly gentleman came to sit at their table and, politely, Emily tried to carry on a conversation with him. But she was constantly craning her neck trying to see who else was going to sit at the table. The man chosen for her was divinely inspired. What would he look like?

"Mr. Greene founded a center for cancer research," Michael was saying to Emily.

"How good of you," she said, looking over the man's shoulder at the dancers. If she turned her head just so and looked through three palm trees she could just see the skirt of one of the dancing women.

"I don't usually come to these things," the man was saying, "but I made an exception tonight because this one is for charity. And I asked for this table to be set up here to keep away from the folderol of the dancin'. Don't approve myself. What about you?" he asked Emily.

"Me? Oh I love to dance." She looked pointedly at Michael and asked in her mind when the man was going to show up.

Michael turned away to look at the older man sitting next to Emily. "And you share the profits of your company with your employees, don't you?"

"That I do. They helped me; I help them."

"And you're a widower, aren't you?"

"My dear wife passed on fourteen years ago. I would have remarried but I never found a modern woman with her morals."

"Emily runs the library in Greenbriar," Michael said, then nudged her with his shoulder, making Emily search for something to say.

"Yes. Uh, ah, maybe you'd like to attend one of our career days, Mr., uh, I'm sorry, I didn't catch your name."

The man chuckled. "Greene. Dale Greene. I'm pleased to hear of a woman who hasn't heard of me. So many women today know more about a man's bank balances than he does. It's refreshing to meet someone like you, Miss Todd. And if I may say so, you are lovely."

It was somewhere in here that Emily began to realize that this old man, a man who was on the far side of seventy, was the man Michael had chosen for her. Slowly, she turned her head toward him, her eyes glittering. "May I see you in private for a moment?"

Michael gave her a weak smile. "Emily, dear, I think—"

"Now!" she said, then lowered her voice. "And I do mean *now!*"

"If you'll excuse us, Mr. Greene," Michael said politely as he followed Emily deeper into the palms.

"Emily, I—" he began once they were alone.

"Don't you say anything to me. You are the lowest of the low. I don't know how I ever had a kind thought about you. How I ever believed that *you* were an angel."

"He's a good man. He—"

"And I bet he's a real firecracker in bed, isn't he? And that's where I'm supposed to get children, isn't it?"

"Look, I didn't have much time so I did the best I could."

"No, you did the worst that you could. You could have found me any number of men who were at least young! But, no, not you. You can't bear any other man touching me, can you? For generations you've done this to me."

"I thought you didn't believe I was an angel," he said with a bit of a smile.

Turning on her heel, Emily started to leave.

He caught her arm. "All right, I apologize. Maybe I didn't mind that he was older than necessary."

"That man is older than my grandfather," she said, her teeth clenched, then smiled at a passing couple. "Look at this," she said. "My one and only chance in the world to go to a party like this and you ruin it."

"You're right," he said solemnly, "and I apologize. I think the evening is ruined and we should leave at once."

"You'd like that, wouldn't you? And what did you have planned for the rest of the evening? A little hanky-panky between you and me?"

Blinking, he looked at her in consternation. "Sex," she nearly spat into his face. "Is that what you had planned?"

"I hadn't thought of that but I am quite willing," he said without a hint of a smile.

Emily could think of no reply so she slammed the high heel of her shoe down on his instep then had the satisfaction of seeing him nearly collapse in pain. "Serves you right," she said in his ear. Then when a passing couple looked as though they might stop and ask if they needed assistance, Emily said, "I think we should get you home, dear. You know how your gout acts up."

While trying to balance on one leg and rubbing his foot, Michael said he thought it would be a very good idea if they left.

"I want to dance and have a good time, and I'm not leaving until I get it."

"I'm afraid I can't allow that. There's a man here who wants to *kill* you."

Emily gave him a little smile. "But isn't that what I'm here to find out about? I thought we came to find out who he is and why he keeps trying to blow me up."

"*I* am to find out those things. You wanted to find a good man you could spend your life with. Mr. Greene is a very good man and you—"

"Could die of boredom, that's what. Did you hear what that man had to say? He doesn't drink, smoke, dance or wear bright colors. He is such a paragon they'd have to create a new wing of Heaven just for him."

Michael didn't smile at her jest. "Emily, you know how you are."

"And what is that supposed to mean?"

"Nothing bad, but you do have a tendency to choose men who are less than virtuous."

"Like you?" she hissed. "You're wanted by the FBI and you have, or, I guess, had an ex-wife who was trying to kill you."

"Neither of those things were caused by me."

"That's true, isn't it? You're just an angel. An angel who interferes in my life until I have no life."

"I'm trying to protect you."

"Protect me from what? From whom? What I want to know is who's going to protect me from you!" With that Emily turned and started to walk away from him.

He caught up with her. "Where are you going?"

"To the dance floor."

"No you're not," he said as he caught her arm in a firm hold. "I can't let you go out there in this state. There's no telling what you'll do out of sheer defiance."

" 'In this state?' " she quoted. "Are you calling me hysterical?"

"I'm saying you're different tonight. I don't know if it's the dress or the rubies but I think you want to do something bad. Or maybe not bad, just . . ."

"Naughty?" she asked, one eyebrow arched.

"Yes, that's the word."

"I do want to do something . . . something outrageous. This is my one and only night to be Cinderella and I want to dance at the ball. Is that so difficult to understand?"

"Of course not. All right then, let's go. I believe I can—"

"Don't do me any favors. I can find my own dance partners." But when Emily tried to move, he blocked her way onto the dance floor. "Would you please move?"

"No, I will not. I don't know what's come over you tonight but I think you should change your thoughts. Maybe this party is overwhelming you." Abruptly, he stopped and stared at her. "Emily, you look like you're about to cry. Should we go home?"

Truthfully, Emily's tears were of rage. This could be

her one and only chance to dress like this, to attend a party like this and he was *not* going to take it from her. She glared up at him. "You don't mind if I go to the rest room, do you? Or is that too exciting for boring little me?"

"No, of course not," Michael said and he had that universal look that men have when they have no idea what they've said or done that's wrong. "I'll wait here for you," he said, giving her a weak smile.

Once in the rest room, Emily tried to calm herself. Did everything have to be a disappointment? She'd loved Donald, only to find out that he wanted her for something other than what she thought. She had come very close to falling in love with Michael, but she knew he wasn't hers and never would be. And now she kept thinking, after he left, what was she going to do?

"You don't look like you're having a very good time," said an older woman sitting beside Emily at the long marble-topped dressing table. She looked as though she'd been to a thousand parties like this and now found sitting in the ladies' room more interesting.

All Emily could do was nod as she reapplied lipstick. She was afraid that if she said anything, she might burst into tears. Her night of adventure was being taken from her. What was she going to tell Gidrah? That she left the party an hour after they arrived?

"Is that big hunk scowling outside yours?" the woman asked.

"Want him?" Emily snapped back, making the woman smile.

"That bad, huh?"

More than anything in the world, right now Emily wanted another woman to talk to. "He's jealous," she said, instantly falling into that camaraderie women often share when they will tell a stranger their most intimate secrets. "He put me at a table in the back and won't let me dance with anyone or even to talk to anyone else. Except to some ancient old man who wants to tell me of all his good deeds."

"You ought to get away from him. I had a boyfriend like that once and he wanted to lock me in an ivory tower."

"What did you do?"

"Got away from him long enough to interest another man. With your face and figure you could get any man you want." She took a pair of glasses from her handbag then leaned forward to look at the rubies around Emily's neck. "And, honey, with those things you should be able to get the attention of any man in the room."

"Really?" Emily asked, feeling a bit better. "Who's the contractor who builds for Wentworth and Mortman?" Emily knew she'd hit pay dirt when the woman drew in her breath sharply.

"You do like to start at the top, don't you? He's David Graham."

As Emily touched up her lipstick again, she tried to sound nonchalant. "Tell me, are any of those three married?"

The woman looked at Emily with new interest, seeming to appraise her. "Look, honey, let me give you some advice. If you're going after any of the Lethal Three you ought to know something about them."

273

Leaning forward eagerly, Emily said, "I have all the time in the world and I'd love to hear everything."

Smiling in a way that let Emily know that the delight of the woman's life was gossip, she opened her mouth to speak, then had to wait while another woman came in, used the rest room, washed her hands, checked her makeup, then left.

"All right, there are three of them and each is unique, or at least different from each other. One is a wolf, one is a nice guy and the third is shy, never married. Keeps to himself. But all three are sharks when it comes to making money."

The woman took a deep breath, glad for the eager audience Emily gave her. "The shy one doesn't say much but when he talks people listen. He loves money, has every penny he ever made. He'll love those stones you're wearing. No one knows much about him—could be gay for all any woman knows about him.

"The nice man is a real barracuda. Smiles as he's foreclosing on widows and orphans. After a meeting with him you leave smiling and it's hours later that you realize he's taken everything you own. He's had three wives and is looking for number four. But I warn you that there are hundreds of applicants to be number four even though the first three wives got not a dime out of him.

"The wolf has never married either. Instead he leads women on, makes them think he's about to propose then one day he doesn't call. No reason and no guilt. He's a cold bastard. I've heard that two women have committed suicide after being dumped by him."

The woman lowered her voice as she heard laughter just outside the door. "The three men are always together. The women they date—if they do—change and if a woman so much as breathes a word of complaint because she has to share her breakfast table with the other two, she's likely to find a dear Jane letter the next day—if she even hears from the bastard ever again, that is."

Abruptly, the woman stopped, checked her makeup and looked as though she were about to leave.

"But which man is which?" Emily asked.

Standing, the woman smoothed her skirt which was a gorgeous opalescent white satin. "I can't give away all my secrets and that one's for you to find out."

"Are you trying to win one of these men?" Emily asked, thinking that a woman her age wouldn't have a chance.

But the woman didn't seem to think that Emily's question was an impossibility. "No. I got a new husband last year. He's eighty-two so I think I'll wait this one out. Where'd you get those blood drops? Inherited?"

"Uh, yes," Emily lied. But then she did receive them indirectly from a person long deceased.

"Well then, go for Wentworth. He likes people to think his father plays polo."

"He doesn't?"

"It's a secret but his father buys and sells slums. Those stones will impress him."

Light was coming back into Emily's eyes. A few weeks ago she'd thought of herself as nothing but a boring little librarian but now that there was a chance for a bit of an adventure, she wanted it. Maybe

Michael was right and this dress and the rubies had transformed her. "But what about . . . ?" she said, nodding toward the door.

The woman opened her purse, took out a vial of pills then shook out three. "When my old man gets feisty I give him one of these and he's snoring in seconds. The next morning I tell him he was fabulous, the greatest lover I ever had. Give that hunk of yours three of these and you'll be free to do whatever you want. But you better get him someplace where he can sleep first, 'cause when he goes, he'll go fast."

As Emily looked at the pills in the palm of her hand, she saw freedom. This would be her one and only chance to play at being a spy or whatever she wanted. If she could meet the men and figure out which one was. . . . Well, she didn't want to think what he was trying to do, but she did want to know *why.* What did a small-town librarian know that could make a rich, powerful man come after her? And it wouldn't be as though she were in any danger because who would recognize her? She looked as different from her ordinary self as a visitor from another planet. Tonight not even her own mother would recognize her. So wouldn't it be nice, just for one night, to be someone glamorous and take on a potentially dangerous job? Just for one night?

"Thank you," she whispered to the woman, her mind full of the possibilities before her.

"If it works out I want a front row seat at your wedding."

"Oh, it's not like that at all," Emily said, grinning. "If it works out you *won't* be invited to my funeral."

With that cryptic remark, she left the rest room and ran smack into Michael.

"Are you all right?" he asked, hovering over her.

"Never better. Shall we go? Oh, wait, could we possibly take a glass of champagne with us? I'd like to have at least one glass." She hoped she looked suitably depressed and that her lower lip was pouting in a pretty way.

Michael narrowed his eyes at her. "You have something in your mind. What is it?"

"Nothing special. There, thank you," she said as she took two tall flutes of champagne from the tray of a passing waiter and handed one to Michael. "Shall we go?" She looped her arm in his and gently pulled him toward the door and the waiting cars.

Fifteen minutes later Michael had drunk his champagne, at Emily's insistence, and was passed out on the back seat of the limo. She tapped the glass behind the driver, and with the world's biggest smile, told him to return to the party.

# Chapter 22

THERE'S SOMETHING ABOUT HAVING ON THE RIGHT
dress, the right jewels and being in the right place to
show them off that does something to a woman's ego.
As Emily walked through the crowd of people she
didn't feel like an imposter; she didn't feel like a
small-town girl mistakenly mixed in with the society
crowd. She felt that she belonged. Irene had always
complained that Emily kept her great figure hidden
under too many clothes, but now nothing was left to
the imagination. Every curve and most of her lush
bosom were exposed; she could see and feel the looks
of appreciation from the men. The women looked at
her in calculation. They looked her up and down, and
stared hard at her jewelry. Emily realized that every
one of these people knew that the rubies were real.

It didn't take a Sherlock Holmes to figure out who

were the three men she'd been told about. They sat together, smoking, drinking, watching the crowd, part of it but separate.

For a moment Emily stood back and looked at them. It was better not to think that one of them had tried to kill her. It was better to think of the present, that she was at a dance and all she wanted to do was find out as much as she could.

She took a deep breath, then was pleased to see a man smile at her since even more of her bosom had edged its way over the top of her dress. She smiled back at him and when he raised his glass in salute to her, she almost laughed aloud.

Feeling full of the power of her newly found abilities, she made her way toward the table of the three men, and as she walked she unclasped her necklace.

"Excuse me," she said as enticingly as she could to the man whose back was to her, then when he moved his chair to allow her to pass (although there was plenty of room) she seemed to trip on nothing and fell forward, catching herself just before she fell into the man's lap. Her necklace unclasped and fell straight down into Emily's bosom.

"Oh my," she said, clutching both the rubies and a great deal of flesh. "I am ever so clumsy."

"I don't mind," the man she'd almost collided with said, rising to help her up. "Would you like me to see to that?"

"Would you? That would be so kind." While the man refastened her necklace, Emily wondered how she should handle the situation. Unless she said something interesting she knew they would not invite her to sit down with them. But what? How does a woman interest such powerful, mega-rich men as these?

"Thank you," she said, smiling at the man, then when he sat back down, she drew in her breath for courage. "So which one are you? The shy one, the wolf or the one who is nice on the outside but terrible inside?"

For a moment Emily thought she'd overstepped the boundaries but then the tall blond man laughed. "I'm the nice one," he said, then motioned to an empty chair. "Won't you join us?"

"Not unless you promise not to foreclose on my house," she said, batting her lashes at him.

"It's a promise. Now, may I introduce my friends? This is Charles Wentworth and Statler Mortman. And I am—"

"David Graham," Emily said, smiling invitingly. "I'd know you anywhere from the description I was given."

Emily's heart was racing as she sat at the table with the three men, one of whom might be a murderer. But just to be around men of such power and mystique was like nothing she had ever experienced before. Charles Wentworth was openly staring at her necklace in a cold, appraising way. "I've never had it appraised. How much do you think it's worth?" she said daringly.

"Half a mill at least," the man said as he took a deep draw on a cigarette.

"If he says that then it's worth twice that much at least," Statler Mortman said, and the way he was looking at Emily made her sure he was the Wolf—and when she looked into his eyes she understood why so many women fell for him. "In fact I'll give you a check for seven-fifty right now."

It took Emily a moment to realize that he meant seven hundred fifty *thousand* dollars. "Oh my," she gasped. "You'll turn my head. I'm just a small-town librarian and this is my first ball ever. Isn't it lovely?" Looking away, she gazed at the dancers as though she were interested in them.

"So, Miss Librarian, where did you get the stones?"

"A ghost told my guardian angel where they were and he gave them to me. The angel, I mean."

Not one of the three men cracked a smile and, suddenly, Emily's blood seemed to freeze and she wished she hadn't drugged Michael, wished she had left the party when he wanted her to.

Charles Wentworth took another very deep draw on his cigarette. "And where is your angel now?"

Better to keep this light, she thought. "He's around here somewhere. You know how guardian angels are, always watching and protecting." No one smiled.

"What's your name?" Statler Mortman asked.

"Anastasia Jones," she said quickly. "My mother wanted something to perk up the last name she married. Now, if you'll excuse me, I need to—"

"But surely, you can't deny me at least one dance with the most mysterious woman here," Statler said, his eyes going to her bosom.

"Me? Mysterious? I couldn't be less so. I'm just—"

"Cinderella at the ball," David said, smiling. "So you must have a dance and let everyone see you in your beautiful dress and your fabulous jewels. Don't you see that every woman here is eating her heart out in envy over rubies like those? I'm sure no woman since Imperial Russia has had jewels like those."

Nervously, Emily put her hand to her throat. For all that the other two men made her feel like something to be served on a plate, this man was so, well, so nice. What was it the woman had said? That he forecloses on widows and orphans, wasn't it?

"Come on, Miss Smith, what would one dance hurt?"

He was so persuasive that Emily took the hand he held out to her—and didn't notice the way he confused her name. What could happen on a dance floor? she thought.

But ten minutes later, Emily was dancing and thinking how she'd leave soon and join Michael in the car when someone rammed into them on the dance floor and she felt a sharp prick in her right hip.

"Oh my, did I do that?" Emily heard a woman's voice say, but Emily was swaying on her feet and didn't connect a voice and face. "Too much champagne," she heard a man say, then felt herself swooped up into strong arms and carried away. Such a lovely dream she was having, she thought as she snuggled her face into the man's strong chest and closed her eyes. She was Cinderella and she was being carried off by Prince Charming.

When Emily awoke it wasn't to a dream but to a nightmare. Her head hurt but when she tried to raise her hand to her forehead, she found that her hands were tied. Groggily, she opened her eyes and tried to focus. She seemed to be in a large, dirty room; there was trash on the floor and what looked to be a couple of rats scurrying across the back of the room. When her vision and her head cleared a bit, she realized that she was seated in a chair and her hands were tied behind her, her feet tied to the chair legs. The only other thing in the room was a beat-up old metal desk. There were no windows, just one heavy metal door to her right.

It didn't take a great brain to figure out that she was in an abandoned building and, unless a miracle happened, no one was ever going to find her.

She was just about to bawl herself out when the door opened and in walked the three men. Daylight came in with them and Emily wondered if it was the day after the ball or the day after that. From the feel of her head, it could be a week later. She was still wearing her beautiful red dress but it was torn and dirty now. She didn't have to look down to know that the rubies were missing.

For a moment the three men stood with their backs to her as though they didn't know she was in the room.

If I'm going to die I might as well find out why, she thought. She wanted to ask an intelligent question, but the only word that came out was, "Why?" and that hurt her throat.

David Graham turned toward her and Emily thought how the woman in the rest room had been right: he seemed so very nice. "You really don't know, do you?" he asked as he held up the set of rubies she'd worn. The large drops caught the light from the single overhead fixture and looked like miniature fires.

"I have no idea," she said tiredly.

"Shall I tell her?" David asked the others, making them turn toward her.

"Can we stop you?" Statler asked, looking at Emily in a way that made her body feel very cold.

There was a sneer on Charles's thin face. "He's the wolf as you so charmingly put it."

At that Emily blinked. Maybe her little jest hadn't been as charming as she'd thought at the time. Saying what she did would seem funny in the movies but in real life it had been rude.

The next moment, her head came up. What was she thinking?! Next she'd be apologizing to men who had tied her to a chair and were probably going to kill her. She glared at them.

"Did you think we'd fall for your insolence, for your . . ." Charles asked.

"That's enough," David said. "She's going to die, what else do you want?"

"Michael," Emily thought. Maybe if she called him in her head he'd hear her and come rescue her. But even an angel needed an address. "Where are we?" she asked, hoping to send that information to him telepathically.

"We're in a state you never heard of," Statler said. This got a laugh from the other two.

"So where did you find these?" Charles asked. "We looked everywhere."

It took her a moment to realize that he meant that they looked through the Madison House attics. "You searched the house? But I saw no evidence that anyone had been there."

"Do you think we're amateurs? Who do you think

spread the story of there being a ghost in that house?"
Charles asked, his hatred of her clear in his voice.

"But there is a ghost in that house. Captain—" she
began.

"Spare us your silly tales. Where did you find the
rubies?"

"My, uh, friend did and I don't know where he got
them. Maybe you should ask him." Maybe she could
persuade them to bring Michael into this then he
could rescue her. As he always did, she thought, and
there were almost tears in her eyes. Be brave, Emily,
she told herself. At least you know for sure that there
is life after death. But even that thought didn't make
her less frightened.

"Is this the friend who's asleep in the limo?" came a
female voice and in walked the woman Emily had met
in the rest room. "Honey, if you gave him all three of
those pills he won't ever wake up."

For a moment all Emily could do was gape in
consternation.

"Did you think you could get the kind of information that I gave you from just anyone?" the woman
asked, her face showing her amusement at Emily's
confusion. Moving toward the desk, the woman put
her arm around David's waist. "This is my dear little
brother," she said as she reached for the rubies. "I do
think they'll look better on me than in your bank
vault," she said, smiling, then turned back to Emily.
"You do look disbelieving. Did you think I just
happened to be in that place and happened to give
you all that information? Didn't you think it was odd
that only one woman came in during the whole time
we were in there? We had someone outside guarding

the door. Oh, and too bad about your friend. He was nice-looking."

At the thought of Michael's death, Emily almost gave up. So now Michael was probably without a body and was back in Heaven, but then she remembered something. "You can't kill him. Not until he finds out what evil surrounds me and fixes it."

At that absurdity, they all laughed. "Baby," Statler said, "there's lots of evil around you."

It was on the tip of her tongue to make a nasty crack to that remark, but a phone rang and Charles pulled a cell phone out of his suit coat pocket. The men were clean and dressed in fresh street clothes while Emily felt as though she'd never had a bath in her life, plus, her bladder was bursting.

"Yeah, uh huh," Charles said into the phone. "Got it. Let's get her out of here."

Statler grabbed her upper arm with one hand and held a knife in the other—whether to cut the ropes or slit her throat, Emily didn't know.

But before she could find out, the phone rang again and Charles put his hand up in that way that powerful men do when they expect to be obeyed. For a few moments he listened, then he put the phone down. "The jail bird escaped." He turned to glare at Emily. "Seems your friend is on the loose again."

At that Emily nearly burst into tears of relief that Michael was still alive, but she got herself under control and tried to remain calm. She had no doubt that Michael would find her; after all, he had contacts in very high places.

"So we've got to wait until tonight to get rid of you," Charles said in disgust.

Emily took a deep breath to give herself courage. "Can't you at least tell me why you've stalked me? You've planted bombs in my car twice."

"I told you that was a stupid idea," David said to Statler. "Stat thought that a car bomb would make everyone believe that your death was connected to the Mafia and that crook you were with. But it didn't work, did it? Somehow, the FBI knew."

Emily was silent. She was not about to tell them that Michael was her guardian angel and could see the auras of cars.

"I can't believe you didn't figure it out, smart lady like you. When we started to find out about you, we were . . ." David looked up. "What were we?"

"Impressed," Statler said.

"Yes, impressed. You were feeding some big news stories to that brainless boyfriend of yours and he was rising in the news world because of it. Too bad you didn't marry him, you could have made him governor."

"But the stories I researched had nothing to do with why you tried to kill me?" she asked and in spite of the horror of the situation, she was very interested now.

"None whatever." Again he held up the rubies.

"You tried to kill me for those?" Emily asked in disbelief. "You could have stolen them. Or, from what I hear, you could have bought them."

"But they are yours," David said and this seemed to be a great joke to him.

Emily was confused. "You could have had them reset, recut, anything and that would have made them yours.

"I thought you said she was smart," the woman said with contempt.

Emily's mind raced. Softly, she said, "What do you mean that they're mine?"

"You own them legally because you inherited them."

"From the captain?" She was getting more confused by the moment but then her head was full of things outside the normal world. For the last weeks she had been living in a world that included both people with and without bodies. If the captain, who was dead, owned the rubies then he gave them to her, did that mean she had inherited them?

"You ought to shoot her just for being so stupid," the woman said, turning her back on Emily.

"What was your mother's maiden name?" David asked.

"Wilcox."

"And her mother's name?"

"I . . . I don't remember."

"Try Simmons."

"Ah, yes, I do believe that was it," Emily said and was even more confused because it was a common enough name.

"And what was Captain Madison's wife's name?"

"Rachel—" Emily's head came up. "Simmons," she whispered. Emily just sat there blinking as thoughts raced through her mind. "You mean that *I* have something to do with Captain Madison?"

"Ever see a picture of his wife?"

"No, after the captain's death she destroyed all pictures of herself."

"Not all of them. My family had a few from when

she was a girl." David put his hand to his inside coat pocket and withdrew a photo which he held before Emily's face.

"But she . . ."

"Looks like you. Yes she does. Just like you. Notice the jewelry in the picture."

"I see," Emily said, recognizing the rubies, but, truthfully, she didn't see anything. "Who are you?"

He knew exactly what she meant. "My great-grandmother was the captain's wife's sister. But you, little Miss Librarian, were the captain's wife's great-granddaughter."

Were. Past tense, as though she were already dead. "I . . . I never knew, never thought. I didn't even know she had a daughter. It's not in any of the records. What do you think drove her mad? I don't know; I hadn't found that out yet."

"But you would have. See, it was a well-kept secret in my family. Young Rachel Simmons got pregnant by her lover then he left her so she was shipped off to an aunt's to have the baby. When she came back her father married her off to the captain. By that time he was the only man in town who'd take her. Did you find out that the captain killed two men in duels who made jests about his wife's virtue in a public bar? No, well, you would have found it out. You always snooped on a story until you found out everything."

"The captain killed her lover," Emily said as she tried to take all this in.

"No, he didn't," David said. "The wife killed him. She loved him with all her heart, the silly cow, then he left her the moment he heard she was pregnant and about to be disinherited. He went abroad then came back years later to find his former lover living in a mansion and wearing rubies the size of lemons. He secretly courted her again. The captain knew but he loved her so much that he let her do whatever she wanted. The captain would have let her lover live with them if that's what she wanted. But when his wife figured out that all the lover wanted was her jewelry, she took one of the captain's pistols and shot him through the heart."

"After she shot him in the genitals," the woman added.

"Oh yes, I forgot that grisly detail. I always forget that detail."

"And the captain took the blame for it," Emily said in wonder.

"Yes. He persuaded his faithful old servant to give evidence against him in a courtroom so the captain was hanged instead of his wife. Later the servant killed himself in remorse and the wife went mad."

"And the baby was raised by a nice family in Iowa," Emily said softly, thinking where her mother's people were from.

"Right."

"And when she grew up she married and gave birth to your grandmother."

"So I guess this means that the captain left everything to his wife and she left a will giving everything to her daughter, wherever she was," Emily said.

"Exactly." David gave his sister a glance. "I told you she was smart."

"But I knew nothing. I—"

"But you were researching the captain's history, snooping into things that didn't concern you and you would have figured it out. Too bad you aren't as stupid as your boyfriend. You wouldn't be in danger if you did. He couldn't find his shoes without help."

"So if you get rid of me then you become heir to the Madison fortune. Is there a fortune?"

"Oh yes, a substantial one," the woman said.

"And there are rumors of hidden riches in that house," Statler said. "His wife had a fabulous jewel collection. It seems that colored stones helped her forget what she'd lost. Besides rubies, she had emeralds and canary diamonds and great hoards of semi-precious stones. All worth millions today. But when she died not one stone was found. She hadn't sold them, so everyone figured they were still in the house."

"Why isn't this known?" Emily asked. "It seems that there would be legends about a house full of jewels."

"There are legends of ghosts. We spent a lot of money putting in a sound system that would scare off bratty kids come to sneak around the place," Charles said, speaking for the first time in a while. "The ghost overrode any stories of treasure."

"But why didn't you just claim the house and do what you wanted to it?" Emily asked. "No one knew about me except you. I certainly didn't know."

"Judge Henry Agnew Walden, is why. We presented our claim five years ago but he said he wanted to know what had happened to the daughter. And he didn't believe us when we said she'd died when she was an infant."

"I told you he wouldn't believe anything you said," the woman said. "My dear brother seduced and abandoned the judge's daughter. The judge learned the hard way about orphaned children."

"So what was I to do? She was offering herself to me," David said with eyes that had no regrets.

"Say no?" his sister asked archly.

"What if I give the place to you?" Emily asked. "What do I want with an old house and a bunch of jewelry? Where would I wear it anyway?"

At that they all turned to look at her and the identical expressions they wore said, We're not fools.

"I'd sign any papers you had," she said meekly. "Couldn't you draw up a contract very fast?"

"What a splendid idea. You sign over millions of dollars' worth of jewels and land to us, then later you don't go to court and try to get it back. Is that your plan?"

"But I'd be too afraid to do anything," Emily said and she could hear the whine in her voice. So much for bravery, she thought.

"Odd thing about money. If there's enough of it it gives the most timid person courage. Believe me, Miss Librarian, a good lawyer could talk you into suing and you'd win, of course. After all, she was your great-grandmother."

"Enough!" the woman said as she looked Emily up and down. "Any more talk and you'll be asking her to marry you."

"That is an idea," Statler said, looking at the upper half of Emily that was hanging out of the dress.

"I say we get her out of here and get it over with. The sooner it's done, the sooner her body will be found and the sooner you can be declared the nearest relative," the woman said. "And give me those," she added as she snatched the rubies from her brother's hand.

"Michael!" Emily said in her mind and wished with all her might that she'd listened to him, obeyed him and not tried to be a femme fatale.

Emily didn't have another thought because a needle was stuck into her upper arm and the next moment she was aware of nothing.

# Chapter 23

WHEN EMILY AWOKE, SHE WAS INSIDE THE TRUNK OF a car. She'd never been inside a trunk before but there was no mistaking the smell, the sounds, the jostling ride, and the tire jack sticking into her rib cage.

For the life of her, she couldn't grasp what was really happening. Being tied up and put into the trunk of a car was something that happened to other people, not to her. Not to boring little librarians whose idea of a good time was to find a first edition in an antique store.

"Michael," she said aloud in her mind. She couldn't speak because her mouth was taped. But if she could talk, she would have liked to say some things to him that she hadn't said before.

First of all, she loved him. She loved him for who

he was, not because he was an angel or even because he loved her. She loved him because he always cared about people, whether those people had a body or not.

And she was so sure of his love for her that she knew she could drug him and he'd still love her the next day. Sure, he'd be angry and he'd shout at her and tell her what a damn fool thing she'd done, but he'd still love her. How many women felt that sure of the men in their lives that they could do that? With Donald, she was always trying to please him, but with Michael, just being herself seemed to please him.

"I love you," she said in her mind and tears gathered in her eyes as she thought that now she'd never get to tell him so. She'd never get to tell him he was right and she was wrong about the party, and she'd never get to tell him how much fun she'd had with him. He was interesting and funny and caring, and all the things that any woman would want, she thought. And I treated him like dirt, she thought, more tears coming to her eyes.

So now she was on her way to her death. She had no doubt of that. And even Michael and all his powers had not been able to save her. What would happen to him when he got back to Heaven and told Archangel Michael that he'd failed, that he hadn't been able to eradicate the evil that surrounded Emily?

So now she was going to die and she'd never see him in human form again. Next life she'd be human and he'd be in Heaven looking down at her. At least he'd be there for a hundred more years before he was transferred elsewhere. Suddenly, a hundred years didn't seem like very long because that was all she was going to have with him.

When the car stopped, Emily wasn't afraid anymore. Maybe it was because since she'd met Michael she'd come to know what awaited her. There was no question of life after death or reincarnation anymore. At least not for her. For her there was only certainty that she'd never again see Michael.

When the trunk was opened, she was not surprised to see that she was in a woods. So, she would become one of those bodies found by children playing and no one would be able to identify her. She'd never even made out a will.

"All right, let's get this over with," Charles said as he grabbed her arm and began pulling her deeper into the trees. She'd already seen that there would be no use asking for mercy from this man; he had no heart.

Please let me die with dignity, she prayed. Don't let me blubber and beg.

With new resolve, she did her best to keep her footing as Charles pulled her across the rough forest floor.

It was David who heard the noise first. "What's that?" he asked, his nerves obviously on edge. The others were so calm that Emily wondered if they'd done this before. They were known as the Lethal Three and maybe with good cause.

Maybe Michael used some sort of witchcraft, or in his case, angel craft, because the motorcycle was upon them almost before they could hear it. It was one of those huge old black Harley-Davidsons that only the meanest hoodlums would ride, and nothing had ever looked better to Emily. If he'd ridden up on a black stallion he couldn't have looked more like a hero of old.

"Untie her," Michael said softly as he got off the big motorcycle.

Charles gave an ugly laugh as he pointed a gun at Michael's head. "Don't make me laugh. Get over here with her."

"Gladly," Michael said as he sauntered toward Emily, then took her from Charles' grip. Michael put his hand on the tape on Emily's mouth and she prepared herself for the pain of its removal, but the tape came off and she felt no pain.

"You can't kill them both," David said, his voice high pitched with nervousness.

"Of course we can," the woman said. "In fact, this is perfect. He kills her then shoots himself. Perfect. It happens all the time."

"I have told the police where you are," Michael said softly as he untied Emily's hands and feet. At least she knew they came untied but Michael didn't seem to move.

"You think we don't pay off the police?" Statler said. "And besides, Donald the idiot has blackened this woman's name enough that everyone will think that she got what she deserved."

The woman gave a cold smile to Emily. "Honey, it's a little late to learn this now, but never trust a man. It was Donald on the phone. He sold you out for a promise of being in the running for governor next primary."

At that Emily gasped and Michael's warm hand slipped into hers, and as always, she calmed. And as she did, she sent thoughts of love to him. He must have read her mind because he squeezed her hand and she felt much better. But then Michael always made her feel safe.

"You can't kill me," Michael said softly, standing just to the side of Emily. "No matter what you do to me you can't kill me until Heaven is ready for me to leave this earth."

Michael was looking at David and his sister so he couldn't see Charles standing to the side. With a smirk on his face, Charles lifted his gun and aimed to fire.

Emily didn't think about what she did. All she knew was that she didn't want to be on the planet without Michael. If he was going to leave this earth, then so was she, and wherever they ended up, they would be together.

Without a thought for her own life, she threw her body in front of Michael's and the bullet went straight through her heart.

# *Epilogue*

MICHAEL WAS STANDING BEFORE ARCHANGEL MI-
chael and the magnificence of the angel was terrifying.
He was a soldier, an angel who had overseen all the
wars in recorded history, and his handsome, com-
manding presence sent fear through his namesake.

"I sent you to do a job," the archangel said, looking
down his aristocratic nose at Michael.

Michael had always wanted to be allowed to see the
face of this most exalted of angels, but now that he
was trembling in his presence, he almost regretted his
wish. "And I failed," Michael whispered. "I admit my
failure and I beg forgiveness."

The archangel looked away toward his friend Gabriel, an angel many thousands of years old. Gabriel
had once ruled the planet earth but long ago he had

turned it over to the younger archangel, Michael. "You have been punished so go now."

But Michael didn't move.

"What is it?" the archangel said, his dark brows drawing into a single line.

"I want to be with her," Michael said, trying to be brave but the words caught in his throat.

"You will be for the next hundred years then—"

"No!" Michael said more sharply than he meant to, then he softened. "I mean that I want to be with her here in this life and now. On earth. In human form."

The archangel looked at Michael with a gaze so piercing that he was sure his soul was being flambéed. "But her earthly body has died."

Michael took a breath then swallowed. "It can be resurrected."

"Only God can do that," Archangel Michael said softly, looking at Michael with curiosity.

"Then I will ask Him," Michael said firmly.

"But there must be a reason for such a resurrection," Gabriel said from behind his young friend.

Michael gathered all the courage he had. "I will give *anything* to bring her body back to life and to be able to be with her."

In Heaven, one did not have to elaborate as the minds of lower-level spirits like Michael were easily read by archangels. "Do you know what you're saying?"

"Yes, I do," Michael said and as he said it, the fear left his body. "Yes, I know exactly what I'm saying."

"Are you saying that you'd give up being an angel for her? You would give up *Heaven* for her?"

"Yes," Michael said without hesitation. "She gave up her life for me so I will give up all for her."

Archangel Michael dismissed that with a wave of his hand. "But she goes on to a better life. She has done well in this life even if it was short so she'll be given better next time."

"I want to be with her in this life and in . . . in all future lives. I will give up Heaven for that," Michael said and tried to keep the trembling from starting again.

Archangel Michael looked at him for several moments. "If you did that you would be taking on all the horrors of human life. There would be pain and sadness, tragedy and—"

"And love," Michael said, and as he spoke he gained courage. "I love her. I have always loved her, I know that now. I'm not good as a guardian angel. I gave too much time to Emily and not enough to the others. And I manipulated lives, something that is impermissible. I even manipulated Emily's lives because I could not bear to see her with other men. What kind of guardian angel am I if I interfere like that? And I bear her a mortal's love. There is nothing holy about my love for Emily. In fact, it is very carnal."

"Ah, then," the archangel said, still looking hard at Michael. "But you must understand that if you give up Heaven you cannot change your mind."

For a moment Michael almost hesitated, but then he smiled. "No, I won't. I have loved her for centuries so my mind's not likely to change."

"You will have no memory of the time when you

were an angel. You will be plagued with all human ills."

"I understand and I am willing to give what it takes. Will you bring her body back to life?"

"If you are determined. You will not change your mind?"

"No. I am sure," and when he said it, he was.

"Then it is done," Archangel Michael said. And it was.

# Epilogue 2

$I$T'S DONE."

"You're kidding," Emily said, holding their eight-week-old son on her knee as she tried to fasten her dress. "No more rewrites?" she asked, teasing him.

"None. Here, let me have him while you change," Michael said as he reached for the baby.

"Change into what?"

"Very funny. Change your clothes because I'm taking the two of you out to dinner to celebrate. It isn't every day that a man finishes a book."

"It isn't every day that a man of thirty-seven writes his autobiography."

"*Our* autobiography," he said, taking the baby and kissing him before snuggling him onto his shoulder.

"Yours," Emily said, smiling as she headed up the stairs of the big old house, and as she went, she thought over the last two years of their life. She thought how she'd met Michael, by nearly running him over with her car, how he'd had a case of amnesia and they had worked together to try to find out who he was. It was during their search, with the FBI chasing them, mistakenly thinking Michael was a wanted criminal, that they'd found out that someone was trying to kill Emily.

For a moment she paused on the landing and looked down at the dark head of her husband holding their baby, gently swaying with him as they listened to the child's favorite recording by Enya.

She remembered how Michael had rescued her from those men, how they got away on Michael's motorcycle and how, behind them, the car containing the three men and the woman had plunged down the side of a mountain. All four had been killed instantly. When it was revealed that Donald Stewart, Emily's television news reporter fiancé had been involved in the plot, he'd been discredited and fired. She'd heard that Donald was now doing weather broadcasts in some small town no one knew the name of.

Afterward, Emily had claimed her inheritance, the Madison house, and she and Michael had married. They had used some of the captain's fortune to renovate the old house until it was a beautiful home which she and Michael planned to fill with children.

Odd, she thought, how such a seemingly unhappy beginning could work out so well. Sometimes she wondered how her life would be different now if she or Michael had not escaped that day when the men held guns on them.

"But we did escape," she said aloud then continued up the stairs. "And thank God and all of Heaven that we did." For a moment she stopped to stare up at the huge stained glass window that went from the top of the house down to the first story. The original had been shattered years ago and when Emily inherited the house the space had been boarded up so when they went to replace it, Michael had said, "Let's have a picture of Archangel Michael made."

"And do you have a photo of him to give the glass maker?" Emily had asked teasingly.

"No, but oddly enough I know just what he looks like."

So now there was a window of a twelve-foot-tall man, an extraordinarily handsome man wearing black armor and scowling down at all who pass by him. But even with the scowl, there was something benevolent in his expression and Emily smiled at the angel every time she passed him.

"Thanks to you too," she whispered, but didn't know why. What did a fictional character like Archangel Michael have to do with their being saved from men with guns?

Having no answer, Emily shrugged and went up the stairs to their bedroom and opened her closet door. "So, Captain, what should I wear tonight?" she said aloud, referring to the ghost that people said haunted the house. But neither she nor Michael had ever seen any evidence of a ghost in the house, and, besides, they didn't believe in them.

Looking down at her belly, which still left a lot to be desired in flatness, she grimaced. "Come on, Captain, have some pity. What do you have that a fat, just-had-a-baby woman like me could wear that would entice her husband? I need *help."*

She said the words in jest, but in the next moment, she heard a sound in the top of the closet. "Not squirrels again!" she said, peering up at the ceiling. She turned on the light, then to her horrified amazement, she saw what looked like the entire ceiling of the closet begin to fall down. Termites? she thought, still staring as the boards fell away. When they crashed down, she ducked, but not before something hit her on the head, and when she put up her hand, she felt something smooth and cold.

When the dust had settled, Emily looked down at her hand and saw that she was holding an emerald necklace and at her feet and on her shoulder and caught on the top of her clothes were what looked to be a pirate's hoard of jewels.

"Oh my," Emily said, eyes wide as she stared at the glittering pieces.

"What was that?" Michael yelled as he came bounding up the stairs, the baby held tightly to him. "Are you okay? It sounded like the roof was caving in."

Slowly, Emily turned toward him and held up her hands. "I think we found the great-grannie's jewels," she said softly.

"I'll be damned," Michael said, picking up a bracelet of what appeared to be yellow diamonds from the floor. "So you have." He looked into a corner of the room. "Thanks, old man," he said, then both he and Emily could have sworn they heard a hearty laugh.

"Let's get out of here," Michael said. Then he took

Emily by the hand and the three of them ran down the stairs laughing.

Gabriel looked up at Archangel Michael and said, "Why *did* you send him to earth?"

"Because over the centuries Michael had fallen in love with Emily. This sometimes happens but in this case Michael was interfering in a negative way. Emily has a very good heart but she keeps falling for rotten men. In the last two lives, rather than see Emily married to a man who treats her like dirt, Michael broke the pattern and prevented the marriages."

"Isn't that good?" Gabriel asked, eyes twinkling because he knew the answer. It was always amusing to him to see such a glorious soldier as the archangel Michael involved in something besides war and peace.

"It would have been except that Michael couldn't bear for any other man to marry her so Emily lived the life of a spinster. For two lifetimes she has died a virgin, with no children, a burden on her relatives, sad, lonely lives. And that was not her destiny."

"So in essence, you sent him to earth to make up his mind whether or not he wanted to be with the woman he loved."

"Exactly."

"And did he do as you hoped?"

"Oh yes. He has pleased me very much. The two of them are good people and they will produce good children. From them will radiate much love and goodness. The earth can always use love and goodness."

"Then our young friend Michael won't be demoted?"

The Archangel Michael looked at his old friend and saw that he was being teased and he smiled. No matter how threatening his countenance, he never frightened Gabriel, or even fooled him, for Gabriel, along with God, knew that Michael had a sweet, soft heart. "Not quite," Michael murmured, then gave his attention back to what was going on in the Middle East. "No, not quite."

**MORE HEART-WARMING
ROMANCES AVAILABLE FROM
POCKET BOOKS...**

## POCKET
### B O O K S

# LEGEND

## Jude Deveraux

Robin, beautiful, bright and very dynamic thinks
that she has it all. A wonderful career as a
successful chef, and a gorgeous and adoring
fiancé. What Robin is not planning for is
upheaval in her well ordered and happy life.

Whisked away from the present back into the
turbulent days of the Wild West, Robin finds
herself being swept into the danger and the
excitement of the time. She is forced to realise
that this is not just a dream that will disappear.
And she struggles to adapt, not only to the
unfamiliar way of dress but to the rough and
tumble ways of cowboy Cole Jordan. In his arms
and in an era that she was not born into, Robin
discovers a destiny that is so strong, she has to
span centuries to fulfil it.

**PRICE £4.99**

**ISBN 0671 85584 0**

# SHADES OF TWILIGHT

## Linda Howard

Roanna Davenport, raised as a wealthy orphan on her grandmother's magnificent Alabama estate, enjoys a passion for horses, a genius for trouble and a deep love for her cousin, Webb. But when Webb marries their ravishing mutual cousin, Jessie, Roanna's desire becomes no more than the stuff of dreams - until the night Jessie is found murdered.

Shocked and bereft, Webb leaves for Arizona, abandoning the legacy that he once believed was all he wanted. When years later a grown-up Roanna walks into a dingy bar in Nogales to bring him home, he doesn't recognise her. For the mischievous sprite he knew is no more. Gone, too, is her fire - in its place is ice that melts at his touch. Webb is drawn back to Davencourt, to Roanna, and to the killer that once destroyed his life and waits only for the chance to finish the job .

PRICE £4.99
ISBN 0671 51642 6

POCKET
B O O K S

# REMEMBER WHEN

## Judith McNaught

Having lost her fiancé to an Italian model, Diana is forced to attend the most lavish social event of the Houston season to save face and to bolster her company's image, Foster's *Beautiful Living* magazine. A woman of gentle grace and kindness, Diana values her privacy and her dignity, both of which are under attack by certain rumour-driven socialites.

Cole Harrison, a man both coolly analytical and arrestingly attractive is being forced to bring home a wife or else he will loose his uncle's share of the business. When Cole sets eyes on Diana Foster she seems to be the ideal candidate. It seems to be the perfect solution to their respective dilemmas, and how could they have known what that slow, bargain-sealing kiss would lead to? Could such a cold hearted match of convenience become unexpected, once-in-a-lifetime love ...?

PRICE £5.99
ISBN 0671 85566 2